P9-DGG-223

Also by Carolyn Brown

THE WEDDING GIFT

CAROLYN BROWN

Published by Sourcebooks Casablanca, an imprint of Sourcebooks
P.O. Box 4410, Naperville, Illinois 60567-4410
(630) 961-3900
sourcebooks.com

The Wedding Gift was originally published in 2020 as an audiobook by
Audible Originals.
A Slow Dance Holiday was originally published in 2020 as an ebook by
Sourcebooks Casablanca.
Summertime on the Ranch was originally published in 2021 as an ebook
by Sourcebooks Casablanca.

Printed and bound in the United States of America.
OPM 10 9 8 7 6 5 4 3 2 1

Chapter 1

"How do you know you are marrying the right person, Granny?" Darla Marshall asked her grandmother.

Roxie leaned in so she could see her reflection better in the round mirror in the middle of the antique vanity. She hated putting on makeup these days, but some days a woman had to gussy up a little, and besides, it gave her a moment to think about what her youngest granddaughter had just asked. Her lipstick ran into the wrinkles around her mouth, and she only had a few gray eyelashes to even try to put mascara on. But makeup was secondary to answering her granddaughter's question. Roxie had babysat Darla from the time she was six weeks old, so they had a close relationship, and she'd always tried to be there for the girl—to be honest with her even with difficult questions.

"Honey, you'd have to ask someone else that question," Roxie said as she applied a little blush to her cheeks. "For the first year of my marriage, I didn't think I had married the right person. There were times that I thought I'd married the devil himself."

"But I always thought you and Gramps had the perfect marriage." Darla plopped down on the bed behind Roxie. "How did you know he was your soulmate?"

Roxie stood up and crossed the room to her closet. She pulled off her gingham-checked snap-front duster and hung it up, took out her dress, and laid it on the end of the bed. "He was not my soulmate there at first, honey."

"Then why did you marry him?" Darla asked.

"Because he was wild and dating him was exciting. Are you having second thoughts, child? Your mama and daddy are out a lot of money for you to be calling off the wedding." Roxie's eyes bored holes into Darla's soul. "Are you going to need me to hide you from your mama? I've got some money put back to buy your wedding present, but if you need it to run away, we can use it for that. But only if you take me with you. I would far rather go to Hawaii or even to the beaches in Florida than to this damned old anniversary party."

"Why would I hide from Mama?" Darla asked.

"Because she's going to throw a pure old southern hissy

fit if you pull one of them runaway-bride things. She told me last week that the wedding had already gone over the budget your dad gave her, and she hadn't even paid the florist yet or the caterer," Roxie answered as she pulled her mauve-colored dress over her head.

"Be careful not to muss up your hair. Mama would have a hissy fit over that too. I'm not planning on running away"—Darla squirmed a little at the lie because she never lied to her grandmother and the idea of calling off the wedding had crossed her mind—"but marriage is until death, and I just want to be sure I'm saying, 'I do,' to the right person." She held up her engagement ring and stared at it for a while. "How do I know for absolute sure, Granny?"

"Gloria is good at hissy fits, but I got to admit, she's been a wonderful daughter-in-law. She and Kevin gave me you three girls." Roxie lowered her voice. "You do know you're my favorite, don't you?"

Darla giggled. "You tell that to all three of us sisters, but since you babysat me so much when I was little, we've kind of got a bond that Sarah and Marilyn don't have with you. A bond"—Darla gave her the old stink eye—"that lets me know when you are evading my question because you don't want to answer it."

"Yes, we do have something special, and yes, I am beating

around the bush, but not because I don't want to answer. It's because I'm not sure how to without going into a lot of detail. Would you zip me up, please?" Roxie turned around. "And you look more like me than the other two, so that makes you extra special."

Darla hopped off the bed and zipped her grandmother's dress. She loved it when folks told her that she looked like Roxie did when she was young. "You look beautiful today, Granny. I wish I'd gotten your red hair, and then we'd look even more alike. Did you have a big wedding when you and Gramps got married?"

"Lord, no!" Roxie went back to the vanity and fastened a strand of pearls around her neck. "We got married on the side of the road. My folks didn't like Claud. The Marshall family lived up in the woods near the Red River just north of Powderly, Texas. They didn't value education very much, and none of the ten boys in the family finished high school. They were Christian people—at least their mother was—and hard-working folks, but the daddy in the family liked his liquor and had a reputation for wasting money on poker games. Back in my younger days, and in my family, that was a bad thing."

"But you fell in love with him even though he was a bad boy, right?" Darla handed Roxie the pearl earrings that matched her necklace.

"I thought I was in love with him," Roxie answered. "There now, we're ready to go to the church. I really do not want this damned party. I'm only going along with it for Kevin and Gloria's sake. I wouldn't let them do anything for our fiftieth anniversary, so when they came up with this idea, I agreed. I'd rather for me and you to go to the bank, clean out my savings account, and head south to Florida. We could be beach bums until the money runs out."

"What do you mean, you *thought* you were in love with him? Didn't you know for sure?" Darla asked.

"As you kids say, that's a conversation for another day," Roxie told her. "Claud is probably already pacing the living room floor, so we'd better get moving."

The two of them walked down the hallway, across the foyer, and into the living room, where Darla's grandfather Claud really was pacing back and forth from the window, around the sofa, and back to the window.

"Don't Granny look beautiful today, Gramps?"

Her grandfather pointed at the clock. "We're going to be late to this shindig if we don't get going. Thank God it's in the middle of the day and don't mess up my television shows tonight."

"Was Granny this pretty on your wedding day?" Darla asked.

"Honey, that was sixty years ago. I can barely remember who won the domino games down at the senior citizens' place yesterday. I don't know if she was as pretty then as she is now, but I imagine she was, or I wouldn't have married her." He headed outside. "Y'all best hurry, or this heat is going to melt the makeup right off your faces."

"Well, that's a romantic thing to say on your anniversary," Darla fussed at him as she slid into the driver's seat of her granny's SUV, started the engine, and adjusted the air-conditioning.

"Honey, sometimes romance takes a back burner to plain old common sense. It's hotter 'n Lucifer's pitchfork. Turn up that air-conditioning so we can cool off and not go to the party all sweaty," he said.

"Gramps, tell me about your wedding day." Darla was determined to get him talking about the past. "Granny said y'all got married on the side of the road. Why would you do that?"

Claud chuckled. "Her folks lived in Paris, right in the middle of town in a little white house with a picket fence, and they went to church every Sunday. The family even had Sunday dinner where they all gathered around the table and passed the food proper like."

"We do that at your house every Sunday," Darla said as she drove down Broadway Street, turned right onto Main, and headed to the Baptist church fellowship hall on the corner of Main and Byrd Streets.

"Yep, but that's not the way I grew up. My mama and daddy had ten sons. I was the youngest. My daddy came from a family with eight boys and two girls. We were those wild Marshall kids from the backwoods up around Powderly. They called us Marshall cousins 'river rats' because we lived on the Red River, and we weren't real smart like your granny's folks.

"Accordin' to your great-grandma, I wasn't good enough for Roxie. She had a scholarship to go to college and was going to make something out of herself. But she said she would marry me, so I bought us a marriage license, and we was going to have us a weddin' in my folks' front yard." He chuckled. "My mama used to say that when you make plans, God just laughs and throws monkey wrenches into the ideas to show you who's boss."

Amen to that, Darla thought as she snagged a parking spot close to the fellowship hall. *God has sure been laughing at my plans lately.*

"Didn't you invite Granny's folks?" she asked.

"You'll have to hear the rest of this story later." Roxie sighed. "Look at all the cars. Folks are already here, so we'd best get on in there and get this over with."

"You know you love a party." Claud got out of the back

seat and opened the door for Roxie. "Even after we got married and made it to my mama's place, you loved the party she had ready for us in the front yard."

"I thought you couldn't remember anything that far back." Roxie got out of the vehicle and headed toward the fellowship hall with Claud right beside her.

"I told you we were going to be late," Claud fussed when he opened the door and everyone applauded.

"Mama told me not to bring y'all until this time so that everyone could greet you when we got here," Darla whispered.

"They're here!" Gloria's voice filled the whole place when she announced their arrival over the microphone. "Happy sixtieth to the best parents Kevin and I could ever ask for!"

"Sweet Jesus!" Roxie gasped.

"It's okay. They're all your friends," Darla said.

"It's not that, honey," Roxie whispered. "I just blew a hole in my pantyhose. A glob of fat has snuck out, and it feels like I've got a chunk of salt pork between my legs. It's sweating and sticking to my other thigh."

"We'll make our way to the bathroom." Darla looped her arm into Roxie's. "You can take them off and throw them in the trash. Nobody wears those things anymore anyway."

They hadn't gone two steps before a whole group of gray-haired ladies circled around Roxie. "You deserve a medal for staying with one man for sixty years," Violet Parsons said. "I'm ten years younger than you, and I've already had three husbands."

"Well, I think it's wonderful," Rosalee Davis sighed. "My poor Frank died just before our fortieth. I wish we would have had twenty more years together."

"Ladies," Darla whispered, "Granny needs to make a quick trip through the bathroom. We'll be right back, but y'all could claim one of those tables for us."

Violet nodded. "We understand, darlin'. When you get to be our age, the bladder has a mind of its own, and if you don't listen, it retaliates. We'll get some punch and cookies ready for you while you're gone."

"If I've got to listen to Violet tell stories about her three husbands and Rosalee whine about her husband that cheated on her the last ten years of their marriage, I'll be ready to go to Florida all by myself." Roxie opened the door and stopped in the sitting room right outside the bathroom. Darla locked the door and then eased down onto a rose-colored velvet sofa.

When Roxie jerked the tail of her dress up, Darla's eyes widened, and her finger shot up to point at her grandmother. "What is that thing you are wearing? It looks painful."

"Do you mean my girdle? A woman is only as well dressed as her undergarments," Roxie said.

"Have you always worn those things? And if so, why?" Darla frowned.

"Ahhh," Roxie said as she pulled it and the pantyhose off at the same time. "Freedom." She sighed. "Now you know why I hate to go to these things. You girls today have life so much easier. Ladies of my generation wear girdles because it's the proper thing to do, like hose or, in today's world, pantyhose. See those little loops on the back and front of the girdle? Those used to hold hooks that kept our nylons up."

"Throw that thing in the trash with the hose," Darla said. "And if that slip is hot, take it off and throw it away too."

"My mama would claw her way up out of her grave and fuss at me if I did that." Roxie shivered. "She always preached that decent women don't go half-naked under their clothing except at home."

"I'll protect you if Great-Granny comes gunnin' for you," Darla said, giggling. "Turn around and let me unzip you. When we leave here, all you'll have on is your granny panties, your bra, and that pretty dress."

"Honey, I just couldn't," Roxie said. "I carry an extra pair of hose in my purse. If you'll get them out for me, I'll put them on."

"Yes, you can, Granny. Violet and Rosalee won't ever know or even suspect. As thin as you are, I don't know why you'd ever torture yourself with a girdle and hose anyway.

Besides, you've always been full of spit and vinegar. Why are you letting society tell you to wear something that's painful to even look at it?" Darla picked up the girdle and pantyhose and tossed them in the trash.

Roxie inhaled deeply and let it out slowly. "I don't suppose it would be proper for me to go barefoot too, would it?"

"This is your party, Granny," Darla said. "You can do whatever you want. I'm going barefoot and wearing toe rings to my wedding instead of shoes. I'm so clumsy, I'd fall if I tried to walk in high heels like the ones you're wearing. Besides, my dress covers my feet."

"Well, mine don't." Roxie removed her dress completely and pulled off the slip. "I feel downright rebellious." She put the slip into the trash can.

"Granny, you've been rebellious your whole life. You eloped with a bad boy, got married on the side of the road, and then had a reception in the front yard of your shady in-laws' place. Throwing away those torturous undergarments is nothing compared to that," Darla assured her, wishing that she had half of her grandmother's spunk.

Roxie laughed out loud. "I can't believe I'm letting you talk me into this. That girdle is at least forty years old. They don't even make them anymore."

"That's because they made women cranky, and probably

caused hernias and fainting spells and all kinds of other ugly things. I bet they were the first birth control ever invented. By the time a guy got that thing off his woman, he was too tired for sex," Darla told her.

Roxie threw back her head and roared with laughter as she turned around for Darla to zip her up. "My mama and my mother-in-law would have both dropped graveyard dead if they'd heard me say the word *sex*. And, honey, I do feel better with just the bare essentials under my dress, but"—Roxie shook her finger at her youngest granddaughter—"don't try to talk me into wearing those thong things you girls call underpants. There's not enough material in a pair of those to sag a clothesline."

"I promise I won't." Darla's phone pinged, and she pulled it out of her purse and read the text. "Will is here and wondering where I am."

"A woman can't hide anywhere, can she?" Roxie grumbled. "Since these newfangled phones have come into our lives, we can't even go to the bathroom and get away from the menfolk. It's a cryin' shame, but it's the gospel truth."

Darla typed in a quick reply and was starting to slip her phone back into her purse when it pinged again. This time the text was from Andy, her old boyfriend from high school: Be there in ten minutes. Can't wait to see you.

Her breath caught in her chest at the very idea of both guys being in the same place. She was engaged to Will, and their wedding was just two weeks away. Andy had come back to town just last week. He had called her to say that he still loved her and asked if there was a chance they could get back together.

Roxie checked her reflection in the long mirror on the back of the ladies' room door and fluffed up her short gray hair that she'd worn in a kinky 'do for the past forty years. "You're right, Darla. I can't tell whether I'm wearing a girdle and hose or not, so what's the difference? Now we'd best get on back out there to the party. Will has sent two of those text things back-to-back. He's needin' to see his lady."

I wish he'd sent both of them, Darla thought. *Things would be simpler and less stressful if he had.* She wanted to be married to Will. He was kind, funny, and so romantic, but wherever Andy went, there was excitement, and he wanted her to leave Tishomingo and go to Hollywood with him.

A rush of cool air met Will Jackson when he pushed open the door to the fellowship hall that afternoon. The first person he saw was Claud standing over in a corner with a group of his old domino buddies from down at the senior citizens' center. Will stopped at the guest book and signed his name, then scanned the room for Darla. When he didn't see her, he sent a text and got one back that said she would be there in a minute. While he waited, he angled over toward the old guys, who looked different in their khaki slacks and dress shirts. Usually they were wearing bibbed overalls or faded jeans.

"Will!" Claud motioned to him with a flick of his wrist. "Come on over here. We was just makin' plans to do some fishin' this week. You should join us Wednesday night. The women will be off takin' care of weddin' plans."

Will shook his head. "Thanks for the invite, but I've got a full day on Wednesday. Maybe next time. Where's Miz Roxie and Darla?"

"Them women is holed up in the ladies' room, primping I'd guess. They was both lookin' mighty fine when we got here, but that's women for you." Claud poured two cups of punch and handed one to Will. "This would be better with a little shot of vodka in it, but Roxie would have my hide tacked to the smokehouse door if I spiked the punch at a church party."

"Thank you." Will took a sip. "Sixty years? What's your secret?"

"No secret to it. You just keep workin' at it because"—Claud nodded over to a couple of chairs in the back corner and lowered his voice as he headed toward them—"marriage is hard work, and you should know something very important, son. I like you, and I think you and Darla will be good together. But that marriage license is forever and ever, amen, like Randy Travis sings about. Once you buy it and they register it at the courthouse, you can't undo it without a divorce."

Will cocked his head to one side and raised an eyebrow.

"Don't go lookin' at me like that." Claud pursed his lips and adjusted his glasses. "It's the gospel truth. I was raised up out in the sticks in northern Texas, and we had to buy huntin' licenses and fishin' licenses every single year. We didn't have to get a driver's license quite as often, but we did have to renew them, or else we'd get a ticket if the police caught us driving without one. So when I went to the courthouse and got a marriage license, I figured it was good for a year or maybe two."

Will chuckled and sat down in one of the two folding chairs. "How old were you when you and Roxie got married?"

"She was just shy of her seventeenth birthday, but she had finished high school. I had just had my seventeenth birthday, but I quit school before the ninth grade," Claud said. "My mama was a Bible-thumpin' woman, and she didn't believe in divorce. She told all ten of us boys that once we was married, then we weren't living in her house, and that if we ever got a divorce, not to come home. I was more afraid of that woman than I was of bullets, red-haired women, and even the devil hisself."

"What happened?" Will asked.

"Roxie was not an easy woman to live with, especially there at first." Claud sighed. "So, after that first year, I took that marriage license to the Lamar County courthouse in Paris, Texas, and told them I didn't want to renew the damned thing. I'd had enough of married life. That's when they told me that I had to get a divorce if I wanted out of the marriage. There I was, betwixt a rock and a hard place. I didn't want to be married, but I sure didn't want one of them divorces, not when it would cause shame to fall on my mother. So, son, you be sure spending your life with my granddaughter is what you really want before you put your name on that piece of paper."

"I'm sure." Will grinned. "I'm in love with Darla."

Claud's brown eyes grew huge behind his glasses. "You be real sure it's love and not lust. Back in my day, we got married because we weren't supposed to do that lust stuff until after the hitchin' took place. Girls who gave in to boys had a bad reputation, and my mama would never have let one of her boys marry a girl like that. So, it was kind of hard to figure out whether you were feelin' lust or love."

"Yes, sir, I will remember that." Will bit his lip to keep from laughing. He was super relieved when he saw Roxie and Darla coming across the floor and started to stand up. "There's our girls."

"Yep, and they don't look a damn bit different than when they went in that bathroom to primp. You remember what I said. Ain't no use in gettin' up yet. See them women about to huddle around our women? It'll take a while for them to shake loose from them."

Will settled back down in his chair. "What did you do when you found out the marriage license didn't have an expiration date?"

"I went home, gathered up my fishin' gear, and went to the Red River. I stayed there until I got tired of eatin' catfish cooked over an open fire. I decided during those two days that Roxie made good biscuits, and her apple pie was the best in Texas, so maybe I could live with her until death parted us," Claud answered.

"You went home?" Will asked.

The circle of women stepped away, and Roxie and Darla headed toward them.

"Yep, but what happened on the way home is a story for another day." Claud stood up, winked over his shoulder at Will, and draped an arm around Roxie's shoulders. "I see that our other two granddaughters have arrived, and they've brought the little urchin great-grands with them."

"Sure is nice to see the whole family here." Roxie smiled up at him.

"Yep, it is," Claud agreed. "You'd think sixty years was a big thing."

"It is a big thing," Roxie told him, "and I deserve a medal for living with you all these years."

"You deserve a medal? What about me?" Claud's voice went all high and squeaky. "Honey, if it wasn't for your cookin', I might have drowned myself in the Red River years ago."

"Well, damn it." Roxie's blue eyes twinkled. "I would have burned the biscuits that whole first year if I'd known that."

"If I can't cuss in church, then you can't either." Claud guided her through the people toward Marilyn and Sarah, their other granddaughters.

Will thought that Darla was absolutely stunning in her cute little purple dress that barely touched her knees. Her long blonde hair floated down her back like a waterfall, and her clear blue eyes mesmerized him, just like they had from the first day he met her.

"I hope that someday we'll have a sixty-year anniversary party right here in this same place, and that we can still tease each other like your grandparents do," Will whispered. "I love you so much, darlin'."

"Love you too." Darla really did love Will, but…

There are no buts *in real love*, the pesky voice in her head scolded.

Chapter 2

I love Will, Darla protested. He is sweet and romantic and never forgets our special days. He's downright sexy with all that dark hair and green eyes. And more important than all that, he loves me.

As if to prove her thoughts were right, Will hugged her to his side and planted a kiss on her forehead. She looked over his shoulder and saw Andy Miller coming through the door with his grandmother. He could sweet-talk the granny panties right off a holy woman. His blond hair was tied back in a ponytail with a strip of leather, and he wore tight-fitting jeans that stopped at his ankles and a shirt that stretched over his chest like a paint job without a single run. He said he loved her and wanted her to go back to California with him when he left in a week. She wasn't sure that he loved anyone but himself, so why was she drawn to him like a fly to a cow patty?

Claud called out to her from across the room and pointed to the lady taking photos. "We need you to be in the family picture. Bring Will with you. He'll be part of the family by the time Roxie picks out which one she wants to hang above the mantel."

Did Will being in the picture seal the deal on what she should or could do? Would she ever get over the way that Andy made her heart do those crazy quivering things? Will took her hand and led her across the room. Everyone turned to watch the photographer do her work, and Darla felt like she was lying to God right there in the fellowship hall.

Roxie and Claud sat side by side on a fancy high-backed velvet settee with carved wood on the front of the arms. Granny looked like a queen, but something that Kevin, Darla's father, had said once about his dad came to mind.

"You can take the boy out of the cornfield or the wildlife refuge, but you can't ever take the cornfield out of the boy. We could put a four-thousand-dollar suit on Dad, and in five minutes, he would look like he had just walked across a plowed field." Her dad had chuckled when he said it.

"Kevin, you and Gloria stand right behind them," the photographer said. "Marilyn, you and Derrick go beside your mother, and Sarah, you and Bryan stand beside your father."

Once they were in place, the lady said, "Now, Will and Darla will sit on the floor in front of Roxie and Claud. Marilyn's two boys will sit beside Will, then Sarah's girls can take their place by Darla. That's perfect. Pretty girls on one side. Handsome boys on the other."

"Maybe we'll have a baby to hold in our laps for the next family picture," Will whispered and slid a sly wink toward Darla.

Darla wasn't sure she was ready for a baby in only a year. She glanced across the room and locked eyes with Andy, who flashed a brilliant smile. Unless he'd changed drastically over the last seven years, he was way too self-centered to ever want children.

The Marshall girls had always been more alike than just their tall height, their blonde hair and blue eyes. All three of them had been good girls who had been valedictorians of their senior classes in Tishomingo and had graduated from college with honors. *Maybe it's time you broke the mold*, Darla's inner voice whispered, *and did something crazy.*

I could never just walk off and leave my job and my students like that. She almost shook her head, but remembered that she was sitting for pictures. *It would break my daddy's and*

mama's hearts as well as Granny's. I'm a kindergarten teacher.
Boring as that might be, it's who I am.

The photographer took half a dozen pictures and said,
"Now we'll take individual shots of Roxie and Claud, then
of each family, and finally one of Will and Darla. That way
our anniversary couple will have new pictures of all of you."

Roxie would never forgive Darla if she ran away after all
this. When Darla dated Andy in high school, Roxie had told
her repeatedly that he was going to break her heart, and she
had been right.

Darla pasted on her best smile when it was her and Will's
turn to sit on the settee for their pictures and decided that
she had to be up-front and honest with her grandmother
about how she was feeling.

Tomorrow.

She and Granny would talk about it after Sunday dinner
the next day while Gramps had his Sunday afternoon nap.
She was still deep in thought when Will stood up and
extended a hand. Her heart told her that this was the man
she should spend the rest of her life with, but suddenly Andy
was right there, not three feet away from them.

"Hello, Will." Andy stuck out his hand. "I don't think we've
ever met. Darla and I graduated together from good old Tish
High seven years ago. We were quite the item back then."

Will shook hands with him. "She told me that she had dated you when y'all were young. Pleased to finally put a face with the name. Have you moved back to Tishomingo? I'm in the real estate business. If you're in market to buy a place, I could help you out."

That was Darla's Will—always ready to help someone out, even her old flame from the past.

"His grandmother told Granny that he's just here for a visit, so I doubt that he's interested in staying around these parts."

"I'll only be here another week, but it's good to see you, Darla, and meet you, Will." Andy flashed one of those brilliant smiles. "We'll probably run into each other again. Maybe in church tomorrow morning?"

"Probably not," Will said. "I have to be in Mannsville at nine thirty to show a home. I usually don't work on Sunday, but it can't be helped this weekend."

"Will you be there?" Andy locked eyes with Darla.

"Right beside my granny and the rest of the family. She asked that we all line up with her on her pew at church tomorrow as her anniversary gift from us." Darla felt like she was babbling, but she didn't have the power to stop. "We couldn't disappoint her. After all, sixty years is a long time to be married."

"My grandmother sits on the pew behind her, so I guess I'll see you there. Don't know that I could ever stay with one woman for the rest of my life." He did a mock shiver. "There's only one lady I can think of that I could manage to do that with, but she's already off the market. Hey, you want to come to dinner with the two of us and talk about old times after church?" Andy asked.

"Sorry, we're all having a family dinner with Granny and Gramps." Darla could feel the blush starting at her neck and creeping around to her cheeks.

"Maybe another time, then. Be talking to you." Andy turned and walked away.

Darla's heart thumped like a bass drum in her ears. She could have strangled Andy and enjoyed watching his pretty blue eyes pop right out of his head, especially when he came off with that comment about one woman for the rest of his life right in front of Will.

Will tucked her arm into his. "That was a little intense. Do I have anything to be worried about? Do you think he was talking about you being that special woman that he could spend the rest of his life with? Do I need to get out the dueling pistols and tell him to meet me at dawn down by the creek?" he teased and shot another of his playful winks her way.

"Maybe so, but only load yours and be sure you shoot

him dead. It'll save a lot of women some broken hearts."
Darla loved Will's sense of humor and the way they enjoyed
teasing each other.

"So he's that kind of man, is he?" Will grinned.

"No one can change a leopard's spots." She rose up on her
tiptoes and kissed Will on the lips.

"For another kiss like that, I'll call off that appointment
to show a house in Ravia in thirty minutes." He grinned.

"Get on out of here." She gave him a gentle shove. "You've
got to make money so we can make the mortgage payments
on that house we're buying."

"Since the family is in for the weekend, are we still on for
tomorrow night? Movie in Ardmore and maybe ice cream
afterward?" Will asked.

"Of course we are," she said. "I love my older sisters and
my family, but by tomorrow evening, I'll be ready for some
downtime with just the two of us."

"Pick you up at six." He gave her a quick hug and walked
away.

Just as Will disappeared out the door, Andy started
toward Darla. Pretending that she didn't realize he had
zeroed in on her, she turned around and hurried into the
ladies' room. She fell back onto the sofa in the small powder
room and put her palms over her eyes.

"Hey, sis, are you all right?" Sarah startled her when she sat down on the end of the sofa beside her.

"Little bit of a headache," Darla answered. That wasn't a lie. Being in the same room with her fiancé and her old flame was enough to give any woman a headache.

"It's just wedding nerves," Sarah said.

"Did you ever wonder if you were marrying the right person?" Darla asked.

"Sure I did. That's normal." Sarah nodded. "Sometimes, when Bryan makes me mad, I still wonder. No one lives with another person twenty-four seven without having disagreements. Doesn't matter if it's roommates, sisters, or a married couple. That's just life." She patted Darla on the knee. "It's all normal, honey. Don't worry."

"Thanks," Darla said, but she couldn't even force a smile.

———————

The church pew was long but still cramped with thirteen people lined up on it, shoulder to shoulder and hip to hip. Darla was sitting on the end and hardly heard a word the preacher said that morning, not with Andy Miller sitting right behind her. The weather had gotten hot—Indian summer, the old folks called it—but the sweat rolling down Darla's neck and into her bra had nothing to do with the temperature outside.

"Sometimes, we just need to pray about our decisions." The preacher's words finally caught her attention. "The devil will test us, just like he did Jesus."

"Amen," Darla whispered under her breath.

"Amen!" Claud said loud enough that the whole church echoed his amen.

"But God will lead and guide you along the right path if you just ask for His help," the preacher said. "Now, in light of the fact that Roxie and Claud Marshall are celebrating their sixtieth wedding anniversary this weekend, and their fifty-ninth year living in Tishomingo and attending church right here, I'll ask Claud to deliver the benediction."

"Sweet Jesus!" Roxie gasped and leaned over toward Darla. "He's never prayed in church before."

Claud stood up and bowed his head. "Thank you, God, for giving me the strength to live with Roxie all these years, and for helping her to live with me. I'm grateful that she's a good cook and a fine-lookin' woman. We've got to get on home now because the pot roast will burn if we don't, so I'll make this short. See you next Sunday if not before. Amen."

Darla nudged her grandmother on the shoulder. "Not bad for the first time."

"'Strength to live with me,' my hind end," Roxie grumbled

as the whole congregation stood up and started moving toward the door. "I could tell you a thing or two."

"After dinner, and when everyone goes home, I'll meet you on the back porch. I'll bring the sweet tea. I need to talk to you," Darla whispered.

"I'll be there soon as he starts to snore." Roxie cupped her hand over Darla's ear and whispered, "He eavesdrops, and, honey, he learns more gossip at those domino games he plays than I do at a dozen Prayer Angel sessions."

"It's not nice to tell secrets in church," Sarah said.

"It's not a secret if you already know what I'm telling your sister." Roxie grinned. "The pot roast won't be worth eating if we don't take it out of the oven pretty soon."

"We'll slip on out," Gloria said, "and get things started for Sunday dinner. Kevin and I are hoping to get back to Denison before too late. I've got to meet at four with the caterer for the wedding." She blew them a kiss, grabbed her husband by the hand, and pulled him toward the side door.

"I'd rather be going with her," Roxie said, "but it would be rude not to shake the preacher's hand since he was so nice to mention us by name. Where's Claud?"

Darla pointed. "Over there with his cronies. The way they've got their heads together, I'd guess that the domino table isn't their only place to gossip."

Roxie marched across the aisle and looped her arm in Claud's. "Unless you want to eat a burnt Sunday dinner, we've got to get going."

"The old ball and chain still holds on tight, even after sixty years," Claud said, chuckling.

"If you want to get rid of that ball and chain, you know where the door is," Roxie said. "Don't let it hit you in the hip pockets."

"She's still full of sass after all these years." Claud laughed and patted Roxie's hand. "See you boys tomorrow morning."

The drive from church to the house took five minutes and would have been less if Darla hadn't had to stop at two of the three traffic lights on Main Street. Her car hadn't even had time to cool down when she parked beside her grandfather's pickup truck. She was on her way from the circular drive to the house when her phone rang, so she sat down on the porch steps and dug around in her purse until she found it. She took a deep breath and let it out slowly before she answered it.

"Hello, Andy," she said.

"Hello, gorgeous," he responded. "My schedule has been changed slightly. I'll be leaving for California a day early, darlin', so you've only got six days to get your things packed. I didn't hear a word that preacher said this morning. All I could think about was how much the camera is going to love you when we get to Hollywood."

"I'm not going with you. I'm getting married in thirteen days." Darla's heart was beating so loud that she could hardly hear anything else.

"You're just punishing me for leaving you behind when we graduated. I deserve it and respect you for it, but, honey, we both know that you're going to leave Tishomingo in the rearview mirror with me, so admit it." Andy lowered his voice to a seductive level. "You weren't made for a life of boredom. You were made for better things, like stardom. With your looks and my connections, you'll be the main attraction in films in no time."

"I have a good job. I'm marrying an awesome man, and..." she stammered.

"And all of it is boooooring." Andrew drew out the last word into several syllables.

"That's a matter of opinion," she argued. "What happens when you get tired of me again?"

"Nothing lasts forever"—Andy chuckled—"but I can guarantee you an amazing, exciting life while we're together. Whether it lasts or not will be up to you."

Sarah poked her head out the door and said, "Hey, sister, we've almost got dinner on the table. Tell Will that Gramps gets grumpy if anyone holds up Sunday dinner."

Darla held up one finger and nodded.

"If you go with me, we'll still be asleep at this time on Sunday." Andy's deep voice was darn near irresistible. "We'll party until dawn when we finish up scenes in our movie, sleep until the middle of the afternoon, wake up, and make wild, passionate love. Life is never dull and boring in my world."

"My answer is still no. I couldn't trust you seven years ago, and you haven't changed a bit, so why should I trust you now?" she asked.

"You shouldn't"—Andy's laugh was brittle—"but, honey, you can believe me when I say that we'll have such a good time together you won't even remember how to pronounce *Tishomingo*."

"Goodbye, Andy." Darla stood up and started across the porch.

"I'm not giving up until the last minute," he said just before she ended the call.

She tossed her purse and phone onto one of the two ladder-back chairs in the foyer and headed straight for the dining room. Claud was already at the head of the table, so she stopped long enough to kiss him on the top of his bald head. "Everything sure smells good. I'm starving."

"Well, scoot on out there and help them women get dinner on the table," he said.

Darla started that way, but then turned around and asked, "Where's Daddy?"

"Helping Sarah's younger daughter get washed up." Claud shooed her away with a flick of his wrist. "I want to get out of these dress britches and this shirt before they chafe me raw, and into my old soft overalls. Roxie puts too much starch in my Sunday shirts, and they make me itch like I've been wallowing in fire ants."

"Why don't you change before dinner?" Darla asked.

"Because I wasn't raised that way. Mama believed in that hymn that said we ought to give of our best to the Master. That meant we had to stay in our Sunday best until after we ate dinner."

Darla stopped. "Did you go to church every Sunday?"

"Yep." Claud nodded. "Mama insisted on that, even if Daddy didn't make it. When he did, he was one of the back-seat fellers who snuck in at the last minute with whiskey still on his breath from the night before and was out of there before the preacher made it to the back of the church to shake folks' hands. All ten of us boys lined up on the front pew with Mama, no matter if we had whiskey on our breath or not."

Kevin arrived in the dining room with Sarah's girls in tow, made sure they were sitting in the right places, and then focused on Darla. "Are you coming down to Denison this afternoon with your mother to talk to the caterer about the wedding?"

Darla shook her head. "Will and I have a movie date tonight. I told Mama what I wanted served, and she said she could handle it without me being there."

"I'll still give you enough to make a hefty payment on your house if you'll elope. We can cancel the flower order as well as the caterer," Kevin offered. "This is your last chance, so why don't you take my check and go to a warm beach somewhere for fall break? Drink them fancy things with umbrellas in them, and work on your tan."

"Mama would shoot me and you both," Darla said. "She's worked too hard on this wedding."

Are you really going to go through with the wedding when you really want to leave with Andy? that pesky voice in her head asked.

"I'm not going anywhere, so leave me alone," she whispered as she whipped around and headed to the noisy kitchen.

Then why are you having doubts? the voice persisted.

"Wedding jitters," she said.

Roxie heard and draped an arm around Darla's shoulders. "We all had them, sweetie," she said.

Chapter 3

DARLA CARRIED TWO GLASSES OF SWEET TEA OUT TO THE screened-in back porch that afternoon. She set them down on a table between two of the four rocking chairs out there, and then took a deep breath. "Football weather," she muttered.

A brisk wind brought down the scarlet, yellow, and orange-colored leaves from the old sugar maple tree in the backyard. She loved this time of year and had chosen the colors in the fall leaves for her wedding. Clouds shifted over the sun and lowered the temperature by a few degrees, finally making it pleasant enough to sit outside that evening.

"Whew!" Roxie said as she slumped down in one of the rocking chairs. She picked up her glass and took a long drink. "Any other Sunday, he would be snoring like an elephant in a matter of minutes, but today it seemed like it took forever for him to go to sleep."

"Can't Gramps go to sleep without you beside him?" Darla asked.

"Not on Sunday afternoon. After the first year when we…" Roxie smiled.

"When you did what, Granny?" Darla asked.

"We didn't do so well that first year. If my mama would have let me, I would have gone home and left him up there in Powderly around his folks. All we did was argue. We couldn't agree on a blessed thing. Then one day while I was visiting my folks, he went into town. I got tired of waiting on him to come and take me home, so Mama drove me back up to my house, and I fumed for an hour or more until he came in," Roxie explained.

"Where had he been?" Darla asked.

"I didn't know at the time, and I damn sure didn't care. He came in madder 'n a wet hen after a thunderstorm, tossed our marriage license on the kitchen table, and gathered up his fishing equipment. Without saying a word to me, he left the house. It was a good thing that it was Friday and he didn't have to work that day or the whole weekend," Roxie said.

"Weren't you worried about him?" Darla could hardly believe what she was hearing. Granny was as protective of

Gramps as an old bear with her cubs. Back five years ago, when he had had colon cancer, she had nearly worried herself into an early grave.

"Not in those days. I hoped he would fall in the Red River and drown. If I'd had the chance, I might have even tied rocks to his feet to help him out a little," Roxie said. "I figured whatever had set him off had something to do with the marriage license, so I called my aunt Tildy, who worked at the courthouse in Paris. She told me what had happened that day."

Roxie giggled, but it came out more like a snort. "Those Marshalls were good people, but some of them didn't understand how things were. Seems Claud got it in his head that if you had to renew a fishing license, a driver's license, and a hunting license, then, after a year or maybe two, you'd need to renew a marriage license. He had gone to the courthouse that day to tell them he didn't want to renew the damned thing and wanted them to throw it in the trash."

Darla had just taken a sip of tea, and she spewed it right through the screen. "Is this a joke?" she finally asked when she could stop laughing.

"It's the God's honest truth"—Roxie held up her hand toward heaven—"and I ain't never told nobody this story before now. It would embarrass him too much, and after that first year, I finally learned to love the old fart. He stayed gone all that weekend and didn't come home until Sunday night. I had my suitcase packed and had already called my sister, your great-aunt Linda Jo, to come get me.

"Mama said that when I eloped with Claud, I'd made my bed, and no matter how hard it was, I would have to sleep in it. That meant I couldn't go back home, no matter what, but Linda Jo knew all my secrets and how Claud and I couldn't get along. She said I could come stay with her anytime I needed to, but I'd have to wait until she got off work from her waitress job at Miss Lou's Café that Sunday night before she could drive up to Powderly to get me."

"What happened then?" Darla was on the edge of her seat.

"Well, it just so happened that one of Claud's buddies had parked his pickup on Main Street there right next to the furniture store. The old guy was selling bushels of peaches off the back of his truck, and the furniture store was open on Sunday because a truckload of television sets was being delivered. Your grandpa stopped with intentions of buying a bushel of peaches to bring home for me to can, but then he got to looking at that television set the furniture store owner had put in the window, and *Gunsmoke* was showing on it. Claud bypassed the peaches and brought home one of those television sets," Roxie said.

"You mean y'all didn't have one before then? When was this?" Darla asked.

"I'm gettin' to it," Roxie scolded. "You got to understand the whole story to know how me and Claud saved our marriage."

"I just can't believe you and Gramps ever had that much trouble," Darla said.

"There's no such thing as a perfect marriage. You got to work together to get one that's even passable, and you've got to want to make it work. During those days, I didn't care if it worked or not," Roxie told her. "But to go on with the story, here he come, bringing in a television. His mama was hardcore religious and called those things 'an abomination unto the Lord,' and she already didn't like me.

"My mama wasn't quite as bad, but there was no way she'd allow one in her house either. No, ma'am! She said that they were nothing but time-sucking machines and would be the ruination of the world, and folks had better things to do with their days, like shelling peas or crocheting doilies, than sit around in front of an idiot box and be entertained all day. I met Claud at the door and told him he couldn't bring that thing in *my* house."

"Oh my!" Darla did the math in her head. "This was in 1961, right?"

Roxie nodded. "That's right, darlin', and we had us a big argument. I told him either it went or I would go. He said he wouldn't miss me a whole lot, and that since I already had a suitcase by the front door, to just go ahead and leave. That made me so mad that I called Linda Jo and told her I was staying with Claud just to teach him that he couldn't tell me what to do."

"Now I understand why he said you'd always been sassy," Darla said.

"I had a temper to go with my red hair." Roxie grinned. "I mellowed a little when it all turned gray."

"I guess you kept the television, right?" Darla asked.

"Oh, yes, and his mother wouldn't even set foot inside our house. I guess she was afraid the devil would jump out of that thing and take her straight to hell. My mother made excuses not to come see me, and I blamed that on the television, but I reckon it was because she didn't like Claud any more than she did the television. Anyway, I've never admitted it to anyone, but it was the best thing that ever happened, because we had to depend on each other, and neither of us could go runnin' home to tattle on the other one.

"I hated that damned TV. Every evening after supper, your grandfather would turn it on to watch the news and whatever gun-totin' western was on: *Bonanza, Have Gun—Will*

Travel, Gunsmoke. I would take a book to the bedroom and read." Roxie went on with the story. "I worried that he'd sit in front of the television all day on the weekend and might not even go to the church on Sunday. His mama would probably drown me in the Red River if we didn't show up for church, so I sent up a prayer that the programs were only on in the evening."

Darla was still having trouble understanding what all this had to do with her grandmother lying down for a nap every Sunday with her grandfather, but she kept quiet and let the whole story unfold.

"That's when I found *As the World Turns*, my first soap opera. I watched that story right up until it went off about ten years ago. When I figured out that there were shows for us womenfolk in the daytime, I scheduled all my housework around them. I ironed many of your grandfather's clothes while I watched *The Edge of Night* and got my dusting done while I drooled over *Young Doctor Malone*. Those shows are what saved my marriage, for sure," Roxie said. "I saved money so that when a color television came out, we could get one, and I didn't give a rat's hind end what my mother or his mama thought of it."

"How did a soap opera save your marriage?" Darla asked.

"The people on those shows had worse troubles than

I did, for sure. When I measured my problems up against theirs, things didn't look so bad. The next year when we moved to Oklahoma so your grandfather could take the job at the wildlife refuge, I told him if he broke the television, I would break his legs and arms while he slept. He told me if I even scratched it, he would make me sleep in a tent out in the yard. It was during that move that one of the characters on the soap opera was having a hard time in her marriage, and her grandmother told her that every Sunday afternoon she and her husband should take a nap together."

Aha! Darla thought.

Roxie took another sip of tea. "The next Sunday, we had our first nap together. Nine months later, we had Kevin, and things began to look up from that point on. We had a baby to raise, and I began to fall in real love with your grandfather after that."

"Oh, *that* kind of nap." Darla smiled.

"Was in those days. Not so much since he had cancer." Roxie held up her glass. "To Sunday afternoon naps. You and Will should always make time for one right from the first week of your marriage. Now, what's got you all in a tizzy about your wedding? Oh, before you tell me, I saw Andy Miller at the party on Saturday. His mama, bless her heart"—Roxie dragged out the southernism and rolled her eyes toward the ceiling—"spoiled that boy so rotten that the garbageman wouldn't have even hauled him off if they'd tossed him in the trash. Then she up and died when Andy was only ten years old, and his grandmother took over the boy's raisin' and made him even worse."

Darla took a long breath and let it out slowly. "Granny, do you remember that he was my boyfriend in high school?"

"Yes, I do, and I was damn sure glad to see him leave Tishomingo." Roxie nodded. "Not that I ever thought he'd make a movie star like he thought he would, and he hasn't. Honey, I didn't care if he went out there to California and picked plums for a living, long as he didn't take you with him. He's as worthless as tits on a boar hog."

"Oh, really?" Darla giggled at the expression.

"From what I hear, what he stars in is them movies that decent people don't watch or even mention out loud." Roxie clucked her tongue like an old hen. "Them porn things that folks do naked."

"Good Lord, Granny, who told you that?" Darla blushed and wondered if that was the kind of movie roles Andy had in mind for her.

"Don't matter who told me, but it came from a good source, from someone that caught her daughter watchin' that stuff on the internet. I swear, if folks thought television and soap operas were bad, they didn't even know the half of it," Roxie answered. "Now what was your problem with these wedding jitters? You don't need to worry about a thing. Your mama might be a little rusty. It's been eight years since she planned Sarah's special day, but she'll come through, and it will be beautiful."

"It's Andy, not Mama," Darla admitted.

Roxie's gray eyebrows drew down to make a single line. "What's that worthless boy got to do with anything?"

"Granny, I loved him so much, and he broke my heart when he left without even saying goodbye or leaving me a note. I looked for a letter from him every day for a whole month. Then he comes back to Tish right before my wedding and wants me to run away with him to California," Darla said.

"Holy smokin' hell!" Roxie slammed her left fist into her right palm. "Don't let Claud know what he's done, or your gramps will be watching your wedding on his cell phone from a jail cell. And, honey, you know how frustrated he gets when he can't get things to work on his phone. You didn't even consider it, did you? Please tell me you didn't."

"No. Well, yes…but not for long… But, Granny, even just longing for a life of excitement…that's not fair to Will, is it?" Darla stammered. "Don't I need to come clean with him?"

"Not just no but *hell no*, my child." Roxie's voice went up several octaves. "I was hoping you'd get past the bridal test, but I guess you didn't."

"What's the bridal test?" Darla dug around in her pocket until she found a rubber band and pulled her hair up into a ponytail.

"I thought I heard you women gossiping out here." Claud yawned as he dragged a third rocker over beside Roxie. "Did you have a good nap?"

"Always," she said. "You usually sleep longer than this."

"I was dreaming about fishing, and that made me hungry for apple pie. Every time I have that dream, I wake up craving apple pie. Where did you hide that last piece that was left over from dinner?" Claud asked.

"It's in the refrigerator," Roxie answered.

"I've got lesson plans to finish for next week, and Will and I are going to the movies later, so I should be getting on back to my apartment," Darla said, even though she really wanted to stay and talk to her grandmother some more. If Gramps got wind of what was happening with Andy, he would either have a heart attack or load his shotgun.

"You should have been stayin' with us these past two years," Claud grumbled. "Just think of how much money you could have saved up if you'd come to live with us when your folks moved to Denison. Why, you could have bought a washer and dryer and a big-screen television. I still don't know how you've managed to live two whole years without a TV in your apartment."

Darla stood up, then bent down and gave her grandmother a hug. "Gramps, watching shows is a whole lot more fun when you and Granny and I see them together."

"Well, you can't come draggin' Will over here every time you want to watch *Family Feud*," Claud told her.

"I expect they'll have better things to do than spend time in front of a television set when they get married." Roxie smiled.

"Yeah," Claud agreed. "But without a television, how are they going to work out all their differences? Honey, you don't know another person until you live with them. I think there should be a live-together license that's only good for one year. You would pay your ten bucks for it, then tear it up and move out if things don't work out. Seems to me like it would be money well spent."

"Why do that?" Roxie asked. "Kids today do that without spending ten dollars on a piece of paper. The rules we lived by back in our day have been replaced, and they can watch anything we do on their tablets and phones."

"Our rules were just fine," Claud muttered. "I'm going to get that last piece of pie."

"Granny, I'll pick you up on Wednesday right after school. Sarah and Marilyn are driving up from Texas so we can all get a final fitting for our dresses," Darla said, wondering the whole time if Will would even want to go through with the wedding if he found out she was having second thoughts. "Gramps, do you want to go with us? I'm springing for hamburgers and milkshakes afterward."

Claud turned around at the door. "Honey, I wouldn't sit through that hen fest for a dozen hamburgers. Me and Ben Rogers is going fishin' out at the refuge that afternoon. I asked Will to go with us, but he's got too much work to do. Ben's wife is packing bologna sandwiches for us, and I'm bringin' the beer, so Will is missin' out on a good time. I hope Will slows down after y'all are married so you can at least see him once in a while."

"Well, y'all have fun. See you later." Darla waved as she left.

She lived about six blocks from her grandparents' place in an apartment complex just south of Murray State College, the community college she had attended before she transferred to OU and finished her education. She parked her car, sucked in the fresh evening air as she slid out from behind the wheel, and walked up the stairs to her little one-bedroom place. The scent of something cinnamon met her when she opened the door and put a smile on her face. She glanced over the rail and saw Will's truck down there in the visitors' parking lot.

"Do I have a burglar in my house?" she called out.

"Yes, you do, sweetheart, and he's stalking you." Will took her purse from her, set it on the dining room table, and led her to the sofa. "Sit down right here. I've got your favorite coffee made, and the snickerdoodles will be out of the oven in two minutes. I've missed you today." He kissed her—long, lingering, and passionate.

The timer dinged in the kitchen, and he stopped the short make-out session to hurry across the living room. Darla slumped down on the sofa and scolded herself for ever even thinking of walking away from a man like Will Jackson. He was always full of surprises, and life would never be dull with him.

But will it be as exciting as it would be with Andy? the devil's advocate in her head asked.

Will returned with a tray holding two mugs of coffee and a plate of fresh snickerdoodles and set them on the coffee table. "Are we okay, Darla?"

She reached for a cookie and held her breath. What had he heard? Did he know what Andy wanted her to do? "Why would you ask that? Do you think we're not okay?"

"You've seemed so distracted this past week. Mama says

that it's completely normal. Please tell me you aren't getting cold feet. We can elope tomorrow if you don't want to go through with all the big stuff." He took her face in his hands and looked deeply into her blue eyes. "I love you so much that it hurts me to see you worrying."

"I love you," Darla whispered and meant it from the depths of her heart. She was speaking the absolute truth.

"Then what's the problem?" Will dropped his hands and picked up his coffee. He took a sip and then reached for a cookie. "I didn't make these from scratch. I bought the dough from one of those kids who came by selling stuff for a school fundraiser."

Honest. Kindhearted. That was her Will.

"They're delicious"—Darla smiled up at him—"and it was so sweet of you to make them for me."

"I would do anything for you, Darla Marshall. Cookies. Coffee. Hugs. Shoulders to cry on. Anything you want or need," Will said.

"Would you curl up with me on this sofa and take a short Sunday afternoon nap?" she asked. "What I need right now is to feel your arms around me until it's time to go to the movies."

"I would love to, darlin'," he said with a smile.

Chapter 4

WEDNESDAY WAS ONE OF THOSE DAYS THAT SEEMED LIKE a Monday. Each second lasted an hour. At eleven o'clock, when it was time for Darla's kindergarten class to go to the lunchroom, she felt like the day had been a week long. The kids were rowdy during their twenty minutes in the cafeteria and couldn't wait to get outside to run off some energy. But as luck would have it, a thunderstorm blew up just as the bell was ringing for them to go to the playground, and they had to go back to the classroom.

When she returned, with the kids grumbling the whole way, there was a huge bouquet of yellow daisies on her desk. She opened the card with trembling hands, expecting the usual love note from Will, since he sent her flowers at least once a month.

She opened the envelope and read: *See you on Friday. Looking forward to good times and seeing your face on the screen.*

She dropped the note, and it fluttered right into the trash can at the end of her desk. "You kids may gather around the puzzle station and see how fast you can put together the one of the United States. I'll be back in just a couple of minutes." She picked up the flowers, stomped down the hallway to the janitor's closet, and tossed them into the trash can. She fumed all the way back to her classroom, alternately cussing herself, for even talking to Andy, and then him, for being so brazen as to think he could waltz back into her life and make her a porn star.

She plopped down in her desk chair and stared out the window.

"Miz Darla, are you okay?" Macy, the tiniest little girl in her class, was suddenly beside her, patting her on the arm.

"I'm fine, sweetheart," Darla answered.

"What happened to your pretty flowers?" Macy asked.

"I shared them with other people." That wasn't a lie since she did share them with the garbage collector.

"I'm sad," Macy said.

Darla draped her arm around Macy's shoulders. "About what, darlin'?"

"My sister is going to run away from home, and I'm going

to miss her, and she said I can't tell Mama because it's our little secret." Macy's lower lip began to quiver.

"Mindy is going to college, isn't she?" Darla asked.

Macy nodded so hard that her little dark braids flipped over her shoulders. "I love my Mindy, and she said she will always love me, but she's in love with a boy named Andy, and she don't want me to tell Mama—" Macy stopped for a breath and then went on. "And she's leaving Friday with that boy, and I don't even know who he is, but I don't like him a'cause he is takin' Mindy all the way to Afornia."

Darla felt like she needed a long hot shower. Damn that Andy Miller for making her doubt her commitment to Will! Maybe she should tell Mindy's father. Bobby wouldn't even think about fancy pistols if he knew what was going on.

You can't do that without it causing so much gossip and rumors in the little town of Tishomingo that Will hear about it, she thought, seething.

"Maybe she won't go when it comes right down to it." Darla managed to keep the anger out of her voice as she hugged Macy tightly. "Sometimes a girl will change her mind."

"I don't want her to go away." Macy's little chin quivered. "It would make me and Mama sad, but Mindy said that Daddy would shoot him if I told anyone. And then our daddy would go to jail."

"Well, then we won't tell, will we?" Darla had heard about Bobby Tisdale's overprotectiveness toward his seven daughters and had no doubt that Macy was telling the absolute truth.

Macy gave Darla a hug and then ran back to the table where the kids were putting together the puzzle. Darla hated for Andy to ruin Mindy's life, but she couldn't figure out how to go about talking to her. Five minutes before the final bell rang, the clouds parted, the sun came out brightly, and the storm was over, but the turmoil in Darla's heart was still boiling hot and furious.

"I wish the guilt I feel over ever even thinking about leaving Will could be gone like that," Darla muttered as she gathered up her tote bag and purse and took her children outside to wait on their parents or the bus monitors to pick them up.

Like always, everything was a madhouse for about five minutes, and then, when the last child had been picked up, Darla was free to leave. She made a beeline for her car and drove straight to her grandmother's house to find Roxie waiting on the porch. She had her big black purse thrown over her arm and was wearing a pair of jeans and a cute little orange sweater set. She waved and made her way down the sidewalk, got into the car, and fastened her seat belt.

"Thank God it stopped raining, or we would have had to

take Claud with us. He's such an old bear in a clothing store, but now that it's stopped, he's convinced that the fish will be biting," Roxie said. "And I've got gossip to share with you. Mindy Tisdale was seen with Andy Miller a couple of nights ago."

"He sent me flowers today," Darla blurted out. "I threw them in the trash. He's been calling and texting and begging me to go with him to California on Friday. I guess he's planning on taking a harem with him, not just one woman."

"Sweet angels in heaven!" Roxie gasped. "Somebody ought to tell Bobby Tisdale. If he finds out Mindy has been conned into going with that rascal, he'll travel all the way out there, and Andy's pretty face won't be fit for them porn films no more."

"Maybe someone ought to leak the news to him." Darla headed west out of town. "Mindy would be mad for a little while, but then she'd get over it."

Roxie fished around in her purse, laying aside a small bag of potato chips, a package of cheese crackers, and two candy bars before she finally brought out her phone. "I'll fix this with one phone call." She tapped the front of her cell phone and smiled sweetly when one of her friends answered. "Hello, Mabel. Did y'all get any rain out east of town?" she asked and then hit Speakerphone.

"Lord, yes. I thought for sure it was going to flood the chicken house," Mabel said. "Did you hear that rumor about Mindy Tisdale and Andy Miller? I heard she was going to California with him and two other women to star in them ugly movies."

"Oh, really?" Roxie acted surprised but winked at Darla. "Who's the other women?"

"One of them is Candace Anderson, but I can't figure out who the other one is," Mabel answered. "But I heard he's run up a flower bill, sending them all three flowers. I bet his poor grandmother is giving him money, God love her soul." Mabel sighed. "She's gettin' senile, so she don't know what's going on part of the time. I just hope that rotten Andy don't get her to sign over her property to him."

Darla's phone pinged, so she pulled over to the side of the road just outside of Ravia and checked to see if maybe Sarah and Marilyn were running late.

The message read: Did you like the flowers?

No, I did not, and please leave me alone. You are one sick bastard, she wrote back, and then eased back out onto the road.

The next ping said: You know you love me, and I love the sass in you. See you Friday.

Roxie tossed her phone back into her purse. "It's done.

Mabel is going to call Betsy. She'll tell her sister, Mary Lou, and Mary Lou is a cousin to Arlene Tisdale. Before bedtime, Bobby will know what's going on, and no one will be able to figure out exactly where the idea started. If that sorry sucker knows what's good for him, he'll hightail it out of Tishomingo before midnight."

"You are amazing, Granny," Darla said.

"Thank you, but I like to think of it as my duty to womankind to save Mindy, just like I saved you seven years ago," Roxie said.

"How did you do that?" Darla frowned.

"I prayed real hard and told God that Andy was going to ruin your life, and I asked Him to make Andy disappear. I told Him I didn't care if it was permanent or if Andy would just leave the state. What I forgot to ask for was that he would never set foot in Oklahoma again. That was my mistake. I hope Bobby remembers to fix that problem when he takes care of it this time. If he needs a little help, Claud keeps two sharp shovels out in the garage, and I'll be glad to help him dig a hole in the ground," Roxie replied.

"Granny!" Darla exclaimed.

Roxie pointed a finger at her. "You know that God does things in His own time and in His own way, right?" She didn't give Darla time to answer, but went right on. "Well,

I prayed for a whole year that you would break up with that kid. I ain't got that kind of time to wait for God this time. I have to save Mindy in two days, so"—she looked upward—"pardon me, Lord. It's not that I don't have faith; it's just that you're mighty busy right now, so I'll use the gossip vine to get the job done."

Darla giggled out loud. "I want to grow up and be just like you."

"You might just do that since I kept you so much when you were little so your mama wouldn't have to hire a sitter," Roxie said. "But be careful what you wish for, honey. You just might get it and then not be able to get rid of it."

"I don't think I'd ever want to get rid of anything that's like you," Darla declared.

They rode along in a comfortable silence until they reached the bridal shop. Darla found a parking spot close to the front of the store and didn't even realize that she had pulled in behind Marilyn's SUV until her sisters got out of it.

"Perfect timing," Sarah called out as she opened the door for Roxie. "We got here about one minute before you did. Y'all ready to go try on pretty dresses?"

"I just hope mine will fit. I threw my girdle and my pantyhose away last Saturday at the anniversary party," Roxie answered.

"Good God, Granny!" Sarah exclaimed. "As thin as you are, why in the hell were you wearing a girdle to begin with?"

"Exactly what I told her." Darla tucked her keys into the side pocket of her purse and followed the other three women into the bridal shop. "I thought Mama might come with y'all."

"She's pulling a double shift at the hospital, and she's already got her dress ready. She bought it in Denison, and it fit perfectly, so it didn't need alterations," Marilyn said.

"Of course it didn't," Darla said. "Mama doesn't gain an ounce or an inch, no matter what she eats. She could probably still wear her wedding dress."

The lady in charge showed them back to a huge dressing room with comfortable wingback chairs, fancy tables, and even an arrangement of chocolate-covered strawberries on a crystal plate. "We have chilled champagne for you ladies to go with the strawberries. My name is Alison, and I'll be helping with your fittings," she said as she poured four flutes full of the bubbly liquid. "Your dresses are hanging right here." She pointed to a rack. "If you'll put them on, we'll see what further alterations might need to be made. I'll give you a few minutes and then I'll be back."

"Well, well, if this ain't uptown." Roxie grinned.

Darla slipped out of her dress slacks and sweater and

removed her white lace wedding gown from the rack. "While we're getting dressed, I want someone to tell me what the bridal test is."

"She got hit by it, girls." Roxie picked up a glass of champagne and took a sip. "This is some good stuff, but getting back to the bridal test, Darla and I didn't have time to talk about it Sunday. Your grandfather didn't take a long enough nap."

"I was hoping you wouldn't have to go through that." Sarah sighed.

"Me too," Marilyn added. "Granny, you go first. Tell us about your test."

"You got it too, Granny?" Darla's eyes widened. "What is this dread thing?"

"It's when an old boyfriend comes back into your life to test you," Roxie said. "In my case it was Jack Sanford. I'd been sweet on him from the time I was fifteen, and we'd even had a few kisses back behind the smokehouse when he and his mama came to visit us on Sunday afternoons. Then he broke my heart when he asked another girl to be his date for the senior dance. He told me that was just to make me jealous, but it made me mad as hell. After that, I started dating Claud, even though my folks thought he wasn't good enough for me, and we eloped that summer."

"Jack came back and wanted you to leave Gramps?" Darla stepped into the dress and pulled it up.

"With romance like I'd never seen before then. He brought me wildflower bouquets and asked me to have a picnic with him on the Red River." Roxie removed her clothes and put on a dark-green dress that reached the floor. "He even asked me to marry him. He begged me to break it off with Claud. He said that we could get an apartment in the married-student housing at the college in Paris, and both of us could get our educations. He made a good argument, and my folks liked him, so I thought about it."

"But you didn't, or you wouldn't be married to Gramps," Darla said.

"Every time I looked at him, I remembered how I felt after he'd kissed me and then turned around and invited that other girl to the dance. I think I married Claud to show him there were other fish in the sea." Roxie turned around for Sarah to zip her dress. "Look at this. No girdle, and it fits like a charm."

"I told you so," Darla said. "Did you have a bridal test, Marilyn?"

"Oh, yes. I fell in love during my freshman year of college, and he broke up with me before the year ended. A month before I got married, he showed back up, and like Granny's feller, he told me what a mistake he'd made. Long story short, his mama hadn't thought I was good enough for him since his family was very wealthy." Marilyn looked at herself in the floor-length mirror. "But between then and the time I was about to marry Derrick, his family went bankrupt. I guess this little country girl from Tishomingo wasn't such a bad match by then."

"And you, Sarah? Don't tell me it was Mitch Fowler." Darla held her arms out. "The sleeves need to be tightened up a little, don't y'all think?"

"Yes, it was Mitch, and yes on the sleeves. Now who has come back to test you?" Sarah answered.

"Andy Miller," Darla answered and went on to tell them the rest of the story. "Do I tell Will? He deserves to know that, just for a minute, I did have second thoughts. He should know, don't you think?"

"Hell no!" Roxie and Darla's sisters all chorused together.

"But married couples aren't supposed to ever have secrets," Darla argued.

Sarah took a couple of steps forward to stand on one side of Darla. Marilyn did the same on the other side. Dressed alike, with their blonde hair cut in the same style, they looked like twins in their orange, yellow, and burgundy floral dresses.

"Well?" Darla asked.

"You are the prettiest bride that Tishomingo will ever see," Sarah said.

Darla stared at her reflection. The wedding dress was exactly what she'd dreamed about her whole life. Beaded white lace with a sweetheart neckline and long fitted sleeves with buttons from her wrist to her elbow.

"Secrets?" Darla was beginning to get worried.

Roxie joined them and peered into the mirror at the group. "Honey, think about what I told you about your gramps and the marriage license. He has no idea that I know that."

"But this is different. It has caused me to doubt my commitment to Will," Darla argued. "Did any of you ever tell your husbands about the bridal test?"

She watched in the mirror as three heads shook back and forth.

Sarah took a step back. "If there was a *How to Pass Tests Book for Brides*, the last chapter, just before the part about walking slow down the aisle, would deal with this kind of thing."

Marilyn hugged Darla. "If there was such a book, it would definitely deal with all the emotions you are feeling right now, and it would tell you to never tell anyone, especially not the love of your life."

Darla turned away from the mirror. "Do you think he's had doubts?"

"Of course he has," Roxie answered. "It's not the doubts that matter. It's whether you let them lead you down the path of destruction and unhappiness, or you listen to your heart and common sense, and someday have a sixtieth anniversary party."

"Do you still love Andy?" Sarah asked.

Darla shrugged. "He's a bastard, but there will always be a special place in my heart for him. He was my first love."

"Are you *in* love with Andy?" Marilyn asked.

"What's the difference between loving and being in love?" Darla asked.

"Simply put, it's like this," Roxie said. "Love is pretty much just lust. *In love* goes deeper and has lust attached to it, but it also has companionship and caring about each other that goes over and above that fifteen minutes in the bedroom."

"Good Lord, Granny, make it half an hour anyway!" Marilyn laughed.

"I'm not *in love* with Andy. I'm *in love* with Will." Darla giggled with her sister.

"Then you have your answer right there," Sarah said.

Darla picked up her veil and handed it to Marilyn. "But not about the honesty stuff."

"You just said you are in love with Will," Roxie said. "Would you break his heart or cause him to worry anytime you got a phone call?"

Marilyn adjusted the veil and then turned Darla back around to face the mirror. "Of course you wouldn't. Are you going to tell him what us girls talk about on our sisters' nights out once a month? Think before you answer. You've heard me and Sarah bitch about husbands lots of times. When we grumble about Derrick or Bryan squeezing the toothpaste from the middle of the tube or not putting toilet paper on the roll the right way, are you going to go home and tell Will what we said?"

"Of course not," Darla answered. "Oh, now I understand."

"Does that finally bring a little peace to your troubled heart?" Roxie asked.

"Yes, ma'am, it surely does." Darla grinned. "Little secrets are okay. Big ones, not so much."

Alison and an older lady with a tape measure hanging around her neck knocked and then came into the room without waiting. "Okay, ladies, let's get these measurements done for the final fitting."

"Thank you all," Darla told Roxie and her sisters. "Knowing that I'm not the only one who's been through this is a big help."

"Wedding jitters?" Alison asked.

"The bridal test," Roxie answered.

"Getting through that is an emotional upheaval. Did you pass it?" Alison asked.

"I hope so," Darla answered.

Chapter 5

WEDDING SHOWERS WERE A BIG SOCIAL EVENT IN Tishomingo, Oklahoma. Invitations went out a month before the date with the registry sites right there at the bottom in script lettering, but folks seldom paid a bit of attention to those. Violet always took a little recipe box full of alphabetized cards with her favorite foods. She even put stars at the top of the cards to show how easy they were to make—one star meant super simple; five meant you had better be prepared to work all afternoon to get it finished.

Molly would bring a crocheted afghan in the wedding colors. That the new couple had decorated their apartment or house in something altogether different didn't matter. Gussie always gave the new bride and groom cast-iron skillets. Then there would be those who wrapped up a piece of fancy crystal—most likely regifting it from anniversary parties of their own.

"You ready for this?" Darla whispered to Will as they made their way up the steps that led into the fellowship hall.

"Yes, I am." He stopped at the landing and drew her into his arms. "But I'm more ready for next Saturday and the week after that when we get to spend a whole week together in the Colorado mountains. I'm sorry that our cruise got canceled."

Darla rolled up on her toes and kissed him. "It doesn't matter where we are as long as we get to have time that's just for me and you."

"I love you, Miss Marshall."

His deep drawl and the way he looked at her made sweet little shivers chase down her spine. Her brief consideration of leaving him behind had been a crazy moment.

"I love you, and next week at this time, I will be Mrs. Jackson," she said.

"I like the sound of that." He grinned as he opened the door for her.

The church's fellowship hall looked altogether different that Saturday afternoon than it had at Granny and Gramps's anniversary party the week earlier. Four wingback chairs were set in the middle of three tables laden with gifts that formed a U at the far end of the room. People were already mingling and visiting when they arrived.

"I've never been to one of these," Will whispered. "You'll have to tell me what to do."

"No worries." Darla smiled up at him. "We'll sit in those chairs and open the gifts."

"We open all of those?" Will looked absolutely bewildered.

"It won't take long with both of us working at once. As we open each one, a hostess will display them over there on the tables against the wall. After we get done, we give a little speech to thank everyone and have refreshments while the folks here look at the presents," she explained.

"Right on time." Roxie met them in the middle of the room. "Before we get this party going, we need to take a picture of the two of you and the hostesses. Come over here and stand behind one of the gift tables, and I'll gather them up."

Darla tucked her hand into Will's and led him to the first table. "The wedding will be a piece of cake compared to this. This is just a test, and we're going to pass it with flying colors."

"I feel like the only rooster at a coyote party," he whispered.

"Honey, every one of these women think you are perfect, and besides all that, I'll protect you if they begin to gather around with a hungry look in their eyes." Darla squeezed his hand.

"I knew I was marrying the right woman." He grinned.

Roxie returned with eight women in tow, who gathered on either side of Darla and Will. Darla recognized the women as members of Roxie's Prayer Angel church group. After Sarah had taken several pictures from different angles, Darla gave each of the women a hug and thanked them individually.

"My turn." Will grinned and went down the line, bringing each elderly woman's knuckles to his lips for a sweet kiss. "Thank you so much for doing this for us," he said eight times.

"Oh, my!" Violet fanned her face with her hands. "Such a southern gentleman. Darla, you are getting a gem of a husband."

"Don't I know it. Are we ready to begin?" Darla asked.

Rosalee motioned toward the chairs with a flick of her wrist. "You'll open gifts first, and then we'll have refreshments while we all look at the display. And, honey, we are honored to do this for you kids. We can't count the number of wedding and baby showers that Roxie has helped us with through the years, and we all just love a good party."

"Well, we sure are grateful for everything." Darla gave her another hug and slipped her arm around Will's waist. "Are you ready to do this, darlin'?"

"Yes, ma'am," Will answered with one of his cute little winks. "With you by my side, I can conquer the world."

Sarah met them at the end of the table and whispered, "A

word of advice. You might both want to make a trip to the bathroom so you don't have to leave during the gift opening."

"Great idea." Will stopped long enough to plant a kiss on the top of Darla's head. "See you at the chairs in a few minutes, sweetheart."

Darla dashed into the first stall, found out too late that the toilet paper dispenser was empty, and noticed feet in the next stall. "Hey, whoever is over there, could you hand me some paper? I'm empty over here."

"Darla?" a husky voice asked.

"That's me, and I'm in a bit of a hurry," she answered.

A hand appeared under the wall with a square of paper. "Just pull and it'll give you as much as you want."

"Thanks a bunch," Darla said. "Who am I talking to?"

"Mindy Tisdale, and I came in here to cry and feel sorry for myself," she said.

"Come on out and talk to me in the sitting room." The presents could wait five minutes if Mindy needed some help.

The door squeaked when Mindy threw it open. "Are you sure? You're the guest of honor today. I thought I was going to get married, but I was a fool."

"I'm sure. Just wait for me." Darla rushed through washing her hands and hurried out into the sitting room.

Mindy looked absolutely miserable when she glanced up

from the sofa. "I made my daddy cry. I've never in my whole life seen tears roll down his cheeks."

Darla sat down beside her. "I heard about Andy Miller wanting you to go to California with him."

Mindy pulled a tissue from the box on the end table beside her and dabbed at her eyes. "I had my bags packed and was going to leave with him yesterday. He told me he was going to marry me on the way, and that he would make me a movie star."

"And then Bobby found out?" Darla asked.

Mindy nodded. "I thought he'd yell at me or threaten Andy, but he took me into the living room, opened up Mama's laptop, and…" She hid her face.

"He showed you exactly what kind of star Andy was going to make you, didn't he?" Darla handed her another tissue and patted her on the shoulder. "I was fooled by his charm when we were in high school. He can lay it on thick."

"My daddy made me watch that horrible thing for five whole minutes. The entire time he just stood there and cried. Then he said that he couldn't bear to think of his baby girl doing something like that," she said between sobs. "How could I have been so stupid?"

"Don't feel like that. Instead, just be grateful that you found out what kind of guy he was before you left town with him," Darla told her. "Now dry your eyes and freshen up your makeup and come on out to the party. Put this all behind you and move on with a wonderful life."

"Is that what you did when he ran out on you?" Mindy asked.

"Pretty much," Darla answered. "After that first month anyway. In circumstances like this, Granny says that I can have fifteen minutes to throw a hissy fit, and then I have to put on my big-girl underbritches and get on with my life. You've had your fifteen minutes, Mindy."

The young lady tucked her long black hair behind her ears and forced a smile. "Thank you. Maybe someday I'll find a good man like your Will Jackson."

"I hope so." Darla stood up and lowered her voice. "And if I locate another one like him, I'll kick him over your way."

Mindy giggled. "If I had a big sister, I'd want her to be just like you."

"Hey, you've got six little sisters, including one in my class named Macy who adores you, so you be the smart, responsible big sister for her." Darla eased out the door.

Sarah and Marilyn were on either side of Will when she made it back to the fellowship hall. Sarah motioned toward the chairs, and she and Marilyn headed that way. Will came over to Darla and draped an arm around her shoulders.

"Are you all right?" he asked. "You were in there a long time."

"Mindy Tisdale needed some help," she whispered.

Will walked with her over to the two empty chairs and waited for her to sit down before he did. "I heard that Andy slunk out of town after Bobby had a talk with him yesterday. Mindy dodged a bullet from what I hear about that guy. I can't imagine *you* ever dating someone like him."

"I was young and stupid," Darla said.

"You're going to be writing thank-you cards for weeks," Sarah told them when she handed Darla the first gift. "This is even bigger than my shower. Marilyn and I will be glad to help you with them this week in our downtime."

"What downtime?" Marilyn asked. "Mama's got a schedule for us every single day starting after church tomorrow. You're the lucky couple that gets to go to your jobs all week. We're going to be making centerpieces and decorating."

"I thought the Wildflower folks were taking care of the decorations," Darla said.

"They are, but Mama has some ideas for little special things, like putting up small pictures of our grandparents and folks who aren't with us anymore on a memory table. Like Mama's folks and Aunt Lucy, and Granny's sister, Great-Aunt Linda," Sarah explained.

"It's the fancy centerpieces that are going to take so much time," Gloria said. "But those sweet folks at the Wildflower venue don't have another event this week, so they said we could work out there. That will give us so much more space than trying to do them in the house." Gloria smiled as she brought a gift from the table and handed it to Will.

"This is bigger than Christmas," Will said.

"Yes, it is," Darla said, glancing over at her mother. "And as soon as school is over every day, I'll be out there to help y'all. And if you don't need me for anything else, Will and I can work on the thank-you cards." She ripped the paper from a crystal ice bucket. "Oh, look, Will! We don't have to use the bathroom trash can to chill the wine in anymore."

Laughter filled the fellowship hall, and several women began talking about what they used for an ice bucket.

"If we get married twice, do we get two showers?" Will opened the card on the top of his gift before he tore the paper away. "Look, darlin', Gramps has given us a tackle box." He opened it and pointed to all the lures and equipment. "And it's full of good stuff."

"That's not for Darla," Roxie said from the front row of chairs that had been set up for the guests. "That's for you. Claud thinks that might save your marriage."

"I'll be sure to thank him." Will chuckled.

"This next gift is from me to Darla. I don't think, I know from experience, that it will save your marriage." Roxie grinned.

Two hostesses slid a huge gift over to Darla. She tore the pretty paper away from the front and giggled when she saw the picture on the box. "Granny! I can't believe you did this but thank you."

"A big-screen television!" Will gasped. "This really is better than Christmas."

"Just doin' my part to help you kids out." Roxie grinned.

"Well, thank you so much." Will shared a look with Darla and gave her a mischievous grin. "Whatever it takes, I hope we make it to our sixtieth anniversary."

"Hope so," Roxie said.

––––––

After the shower, the wedding gifts were loaded into Sarah and Marilyn's vehicles, the back of Will's pickup truck, and the trunk of Darla's car. Will's mother, Vicky, and his sister, Susanna, along with Roxie, Sarah and Marilyn, and Darla and Will, all caravanned north of town to the house Will had recently purchased.

Darla still couldn't believe that she and Will were starting out in their own home. Even if the bank owned eighty percent of the little three-bedroom white house with a porch that wrapped around three sides, they would be paying on something that would be theirs someday. Will backed his truck at the end of the row of all the other vehicles, got out, and then jogged over to Darla's car and opened the door for her.

"It will take hours to get all this put away." He grinned.

"Yep." She nodded. "With what we've both accumulated in our apartments and all this, we won't have to buy anything."

"What did your granny mean about the fishing stuff and the television saving our marriage?" he asked.

"Long story that I'll tell you later," Darla answered.

"Maybe on our honeymoon?" He wiggled his eyebrows.

"Oh, honey, I've got far better things planned for the honeymoon," she teased. "And it doesn't have anything to do with a television or a tackle box, although I appreciate both of those things."

"This is going to be a long week," he groaned.

"Yep, it is." Darla looped her arm in his. "But after this week, it's a little cabin in Colorado, and maybe even some skiing if I decide to put on clothes."

"You are killin' me." He scooped her up in his arms and carried her across the yard and onto the porch. "I'm not taking you over the threshold until after we're married."

"Good idea." She wiggled free of his arms. "I'd have to ask Granny, but it could be bad luck, and, honey, we don't need any of that."

"Amen!" He opened the door and stood to the side. "Let's go put those gifts away. When are you planning to pack up your apartment?"

"Rent is paid until the first of next month, so I thought maybe we could take care of that after the honeymoon," she answered.

"Have I told you today how much I love you and how beautiful you are in that dress?" Will whispered seductively in her ear.

"Only about four times, but a dozen wouldn't be too many," Darla answered.

"Then, darlin', I love you with my whole heart, and you are absolutely gorgeous," Will said.

"Much more of that, and I'm going to forget about unpacking presents and drag you off to my apartment to my bedroom," she told him.

Sarah appeared in the small foyer and motioned for them to come into the living room. "There's no furniture in here, so we need some direction as to where to put the television. Marilyn is ready to hang it on the wall and get it all hooked up, but she needs to know where."

"Later?" Will muttered.

"We missed our chance." Darla took him by the hand and pulled him into the living room.

Just as Will's sister and Darla's two sisters were putting away the last of the pots and pans, Will came into the kitchen and said, "I'm sorry, darlin', but I've got to go help Dad. He's got a spare but no jack, and he's had a flat out north of Milburn."

"No worries," Darla said. "I'll see you tomorrow in church, and we're having dinner at Granny's place, then working on thank-you cards all afternoon."

"We should have eloped," Will groaned.

"You are probably right, but then we wouldn't have fishing tackle or a television." Darla walked him to the door, and when he was gone, she slipped into the master bedroom. She loved the huge walk-in closet and had just sat down on the floor in the corner of it for a moment of peace when her future mother-in-law and sister-in-law, Vicky and Susanna, came into the bedroom. She started to call out and ask if they wanted to share some floor space with her before they all left.

"Are you sure he's okay?" Susanna asked in a low voice.

Darla leaned forward as far as she could so she could hear her better.

"I think so, but it's been touch and go for the past couple

of days. He loved her so much, and she broke his heart when she"—Vicky sighed—"broke up with him."

"She's got a lot of nerve showing up after three years," Susanna said. "Right now, when he's got the perfect woman for him in his life and just days before their wedding. She better stay out of my sight. I didn't like her even back then."

"Of course you didn't." Vicky sighed again. "You are his big sister, and you could see right through her narcissistic ways. Your father and I did our best to be nice, but it wasn't easy. Believe me, it took every bit of my willpower not to kick her off our porch when she showed up at the door."

"If Will hadn't been there, you could have said he was living in Alaska," Susanna said. "Today he seems genuinely happy, though, so maybe all our worry has been for nothing. Please tell me she's gone back to Dallas."

"She told Will she was leaving this morning. She had a room out at the motel west of town and said she would give him until today to make up his mind about calling off the wedding and moving out of this hick town," Vicky said.

Darla's heart pounded so hard that she just knew the two women would hear it through the wall. Since, evidently, guys had to go through the same thing, the test shouldn't be referred to as the bridal test, but as the wedding test or maybe even the marriage test.

"I'm glad she's gone," Susanna said, "and that Will could see that Darla is a much better choice than that self-centered hussy."

"Enough about that. Let's go make sure the back door is locked and then go on home. I don't remember anyone leaving that way, but we'll check to be sure," Vicky said.

Darla gave them a few minutes, and then she rushed out the front door and sat down on the swing at the end of the porch. Her heart was still pounding, and her hands trembled. In what seemed like seconds, Vicky and Susanna came out of the house, and both of them looked surprised to see her.

"Hey, I thought you left with your sisters," Susanna said.

"This has been such a big day that I just wanted a minute or two to collect my thoughts," Darla said. "Have I told y'all that this is my dream home? If I have my way, Will and I will still be living right here when we've been married fifty years. I've always wanted a white house with a big porch and a swing. I can see Will and me spending lots of hours out here."

Susanna shot Vicky a knowing look that Darla interpreted to mean she was glad her brother was marrying her instead of some woman who had tried to sweet-talk him into leaving town.

"That's so sweet," Vicky said. "Well, we've had a big day

too. We'll see you in church tomorrow morning, and we'd like to invite you and Will to supper at our house. I know you have Sunday dinner with your grandparents, but we'd like to start a tradition of our own for Sunday supper."

"That would be great," Darla agreed.

She watched them drive away and then got into her own car and was about to back up when Will pulled in right behind her. She put her car in Park and got out before he could open the door for her.

"I was halfway there when Dad called and said that an old farmer came by and helped him change the tire. Can we talk?" he asked.

"About what?" She had a sudden fear that he was going to say he had cold feet and wanted to call everything off.

"Come sit on the porch swing with me." He took her hand in his. "I need to tell you something because I don't want us to ever have secrets from each other."

"Al-l-l-l…right," she stammered.

"I was in love back in college with a girl named Teresa. She came to Tishomingo two days ago and said that she'd never gotten over me and wanted us to get back together. She had heard that I was getting married, and she said she wanted to—"

Darla put her forefinger over his lips. "I don't need to

know the details. I love you, Will Jackson. And just so you know"—she realized she was about to break the bridal test rules, but this was Will, and she was going to spend the rest of her life with him—"Mindy wasn't the only one that Andy Miller was trying to cajole into going to California with him. Somehow he got ahold of my cell phone number, and he sent texts and called and even sent flowers, which I threw in the trash." She removed her finger and leaned over to kiss him on the cheek.

"Did you consider it?" he asked. "He does live in an exciting world, and I'm just plain old Will who helps his folks run a real estate business."

"Did you think about going with Teresa? After all, I'm just a kindergarten teacher in Tishomingo, Oklahoma. I'm not all that fancy either," she said.

"For about a split second, I thought about the big city life," he admitted.

"So did I, and I thought because of that, I wasn't worthy of your love." She had to be honest. "Granny and my sisters called it the bridal test."

"My dad and mama said it was a minor test compared to others that will pop up in our married lives. Right now, it may seem big, but when we look back, we'll realize that it just helped us to be sure that we were in love."

"That's basically what Granny said." Darla scooted over even closer to him and laid her head on his shoulder. She was crazy, she realized, to have even thought about leaving all this behind for a moment of excitement. "Is that all that we need to talk about?"

"Not really." Will tipped up her chin and studied her face.

She felt as if he could see past her heart and into the depths of her soul. "What else do we need to...?"

He gently pushed a strand of her blonde hair away from her face. "I want you to tell me the story behind the fishing stuff and the television set."

"I don't think we're going to need either one of them like Granny and Gramps did, but here's the story..." She went on to tell him and ended with, "Are you going to watch *Bonanza* every night?"

Will's chuckle turned into full-fledged laughter that rang out across the yard. When he stopped laughing, he wiped his eyes on the sleeve of his shirt and said, "That should be written down in a journal for our kids and grandkids to read, not that I'm in a hurry for either one. I want to have you all to myself for a couple of years before we start a family."

"Then we'll have to be very careful with our Sunday afternoon naps," she teased.

Chapter 6

"WE CAN BE IN FLORIDA ON THE BEACHES BY MIDNIGHT." Roxie finished off her coffee at breakfast on the day of the wedding. "All you have to do is say the word."

Sarah pushed back her chair, stood up, and refilled everyone's mugs. "Toes in the sand does sound good."

"A nice margarita while we sit in a hot tub," Marilyn joked.

"Maybe even some fresh boiled shrimp," Gloria chimed in.

"If this is another one of your tests, you can forget it," Darla told them as she reached for two more pancakes. "I'm getting married in seven hours, and tomorrow morning, I will be having breakfast in the Colorado mountains with Will."

"She's serious," Roxie sighed. "And I had my heart set on sitting in the sand tomorrow."

"You'll have to talk Gramps into taking you," Darla said

between bites. "Thank you for making my favorite breakfast today, Granny. With a two o'clock wedding, I'll be way too busy to eat lunch."

Gloria shook her head. "Oh, no, you will not be too busy or too nervous. I've ordered a fruit and cheese tray. I will not have you fainting at the altar. Rumors will spread like wildfire that you're already pregnant if that happens."

"Not that we would mind." Roxie winked from across the table. "It's been a while since we had a baby in the house."

"We're both done with babies." Sarah nodded toward Marilyn and then turned her attention back to Darla. "It's up to you to keep Granny happy now, little sister."

"Wedding first. Marriage second. Babies later." Darla finished her breakfast and stood up. "Let's get this kitchen cleaned up and get on out to the Wildflower. I don't want to be rushed, and our beauty operator and makeup specialist will be arriving at ten o'clock."

Darla had fallen in love with the Wildflower venue when she and Will attended a wedding out there just before they had gotten engaged back in the spring. The weather in Oklahoma, especially in the fall, is about as predictable as a woman who is eight months pregnant. The backup plan was to be married in the church if it rained or, heaven forbid, even snowed, but that morning turned out to be beautiful.

"Oh. My. Goodness!" Darla squealed when she and all the women had arrived and she saw the white chairs arranged outside on a carpet of green grass, with an aisle down the middle and a decorated arch at the end. "It's even more beautiful than I remembered. Look." She pointed at a van pulling up in the driveway. "There's our makeup and hair ladies. Thank all of you so much for working so hard to make my day perfect."

"I wish this place had been here when I got married." Sarah sighed.

"Me too," Marilyn added. "But the past is the past and can never be changed. This is Darla's day. Let's go inside to that gorgeous bridal room and get beautified for the ceremony. It's been ages since someone else has done my makeup, and my nails are a fright from working with flowers all week."

Darla's eyes welled up with tears. "I have the best family in the whole world."

"And now you're getting good in-laws," Sarah said. "We all love Vicky and Susanna and Robert like they were family."

"Did we hear our names?" Vicky asked as she followed them into the bridal room.

"I was just telling everyone that I have an amazing family, and that includes all y'all as well," Darla said.

"Honey, getting you in our family makes us the blessed

ones," Vicky said. "Now you sit down in front of one of those mirrors and let everyone wait on you. Today you are the queen, and we all intend to make you feel like one."

"Yes, ma'am," Darla said with both excitement and peace in her heart.

———

Will took his place under the arch with his sister and his best friend standing beside him, serving as best woman and groomsman. He had worked on memorizing his vows for days, but he had thrown away his notes ten minutes before the ceremony and decided to speak from his heart.

"Don't be nervous," Susanna whispered. "Think of that cabin up in the mountains."

"I'm trying to," he said out the side of his mouth.

"We've got everything covered," Susanna replied.

The music started, and a white horse-drawn carriage came into view. Sarah opened the door and helped her older little girl out, and then Marilyn's younger son, Dustin, jumped out on his own. Sarah handed him the pillow with the wedding bands tied to it and gave her daughter Ivy a basket. Ivy scattered fall leaves as they walked down the aisle together and then took their places beside their fathers, who were sitting on the front row of chairs.

To Will, it seemed like Sarah took hours to get from the carriage to the arch. He wished a thousand times that he and Darla had eloped by the time Marilyn made her way down the aisle. Then Kevin stepped out of the carriage and helped Darla out.

From that instant, everyone and everything disappeared. Will was speechless as he watched Darla coming closer and closer—gorgeous in all that white lace. His hands began to sweat, and he forgot the vows he had labored over. He didn't even realize that everyone was standing until the preacher told them they could be seated. He came out of his trance and stepped forward.

Darla handed her bouquet to Sarah and slipped her hands into Will's.

Kevin laid his hands on theirs.

"Dearly beloved, we are gathered here this fine day to celebrate the union of Will Jackson and Darla Marshall in holy matrimony. Who gives this woman to this man?" the preacher asked.

"Her family and I do. I will share my daughter with you, Will, and I will accept you as one of our own children. Take care of her and love her, son." Kevin gave Will a hug.

"I promise I will," Will said.

"I understand that the couple have written their own vows," the preacher said. "Will, you may go first."

Will gently squeezed her hands. "Darla, I think I fell in love with you from the first time I laid eyes on you. You stole my heart that very day. I vow that I will love, honor, respect, and protect you with all that I am and all that I have from now until eternity. We've passed the wedding tests thrown at us, and with our love, I'm sure that we can survive any hurdles that life sends our way."

"That was beautiful." The preacher smiled. "Now your turn, Darla."

"Will, I give you my heart this day. I vow to love, honor, and respect you with all that I have and all that I am from now until eternity. If you take that step from this life to the next without me, then wait on the bench outside heaven's door. I'll be along real soon because a person can't live without a heart, and you'll be taking mine with you. If I go before you, then take care of my heart, and I'll wait for you. No obstacles or tests of time will ever separate us," Darla said.

The preacher dabbed his eyes with a handkerchief that he pulled from his pocket. "I don't believe I've ever heard such heartfelt vows in a wedding ceremony..." He went on to do a traditional service with the exchange of rings and then pronounced them man and wife. "Now you may kiss your bride."

Will bent her over in a true Hollywood kiss to Clint Black's song "When I Said I Do." Then he two-stepped down the aisle with her to the carriage as the guests applauded and cheered.

The lyrics said that it didn't matter if they were side by side or a million miles away; nothing would ever change the way they felt when they said, "I do."

"I mean every word of this." He kissed her again as the carriage began to move.

"Me too." Darla sang along to the words that said when she said, "I do," it meant that she would be faithful and true until the end of time.

"We should play this song as we fall asleep on Sunday afternoons," Will said.

"Who says we're going to sleep?" She pulled his face down for another kiss.

THE END

Can't get enough of Carolyn Brown's sultry,
small-town romance? You're in for a real treat!

Roll through the seasons with two complete novellas
from this beloved bestselling author

A SLOW DANCE
Holiday

Chapter 1

JORJA JENKS HAD NEVER BEEN ONE TO TAKE RISKS.

She wasn't the type of woman to quit her fantastic job in Nashville, Tennessee, on a whim to move to Mingus, Texas (population two hundred), but she did. She had worked in the accounting department of a big record company ever since graduating from college eight years before. She had never even thought about owning and operating a bar, but she was about to do just that.

When her mama and daddy found out what she had done, they were going to have a hissy fit that went way beyond the one they'd had when her grandparents took her to the Honky Tonk on her twenty-first birthday. She was a preacher's daughter and she didn't belong in bars—according to what they thought.

She dreaded telling them that she was now the half owner of a bar, that she'd left a lucrative job in Nashville and moved to Mingus, Texas. She would have to come clean with them within the next week, because they would be expecting her to come home for the holiday. Guess what? She wasn't going to be in Hurricane Mills, Tennessee, for Christmas dinner.

She'd only been to Mingus one time in her life, and that was on her twenty-first birthday. Her maternal grandparents had taken her out for what they thought was her first legal drink. The Honky Tonk was a pretty neat little place back then, but that had been nine years ago. If the bar had changed as much as she had, there was no telling what it looked like now. Back then, she had danced with a couple of good-lookin' cowboys, but that wasn't anything new. In Nashville, where she went to college, she could have kicked any bush from Church Street to the Ryman Auditorium and a dozen cowboys would come running out wanting to sing a sad country song.

Jorja had been wishing for months that she could get away from the big city and do something less stressful with her life. When her grandparents, George and Lila, and their friend Merle Avery had come to Nashville, and Merle had told her that she was retiring and wanted to give her half rights to the Honky Tonk, Jorja had thought she was kidding. The offer of owning her own business, even if it was a bar in the little bitty town of Mingus, seemed like an answer to a prayer. She could leave the city, live closer to her grandparents, and she'd own her very own business. The only problem was that she had no idea what all was involved with securing ownership. She had thrown caution to the wind and signed the papers on impulse. Now that she was minutes away from Mingus and driving in a mixture of sleet and snow, she wondered what in the hell she had done.

"I don't take risks," she whispered.

But you did this time, her grandmother's voice singsonged in her head, *and you did it without batting an eye or asking a single question about Cameron Walsh, your partner in this new adventure.*

"I just hope the co-owner makes a good roommate, like my old high school friend, Cam. I should call her this week and tell her about moving here. She'll never believe it." Jorja heaved a sigh of relief when she eased into a parking space. Her SUV was loaded with everything she owned these days. She located the key to the back door in her purse and pushed the driver's door open. Icy-cold wind whipped through the car, and sleet stung her face when she stepped out onto the slippery concrete parking lot. Her red hair blew across her face as she hurried to unlock the back door. She brushed it away and attempted to insert the key into the lock, only to find that it was filled with ice.

"Dammit!" She swore and ran back to her vehicle. Sitting in the driver's seat again, she glared at the door, but her go-to-hell looks didn't melt the ice caked around the keyhole. Finally, she remembered the cigarette lighter in her emergency kit. She opened the console, found it, and said a silent prayer that it still had some fluid in it—the thing had been in the bag of unused items her father had given her for at least ten years.

"One more time," she muttered as she opened the door and braced herself against the cold. She tried to jog from vehicle to door, but the second time her feet slipped out from under her and she almost fell, she slowed down the pace. She held the flame close to the lock, but the sleet kept putting out the tiny bit of fire. Finally, after a dozen tries, a bit of water trickled from the metal hole, and she was able to unlock the door. She reached inside and found the light switch, flipped it on, and stepped inside her new apartment.

"Holy damn hell!" She hadn't known what to expect when she swung the door open, but it damn sure wasn't what she was looking at. Merle had told her the apartment in the back of the bar hadn't been lived in for ten years, but that had to be wrong. No way could that much dust accumulate in only a decade. Jorja was looking at forty years' worth of stuff, at the very least.

Two twin-sized beds were shoved against a far wall to make one bed. That would never work. Jorja would share an efficiency apartment with another woman, but she wasn't going to share a bed. At the far end of the room was a small kitchenette with barely enough space on the right side of the sink for a dish drainer and on the left side for a coffeepot. The apartment-sized stove sat on one end, and a small two-door refrigerator on the other. She walked across the floor, leaving footprints in the dust behind her, and found that the stove worked, but the refrigerator was unplugged. She pulled it out enough to get it going, killed two big-ass spiders that ran out from under it, and then pushed it back in place. When she opened the doors, she found it empty but at least clean.

She opened several doors—one to a big closet, another to a bathroom, and finally the last one got her the utility room with a stacked washer and dryer combination and cleaning supplies and another door at the far end that led into the bar. She peeked inside and found it hadn't changed since she'd been there all those years ago. She filled a bucket with water and another one with cleaning supplies, and carried both out into the apartment. When it was spotless, she'd bring her things inside. If it wasn't clean enough by bedtime, she'd drive back over to Mineral Wells and spend the night with her grandparents.

"Where are you, Cam?" she groaned. "If I get this all cleaned before you get here, then you have to do the weekly cleaning for a month."

———

Cameron Walsh was a big risk-taker.

He didn't care what other people thought about his decisions. He made them. He lived with the consequences, so basically whether they were related to him or not, it was none of their business.

He didn't hesitate about quitting his job or moving from Florida to Texas—not one minute when his grandparents, Walter and Maria Walsh, called and told him that their friend Merle wanted to give him half ownership of the Honky Tonk.

God, he loved that old bar, and when he visited his grandparents in Stephenville, he had spent too many nights there to count. To be half owner of his own bar was a dream come true. He could live in the apartment behind the Honky Tonk with some guy named JJ. His favorite cousin, Jesse James, was nicknamed JJ, and they'd shared too many hangovers and good times together to count on their fingers and toes combined. He only hoped this new co-owner was half as much fun as his cousin had been. Just thinking about him being gone put a lump in Cameron's throat that was hard to swallow down.

The digital clock on the dashboard of his truck turned over to 11:11 when he rounded the back corner of the bar and nosed his vehicle in beside a bright red SUV. "So, you're not a cowboy, JJ." He chuckled. "I sure hope you at least like a beer now and then."

When he stepped out of the truck, the wind whipped his cowboy hat off and sent it rolling like a tumbleweed across the snow- and ice-covered parking lot. He chased it down and settled it back on his head. Another gust sent it flying across the lot again. This time it came to rest on a low limb of a huge pecan tree. He retrieved it a second time and held it tightly in his hands all the way to the back door of the Honky Tonk.

Merle said that the apartment hadn't been used in years, so he wasn't expecting much. Hopefully, it wouldn't take long to clear off his bed and throw a set of sheets on it. Cameron was dog tired after driving for more than eighteen hours. Using the key Merle had sent him in the mail, he opened the door and stepped into a small apartment that smelled like lemon-scented cleaners. From the looks of the place, JJ was a neat freak and had chosen the twin bed across the room. Red and green throw pillows were tossed onto an off-white comforter, and the chest of drawers on that side had a doily on it.

"Sweet Jesus! What have I gotten myself into?" Cameron muttered as he crossed the room and opened the first door to find a utility room. The second door opened into a bathroom that was complete with the standard toilet, a wall-hung sink, and a deep claw-foot tub with a shower above it. He groaned when he realized he was looking at a shower curtain that had a Christmas tree printed on it. He turned around, bewildered. Cowboys didn't decorate, and they damn sure didn't use doilies under cute little lamps like the one sitting on the chest of drawers on JJ's side of the room.

He shook his head, stepped into the bathroom, and closed the door. When he finished getting rid of two cups of coffee and a big bottle of root beer, he washed his hands and opened the door to find a woman standing in front of him with a pistol pointed at his chest.

"Who in the hell are you, and how did you get in here?" Her cornflower-blue eyes didn't have a bit of fear in them. She had flaming-red hair that hung in curls down to her shoulders, and even though she was short, her stance said that she would be likely to shoot first and ask questions later.

He raised both hands and said, "I didn't know JJ was bringing a girlfriend, but that explains all the foo-foo crap."

"Are you drunk or crazy?" the woman asked. "No one calls me JJ except my grandparents, and I damn sure don't have a girlfriend."

"*You* are JJ?" Cameron felt as if his eyeballs were going to flip out of their sockets and roll around on the floor like marbles at the toes of his cowboy boots.

"I am Jorja Jenks," she said, and her grip on that gun was firm and her hand was steady.

"I'm Cameron Walsh," he said. "You can put the gun away. Looks like we're going to be roommates and co-owners of the Honky Tonk."

"That's not possible. Cameron is a g-girl," she stammered.

"And JJ was my favorite cousin, and believe me, he was all cowboy," Cameron chuckled. "I think our grandparents and Merle Avery have pulled a good one on us. Would you please lower that gun? Talkin' is a little tough with that thing pointed at my heart, and, honey, we definitely have a lot to talk about."

"I'm callin' my granny." She laid the gun on her chest of drawers and picked up her phone.

Cameron crossed the room, sat down on the bare mattress of the other twin bed, and slipped his phone from his back pocket. His grandmother answered with a question, "Are you at the Honky Tonk yet? We just got word that bad weather was coming that way. Y'all may get two or three inches of snow tonight."

"You've got some explainin' to do," he said. "JJ is a woman."

"Yep, and you're a cowboy." He could visualize his grandmother's brown eyes twinkling. "All of us thought it was best not to tell you until you'd signed the papers."

"I'm not living in a one-room apartment with a strange, pistol-toting woman. I'm not even unpacking. I can drive from your place in Stephenville every day," he said.

"Nope, you can't. We're in Fort Lauderdale tonight. Tomorrow, we set sail on a long cruise that will last until after New Year's. I forget what it's called, but we've let out our house on one of those things where folks can come and stay while we're gone," Maria Walsh told him sternly.

"Y'all are at the top of my shit list," he grumbled.

"Call it payback," Maria giggled. "You were on the top of ours when you went and quit the college education we'd paid for without a degree and went to Florida to manage a bar. You have a brilliant mind, Cameron. You could have been an astronaut or a doctor or a lawyer, or even the governor of the great state of Texas or Florida if you'd set your head to it, but oh, no, you wanted to be a bartender. So, now you are one and we're even. We'll see you after New Year's, and if you don't like the arrangements there, then why don't you go back to Florida and give your half of the Honky Tonk to Jorja?"

"Or maybe she'll go back to wherever she came from and give her half to me," he said.

"Don't underestimate that redhead. From what Lila told me, she don't back down easy," Maria told him.

"We'll see about that," Cameron said. "Have a good cruise, and this isn't over."

"Don't expect it is. Glad you made it to Mingus and that you've met Jorja. Y'all play nice now and share your toys." Maria's laughter was cut off when she ended the call.

Jorja tossed her phone on the bed and flopped down beside it. "Our grandparents have pulled a sneaky one on us. What would they do if we just walked out of here this evening and didn't open up for business tomorrow evening?"

"You ever worked in a bar?" Cameron asked.

"Nope," she answered. "Have you?"

"I've managed one for nine years. If you've got a mind to leave, then pack up your pretty little pillows and your Christmas tree shower curtain, and sell your half to me." Cameron met her cold stare and didn't blink.

"I haven't worked in a bar, and only know how to mix up a daiquiri and a margarita, but I have a degree in business management, cowboy, and if I can take care of a multimillion-dollar corporation for eight years, I expect I can run the Honky Tonk," she answered with a definite sharp edge to her tone. "That said, if you don't want to own this bar with a girl,"—she put air quotes around the last two words—"I will gladly buy you out, and you can scoot right back to the beach."

"I didn't mention that I managed a tiki bar on the beach in Florida." He eyed her even more closely.

"Granny just now told me. She thinks this predicament they've put us in is funny. I don't," Jorja told him.

"Neither do I, but I'm damn sure not selling my half of this place to you." Cameron's stomach grumbled, reminding him that he hadn't eaten since noon, and it was now nearing midnight. Mingus didn't have a café, and the one in Thurber, just a mile or two down the road, had been closed when he came past it. "I'm hungry, so before I unload my things, I'm going into the bar to grill a burger or make an omelet." He stood up and headed toward the door he figured went out into the bar, but the one he opened was a walk-in closet, and her things were all lined up on the left-hand side. Shoeboxes five deep were stacked on the shelf above her clothing, and there were at least twenty more pair on the floor. "You figure you've got enough shoes?"

"That's my business, not yours," she smarted off at him. "And you can keep your dirty old boots on your side. If I find them mixed in with my things, I'll toss them in the trash."

He shut that door and tried another that opened on the bar. He reached around the wall and flipped on the light switch. A single bulb above the grill lit up, and he headed in that direction.

"How did you even know that they'd installed a grill?" Jorja asked. "And we have a kitchenette in our apartment." She followed him and switched on another light that showed tables with chairs turned upside down on them, two pool tables, and a jukebox over in the corner.

"I was here last Christmas, and the bartender made me a burger and some fries. Is there food in the apartment refrigerator?" he asked as he turned the knob to heat up the grill.

"It's empty," she admitted, "but I checked things out when I arrived, and there's food in the refrigerator in the bar. Evidently, the last managers were here until closing last night from the look of things."

"No use in taking the food from here to there, and besides, the grill is bigger than that tiny stove I saw in there." He went to the refrigerator and brought out bacon, eggs, cheese, and a bag of onions and peppers chopped up together.

Jorja hiked a hip onto one of the barstools and watched

him like a hawk. *Did she not know how to make an omelet or use a grill?* Cameron wondered. *Dammit! What kind of partner had Merle stuck him with?*

When the green light said the grill was ready to use, he cracked four eggs into a bowl and whipped them with a fork. Before he could pour them out on the grill, Jorja hopped down, rounded the end of the bar, and headed for the refrigerator.

"What do you think you're doin'?" he asked.

"I'm going to make myself an omelet, but I want bacon in mine, and maybe a hash brown and some grilled toast to go with it. If I'm going to eat this late, I'll just call it breakfast, so move over and let me have my half of the grill," she said.

Granny had damn sure been right when she said the redhead could hold her own. She'd be a force to deal with for sure, but after ten years of bartending, Cameron figured he'd seen about everything. One curvy, feisty little lady didn't scare him, not unless she was pointing a pistol at his chest, anyway.

Chapter 2

JORJA WHIPPED THE EGGS IN HER BOWL AS IF SHE WERE trying to beat them to death, but then she was still fuming inside at her grandparents and Merle for putting her in this situation. Not only was she going to have to share the Honky Tonk with the sexiest cowboy she'd ever seen, but their beds were going to be only ten feet apart.

She glanced over at him in time to see one little jet-black curl escape his otherwise perfectly cut hair and come to rest on his forehead. When she finished with the bacon, he reached across to her side of the grill and started to pick the package up, but she slapped his wrist.

"What's that for?" he asked.

"I'm not finished with that," she informed him.

"You've got half a pound on the grill," he said. "How much are you planning to eat?"

"Two more slices, and the package only weighs ten ounces, so half of that is five ounces, which is a far cry from eight. Don't judge me. I like bacon." *Does he think I'm fat and shouldn't be eating so much?* she wondered. The aroma of frying bacon filling the air made her stomach grumble, so she added another egg to her bowl.

"Besides, if you'd have been here earlier and helped me clean up that room, you would have worked up an appetite too." She peeled off two more slices of bacon, laid them out on the grill, and then handed what was left of the package over to Cameron. He damn sure didn't look like any Cameron she'd ever known, with those brooding brown eyes and that jet-black hair. His name should have been River or Creed, something totally masculine, certainly not a name like Cameron that could belong to either a man or a woman.

"I take it from your attitude and the smudge of something gray on your forehead that it did not smell all clean and nice when you arrived." He grinned.

He had one of those thousand-watt smiles that reminded her of a used-car salesman. He could probably sell a forty-dollar shot of whiskey to a poor old cowboy who had to count out his last pennies to buy the drink. Eli Smith had fooled her with a smile just like that five years ago, and she had promised herself that she would never be duped again.

Her heart had been broken into too many pieces to ever be put back together.

She wiped the back of her hand across her forehead. "There were dust bunnies as big as baby elephants in there, and a dead mouse under your bed. I should have left your side of the place for you to clean."

"But you didn't because you thought I was a female, and you were trying to start off on the right foot."

If his smile got any bigger, she would have to drag out her sunglasses. "I figured if I left your side, then you'd stir up all the dust that I left, and it would float back over to my part of the apartment."

"I suppose I owe you a thank-you." He flipped his bacon over so it would get crisp on both sides.

"No, you owe me more than that," she told him, "and I will collect someday."

A dozen ways to make him pay came to mind. The first and foremost was to make him drag the mattress off his bed and sleep out in the bar rather than in the apartment with her. That would make him think she was afraid of him and give him power over her. After Eli, there was no way in heaven, hell, or on earth that a man would ever again have that kind of control in her life.

"Just tell me when, darlin'," he drawled.

"I'm not your darling and never will be. We are partners and roommates, and that's where it ends." She shook a fork at him.

"Yes, ma'am, but I'm wonderin' how we're going to manage it when I pick up a bar bunny for the night. Do I hang a towel on the knob or what?" His grin was enough to cause a sworn Sister of Mercy to hyperventilate.

Her hands began to sweat, and heat crawled up her neck all the way to her cheeks at the vision that popped into her head—he was naked and tangled up in the sheets on his twin bed. She dropped the fork, tried to catch it before it hit his foot, but failed.

"Good thing I didn't kick my boots off before we came in here." He bent over to retrieve the fork, and she got a full view of his butt in tight jeans. She was way too young for menopausal hot flashes, but right then, she sure could have used one of those church fans with Jesus on one side and that psalm about lying down in green pastures on the other.

When she thought of that, another picture of Cameron wiggled its way into her mind. He was lying beside her on a quilt with pretty green grass all around them. She could hear the quiet sound of a bubbling brook nearby.

That's close to sacrilege, a niggling little voice in her head said loudly. She shook the image from her mind and concentrated on finishing her breakfast.

When everything was done to her satisfaction, she put it all on a platter and set it on the bar. Careful not to brush against Cameron on her way around to the other side, she gave the swinging gate a shove and thought she was doing well until it stuck. She lost momentum and started to fall, then two strong arms caught her and set her upright.

"Now we're even," Cameron said.

With both hands on the edge of the bar and adrenaline still rushing through her veins, she shot him a look of appreciation. "Thank you, but how come you think we're even?"

He shrugged. "You cleaned our apartment. I saved your life."

"I almost fell, but I didn't almost die," she smarted off.

"If you'd have hit your head on this hard floor, you might have died," he answered. "Or worse yet, had brain damage and couldn't help me run this place. Cleaning the apartment is a small price to pay for your life, darlin'. . . I mean Miz Jorja."

"Just Jorja," she said through clenched teeth as she kicked the gate open. "Tomorrow, we'll have to put some WD-40 on that thing." She continued around the end of the bar and sat down on the barstool in front of her food. "And speaking of tomorrow, I found all kinds of Christmas decorations in the utility room, so I thought we'd make this place look a little more festive."

"Mistletoe?" he asked.

"What about it?" She picked up a piece of bacon with her fingers and bit off the end.

"Maybe we'll hang two or three pieces so the poor old cowboys will have an excuse to kiss the pretty ladies." He went back to the grill and finished making his omelet.

"Cowboys don't need excuses for that," she told him.

"Some of them might be shy, like me," he teased.

She almost choked on a bite of omelet. "Honey, I've known you less than an hour, and I already know beyond a shadow of a doubt that there's not a shy bone in your body."

"No endearments, remember?" He shook an egg turner at her. "We are just roommates and business partners."

She gave him a curt nod and went back to eating.

You'd do well to remember that, the voice in her head reminded her.

———————

Cameron had lived alone for the past ten years, and he'd slept in the nude every single night of that time. Even when he was in one of the two relationships he'd had over that decade, he had not worn anything to bed at night. He had a pair of running shorts among his clothing that he could wear, but as he got out of the shower, he groaned at the thought of elastic binding his waist. Add that to the idea of decorating the bar with someone as obviously OCD as Jorja was—doilies, for Pete's sake, and a fancy shower curtain—and he was tempted to make a run for it. If the roads hadn't been so damn slick and Florida hadn't been so far away, he might have gotten into his truck and headed back south.

But that would mean admitting that Jorja had gotten under his skin, and he'd already let a couple of lovely ladies do that job in the past. Now his policy was to love them for a night or a weekend at the most and leave them with a smile on their face and some happy memories. No more commitments for him. He had been burned badly the last time around, and now he steered clear of the fire.

When he left the bathroom and padded barefoot across the cold wooden floor, he noticed that she was already in bed and facing the wall. Her red hair was splayed out on the pillow. Thick red lashes that he had seen earlier proved that her flame-colored hair didn't come from a bottle. Like stars in the sky, freckles were scattered across her nose, reminding him of what his grandmother had told him about the freckles on his sister's face.

"That's where the angels kissed her before she was born," Nana said.

Evidently, the angels didn't think a tough old cowboy who'd grow up to be a bartender needed any kisses. He stared his fill of Jorja and then crawled into his own bed. He'd driven long, long hours that day, and it was almost two o'clock in the morning, but tired as he was, he couldn't fall right asleep. He laced his fingers behind his head and stared at the dark ceiling for a long time before his eyes finally got heavy enough, and he drifted off. When he awoke, the clock on her chest of drawers across the room clicked over nine thirty, but the window above his bed was foggy gray. For a few seconds, he was disoriented and unsure where he was. Had he spent the night in some woman's house?

Then everything came back to him in a flash. He cut his eyes across the room. Janie's bed was made, and the red and green pillows—no, that wasn't right—it was Jorja, not Janie. Jorja Jenks, hence the JJ that he'd thought would be a guy. He heard a noise, and then cussing loud enough to blister the paint right off the walls filtered across the room. The door to the utility room opened and Jorja dragged out a box with a picture of a Christmas tree on the front of it. His eyes left the box and focused on the fuzzy black spider crawling toward her arm. He started to yell, but words wouldn't come out of his mouth. The critter hopped from the box to her arm, and she simply slapped it away.

Cameron could tolerate snakes, wild bulls, mice, rats, and even redheaded women, but spiders gave him hives. When the black furry thing flew through the air and landed on his leg, he came up out of the bed with a yelp and began dancing around the room.

"Good God! What's the matter with you?" Jorja stomped the spider, gasped, and spun around.

He felt a cold breeze on his naked body and scrambled for his sleeping shorts, which were lying on the floor. "Sorry about that. I must've kicked these off in the night," he muttered as he pulled them on.

"Rule number one," she said. "You have to wear clothes to bed."

"You can turn around now," he said.

"Are you sure?" she asked.

"Do I have to wear a shirt too?" He glanced at the black spider she had smashed and shivered.

"That would be nice." Her face was still scarlet when she turned around. "So, you're afraid of spiders? Anything else going to make you do your rain dance?"

"Nothing like a spider touching me." He jerked a shirt down over his head. "Where did that sorry little bastard come from? What are you scared of?"

"Probably out of the storeroom where the Christmas tree

was put after last holiday season. There's probably another one hiding up under your sheets, and to answer your question, I'm afraid of commitment," she answered.

"Too bad I can't wipe away a dead commitment to repay you." His eyes shifted over toward his unmade bed. He wouldn't be able to crawl between the sheets until he was sure all spiders were gone. The only good spider, in his estimation, was a dead one, and there was no wrong way to kill one of the evil varmints.

"If you could do that," Jorja told him, "I'd rent you out and we'd make a million bucks within a year. Are you ready to get busy with our decorating?"

"Coffee first," he muttered. "Maybe I'll help with decorations after that. Are you obsessed with Christmas or something?"

"What makes you think that?" She slid the box forward a few more feet with her foot.

"Red and green pillows, Christmas shower curtain, and now decorating a honky tonk? You think the people who come in here will give a damn if there's a Christmas tree in the corner or lights all around the bar?" He covered another yawn with the back of his hand.

"I'm not obsessed with the holiday, but I do love the spirit of Christmas." She sat down on the edge of her bed and wiped sweat from her brow with her shirtsleeve. "I enjoy decorating, and it's the smart business thing to do. Folks will come in here tonight and see everything all festive, and they'll be more apt to buy their neighbor a drink or a beer. Trust me, we'll have more business when folks are in a giving mood."

"Bull crap," he muttered. "But if you want to go to all the trouble, I ain't got anything else planned for today, so let's get to it. I'll bet we don't have half a dozen folks tonight anyway."

"Why?" she asked.

"It's Monday, and the weather is horrible. Look out the window." He pointed.

"That's all the more reason for them to be here," she told him. "The guys will be tired of their wives nagging them to fix this or that, and the women will be tired of their husbands sitting around in their recliners watching television. The parking lot will be full. What do you want to bet?"

"Whoever loses has to take down all this crap after New Year's without gripin' or beggin' for help from the other one," he said.

She stood up, crossed the room, and stuck out her hand. "It's a deal."

He wasn't prepared for the jolt of heat that rushed through his body at her touch. He'd kept her from falling the evening before, and their bodies had brushed against each other several times during the cooking process. He hadn't felt chemistry then, so why now?

Another spider reappeared right at his toes, and he took a couple of steps back. His knees buckled when they hit the edge of the bed, and he fell backward and then bounced back up so fast that it made him dizzy. How many of the damned things could infest one box of Christmas decorations?

Jorja stomped the spider and then calmly pulled a tissue from the box on her chest of drawers. She cleaned up the dark spot from the floor and said, "There now. That mean old spider is gone. I'll meet you in the bar, and you can bring that box out to me. I'll start getting the lights out of one of the lighter boxes." Her face was still scarlet red when she closed the door behind her.

Surely to God, she'd seen a naked man before, he thought, and he *had* apologized. What more did she want?

When he finished brushing his teeth, running a razor over his face, and getting dressed, he scanned every inch of the Christmas tree box for more spiders, and then picked it up and carried it out of the apartment. Jorja was busy hanging lights around the edge of one of the pool tables. He could imagine some old cowboy making a wrong shot with a cue stick and breaking one of the bulbs, but he didn't say a word.

He dropped the box on the floor and followed his nose to the back side of the bar and the coffeepot.

He poured a cup and sat down on a stool with his back to the bar. He expected her to bring up his nakedness again, but to his surprise, she just turned around and said, "When you finish that cup, you can take the tree out of the box and put it together. It's one of those old ones that you have to stick every branch in a separate hole. We don't have time to buy a new one for this year, so it will have to do. I vote that when we take it down, we trash it and hit an after-Christmas sale for a new one for next year."

"You plannin' on stickin' around that long, are you?" he asked and then took his first sip of coffee. "This is really good. You know how to make a decent brew."

"My granny says that if you can see the bottom of the cup, it isn't nothin' but murdered water. Good coffee is black and strong," she said as she started stringing lights around the second pool table. "When you get the tree out and ready to decorate, then you can put tinsel up over the bar. I'm too short to do that."

"Your granny is a smart woman." He glanced out the window. Snow was coming down even harder now. She'd be disappointed later when no one showed up, but he damn sure wasn't going to argue with her about it right then.

Besides, he hoped a few folks would come out since she was working so hard to decorate the place.

"Yep, she is," Jorja said.

———————

Jorja's face was still hot when Cameron brought the tree out into the bar area. She didn't even have to close her eyes to envision his sexy naked body, but she damn sure wasn't going to say a single word about it. That would be opening a can of worms that she wasn't sure she wanted to deal with. No doubt about it, he'd ask her if she liked what she'd seen, and then she'd have to tell a lie. He'd think she was flirting if she said, "Damn straight!" She could tell him that she'd seen better on a twelve-year-old boy, but the devil would claim her soul for a lie that big. She thought it was best to leave the whole incident completely alone.

He finished his coffee, slid the pitiful-looking tree base out of the box, and set the trunk in place. "There, I've done my part," he said.

"In your dreams, cowboy," she told him. "Now you get out the limbs and match the color on the stems to those holes in the base. We might have this place looking like Christmas by the time we open the doors tonight."

Someone rapped hard on the outside door before he

could say anything, and he left the bare pole and headed that way. He unlocked the door and eased it open.

"Beer delivery," a deep male voice said.

Cameron slung the door wide open, and for a minute, Jorja thought she was looking at the abominable snowman. The guy pushing the dolly in with cases of beer on it was taller than Cameron and covered with snow from the hood on his head down to his rubber boots. He stood on the rug just inside the door, removed his coveralls, and hung them on one of the hooks meant for hats. Then he jerked a bright-red stocking hat off his head, revealing a mop of gray hair that hung on the collar of his red flannel shirt.

"For a cup of that coffee, I'll gladly get y'all all stocked and put the rest in the storage room." He pushed the dolly across the floor to the bar. "I'm not making any more deliveries today. My boss thought I could make my run, but if I get home to Gordon, I'll be doing good, and that's less than four miles from here. I stocked up my truck in Stephenville a couple of hours ago and dropped off my first load at the convenience store in Huckabay."

Cameron poured the guy a cup of coffee and set it on the bar. He warmed his hands with it before he took the first sip. "My name is Frankie Dermott. Me and my girlfriend, Chigger, come in here pretty often on the weekends. This coffee damn sure hits the spot. Y'all the new owners? I heard Merle was havin' a tough time gettin' folks to manage the place and was sellin' out to new owners."

Jorja stuck out her hand. "Do you know George and Lila Jenks? I'm their granddaughter and the new co-owner."

Frankie shook hands with her and then extended his to Cameron. "And you are Mr. Jenks?"

Cameron smiled and shook his head. "No, I'm Cameron Walsh. My grandparents are Maria and Walter Walsh from down around Stephenville. You might have met them here at the Honky Tonk. They're good friends of Merle's."

"Yep, know them very well. Me and Chigger know most of the folks that come around here. Years ago, she managed this place, but that was back before me and her got together. She was married to Jim Bob back then. They had a couple of kids, but Jim Bob got to take them to his place this Christmas, so she's down and depressed," Frankie said. "Guess we'd better get after puttin' this beer away. She's goin' to be worried about me. I called her an hour ago and said after this delivery I was on my way home."

Jorja took over the job of putting the Christmas tree together, while Frankie and Cameron situated the beer in the right spots. She had sorted all the limbs by the color on their tips when she heard Cameron call out to her.

"Hey, business lady, where's the checkbook?" he asked.

"In the office," she answered.

"Where would that be?"

She laid down the limbs she was holding and headed across the floor. Merle had sent her a hand-drawn map of the place. Too bad she didn't have an eye for size. From the drawing, Jorja had figured the apartment would be twice the size it turned out to be. The office could be anywhere from the size of a broom closet to as big as the entire Honky Tonk.

When she swung open the door, she found a nice-sized room, but it made the apartment look like a five-star hotel suite. Papers, invoices, and unopened junk mail covered the top of a huge oak desk. The antique chair pushed up under the kneehole was stacked high with newspapers and magazines.

"Hallelujah!" Jorja shouted when she saw the checkbook lying on the top of a four-drawer file cabinet in the corner. She latched onto it like it was a lifeline and carried it out to the bar. Frankie handed her the invoice for the beer, and she wrote out the first check that had both her name and Cameron's on it.

"That's why the checkbook was on the top," she muttered.

"What was that?" Frankie was busy tugging his coveralls up over his beer belly.

She handed him the check. "Nothing, just thinking out loud."

"Thanks, honey. Me and Chigger will be in soon as this weather clears up a little. We don't mind drivin' when the snow is on the ground, but Chigger don't like to get out in it when it's blowin' her hair every which way." He tugged his stocking hat down over his head, waved, and rolled the dolly out of the bar.

"We'll look forward to seeing you," Cameron said before Frankie closed the door.

"What was that squeal I heard out of you when you went into the office?" Cameron asked.

"Go look for yourself," she told him as she headed back toward the Christmas tree. "Since I cleaned up the apartment, it's only fair that you do that room."

"Holy crap!" he gasped when he peeked inside. "I wouldn't even know where to start, and besides, you're the one with the business degree. You'll know what to keep and what to throw away."

She shot a smile his way. "But you've managed a bar for years. You'll know what's important."

"How about we tackle it together?" he suggested as he shook his head. "But where do we even start?"

"I suggest that we get these decorations up and worry about that mess tomorrow," she told him.

He eased the door shut and nodded. "Great idea. You

wanted me to hang some garland over the bar, right? I'd rather do that than face off with cleaning that desk on our first day. Which box do you figure it's in?"

"I can't know. Just start opening them," she answered. "The only one I'm sure about is the tree. The others just say *Christmas decorations*. I was lucky enough to find the lights in the first one I opened."

He reached into a front pocket of his jeans and brought out a pocketknife. The first box was strings of lights that needed bulbs, the next held strings of bulbs that had the big old-fashioned lights in them, and the third one was filled with garland—red, blue, silver, gold, and even pink. Right there, on the top of the garland like they were in a nest, two cute little white doves were sitting inside a silver circle.

"Which color?" he asked, holding fistfuls of garland up. "Do you reckon this is for the top of the tree?"

She turned from the tree and said, "Blue and silver roped together for the bar. I'll use the gold and red on the tree. And that's not for the top of the tree. It's going right above the bar with garland coming out from both sides. I wonder where they used that pink stuff."

"Probably in the bathroom." He chuckled.

"Great idea!" She smiled. "We'll drape it over the mirror

in the ladies' room, and if there's any left, I'll use it in our apartment bathroom to spruce it up for the holidays."

"You can't be serious," he groaned.

"Of course, I'm not." She turned back toward the tree. "Pink wouldn't match the shower curtain. If we have any red left over, I'll use it."

If Cameron Walsh thought he could get ahead of her, then he wasn't nearly as smart as he was sexy.

Chapter 3

CAMERON ROLLED UP HIS SLEEVES, PLUGGED FIVE DOLLARS into the jukebox to get the music started, and opened the doors at exactly six o'clock. He fully well expected the parking lot to be empty, even if the blizzard-like conditions earlier that day had moved on toward the east. Six inches of snow covered the ground. The state folks would make sure Interstate 20 was graded, but Palo Pinto County wouldn't have the resources to clear off all the back roads around Mingus and Thurber.

He and Jorja had worked hard all day long, barely stopping long enough for a sandwich in the middle of the afternoon. He hated to admit it, but the Honky Tonk had taken on a brand-new look with all the decorations. She had plugged in all the lights. Mistletoe hung from the ceiling in four places, and the eight-foot tree looked like something out of a magazine. He'd made damn sure every inch of garland was strung up somewhere in the bar so he wouldn't have to fight with the stuff in the apartment bathroom. The room was tiny enough and already had a Christmas shower curtain. He could imagine getting tangled up in garland every time he got out of the shower.

"We are officially open for our first night of business," Jorja said from behind the bar.

"Yep, and I don't see people rushing through the doors, even though we've got music and plenty of beer and bourbon," he told her.

Jorja moved around the bar to sit on a stool. He followed her lead but left a seat between them when he chose a place to sit. If they did get customers, he'd be on his feet for the next eight hours, and he'd learned long ago to rest a few minutes when he had a chance.

"You ever worked in a bar?" he asked.

"Nope, but I've been in my fair share of them in Nashville," she answered. "If you can hold down the back side, I reckon I can run the grill and ring up charges."

"Hey, we made it." Frankie pushed his way through the door behind a tall redhead who was all decked out in tight jeans and a sweatshirt with Rudolph on the front—and his nose was lit up. Two big bluetick hound dogs ran in with

them, and both the animals were wearing Rudolph antlers. "This here is my girlfriend, Chigger. That's Jorja"—he
pointed across the room as they hung up their coats and
hats—"and the guy beside her is Cameron. Them dogs don't
belong to us. They're Luke Thomas's huntin' dogs."

Frankie whistled shrilly and the dogs ran out the door as
if they'd caught the scent of a coyote out in the parking lot.
"They come by the bar every few days to see if anyone will
buy them a beer."

"You're kiddin', right?" Jorja asked.

"Nope," Chigger answered for him. "Luke says that they
hunt better after they've had a beer. He likes to dress them
up, even when he takes them huntin'." Chigger turned and
winked at Cameron. "Oh. My. Goodness. It's a good thing
I'm not twenty years younger, or I'd take that cowboy away
from you, Jorja."

"You can have him, but not until after closing time." Jorja
slid off the stool. Not only did she not usually take risks, but
she also didn't believe in signs and omens. Yet, there had
been two doves and then, of all things, two hound dogs. She
shrugged off the idea that the universe might be trying to tell
her something and asked Chigger, "What can we get you?"

"We want bacon cheeseburger baskets and two beers—
Coors, longnecks," Frankie answered. "And me and my girl

here will do some two-steppin' while you get it ready. She said she was bored, so we got out the four-wheeler to get here tonight. If Mama ain't happy, ain't nobody happy, most of all this old bowlegged cowboy."

He grabbed Chigger by the hand and swung her around, then brought her back to his chest for some fancy two-stepping to "Anymore" by Travis Tritt. For such a big man, Frankie sure was a smooth dancer. While Cameron filled a basket with french fries and lowered it into the hot grease, he wondered how it would be to dance with Jorja. Did she even know how to two-step, or was she one of those city girls who went to bars that played loud rock music?

When the song ended, Frankie kept Chigger's hand in his and led her to a nearby table. The burgers and fries were done, so Jorja arranged them in baskets, set them on a tray with two bottles of Coors, and carried them out.

"Y'all enjoy," Jorja said.

"You ain't busy yet, so sit with us a spell." Chigger motioned to an empty chair.

"Yet?" Jorja asked.

"Like Frankie said, I was bored today so I talked to lots of the folks around here on the phone. You'll have a full house by eight o'clock. Tell me about yourself. Frankie tells me that Lila and George Jenks are your grandparents. They talk about you all the time when they come up here for some dancin'. But"—she dipped a fry in ketchup—"I can't imagine why you'd ever leave Nashville and move to Mingus."

"I was tired of the rat race and needed a change of scenery," Jorja answered.

"Well, honey, you can see all of Mingus in a two-minute tour." Chigger giggled and then lowered her voice. "But if I was you, I'd just park my butt in this place and stare at the scenery in here." She glanced toward Cameron and chuckled again. "That is a fine hunk of cowboy behind the bar, and you'll have to keep a tight rope on him, or else all the single women in Palo Pinto County will be findin' a way to get next to him. I been down in the dumps all week because this is the year my ex gets my kids for two weeks, but I'm already feelin' better now that I'm here."

"I'm sorry, but I'm glad you're feelin' better now, and just how many women would that be?" Jorja teased.

"I'd guess maybe a lot, because some of them that ain't single right now might be by the time New Year's gets here once they get a look at him," Chigger answered.

"Well, that's between him and them," Jorja said, but a little rush of jealousy filled her heart. She told herself it was because she damn sure didn't want to sleep on the sofa in the office if he had a woman in the apartment, but the voice in her head said that wasn't the only reason.

"Honey, there won't be nothing between him and them but sweat if the women I know have their way about it," Chigger said.

"Is Chigger your real name?" Jorja changed the subject.

"No, it's not," Frankie answered for her. "But she says that only her mama—who has been dead for years—and God know what name is on her birth certificate. That's why she won't marry me. She's afraid I'll find out her real name."

She raised an eyebrow at Frankie. "My name is Chigger. I gave myself that name when I was a teenager and figured out how much fun sex could be. Until I got a little older, I could put an itch in a man's britches that made him feel like he'd been in a patch of chiggers, but I could relieve that itch with a romp in the sheets."

Jorja's cheeks burned for the second time that day.

"Don't blush, darlin'." Chigger giggled again. "I was ownin' my sexuality long before women figured out they had the right to like it every bit as much as a man. I hear a couple of doors slammin'. Things are about to start hoppin' in here. Nice visitin' with you, and any time you want to get away from here, you just give me a call, and I'll make supper for you and the cowboy."

"Thank you." Jorja pushed the chair back and headed toward the bar.

"You're blushin'," Cameron said. "I don't see that often in women your age."

"Just how old do you think I am?" She picked up an apron and tied it around her waist.

"You want to bring the ties to the front," Cameron said.

"Why?" she questioned.

"Because a feller won't mess with them if they're in the front. That's too personal. But if they're in the back, you'll spend half the night pickin' up your apron. They'll untie it every chance they get," he answered. "And you'll want to hang a bar towel out of your hip pocket. It's a lot easier to grab for it and wipe up a spill than to try to find one," he told her. "As far as your age, honey, I'd guess more than twenty and less than fifty."

"I'm thirty as of last October, so you're right, and I was blushing because of what Chigger said about her name." She told him exactly what the woman had said.

He turned his back to the bar and laughed so hard that he had to wipe his cheeks with the bar rag hanging out of his hip pocket. "That woman is a hoot. I bet she could tell tales that would fry Lucifer's eyeballs right out of his head if she'll tell you that kind of stuff the first time you meet her."

"Amen to that," Jorja said. "And she also said we're going to have a full house because people are bored with this weather, and I get the impression this is kind of like that old television show *Cheers*, where folks come to drink, visit, and eat burgers."

"Where everybody knows your name," Cameron sing-songed. "And maybe in a few weeks we'll know all of *them* by name."

"Bet we don't forget Chigger, even for a minute, though, will we?" she said as the door opened, and half a dozen cowboys came inside. They didn't even slow down but hurried across the floor to claim the barstools. The two dogs made another race through the bar, their antlers now hanging off to the side.

"It's colder'n a mother-in-law's kiss out there," one of the cowboys said as he hung his coat on the back of his barstool. "Luke's on his way to get them dogs of his. He shouldn't have named them Miller and Coors if he didn't want them to beg for beer every time they get out of their pen. I'll have an order of french fries and a Coors in a can. I heard Merle had turned the place over to some new owners. I'm Billy Bob Walters. Got me a little spread a few miles north of Mingus. Who are you, darlin', and can I have the first dance of the evenin' with you?"

"I'm Jorja Jenks," she answered, "and thank you for the offer, but rules say that we don't dance with the customers."

She leaned over the counter and whispered, "That would make all the other folks jealous, and we wouldn't ever get our work done back here."

Cameron bumped her with his hip. "What rules?" he whispered.

"I'm making them up as we go," she told him. "You already know the first one, and the second is that we don't stop work to dance with customers."

"What if there's only one customer in the Honky Tonk, and she's really cute?" he asked.

"From six to two we are working," Jorja answered as she helped get bottles of beer from the refrigerator and set them on the bar. "If you want to dance with a bar bunny, then you have to wait until the doors are locked, and just so you know, if you want to keep one overnight, you can use the couch in the office or the floor in the bar. The apartment is off-limits."

"Well, ain't you the bossy one." Cameron chuckled.

"Been accused of it many times." She nodded.

Before either of them could say another word, the doors opened and every table was filled, folks were on the dance floor, and customers were lined up three deep at the bar asking for burgers, beers, and double shots. Jorja was kept busy at the grill, but from what she heard, it didn't take a rocket-scientist genius to be a bartender. She could draw up a draft beer, or take a longneck or can from the refrigerator. She could also pour a double shot of whiskey and even make a daiquiri or a margarita.

"Hey, Red," a cowboy with a deep drawl said above the normal noise. "You makin' them burgers for me?" When she didn't respond, he asked his question again.

Jorja glanced over her shoulder.

"You're 'bout as cute as a newborn kitten. What're you doin' after you close this joint? Want to go look at the stars with me?" He grinned.

He wasn't a bad-looking guy—a little on the lanky side, and his hat had flattened his thin brown hair. He had a nice smile, but not one thing about him made her want to get out in the cold and look at the stars with him.

"Sorry, I've already got a date." She turned back to the grill. "And don't call me Red. I hate that nickname."

The guy laughed, picked up the double shot of Gentleman Jack that he had ordered, and threw it back. In Jorja's eyes, that alone was a sin and testimony that he was a wannabe cowboy—just a guy who got dressed up in jeans and boots to go to the Honky Tonk with hopes of getting lucky. The next morning, he would put on his dress slacks and go to work at a bank, a law firm, or maybe even an oil company. A real cowboy would sip Gentleman Jack. He would never act all tough and toss back such a smooth whiskey just to impress a woman.

"What are you thinkin' about?" Cameron asked. "You look like you could go to the apartment, get your gun, and shoot someone. I hope it's not me."

"You've got nothing to worry about." She managed a smile. "I was thinkin' about wannabe cowboys."

"Is that something like a wannabe surfer?" He grinned back at her.

"I imagine it's pretty much the same kind of animal." She put together four burger baskets. "Are you a surfer?"

"Nope," he answered as he drew up a pitcher of beer. "I love the sound of the ocean, but I'm a cowboy through and through. I lived in a trailer on my grandparents' ranch in Florida. Little place north of Laguna Beach. I helped them out on my days off and in December and January when the bar was closed."

"I thought your grandparents lived here in Texas and were friends with Merle and my granny and grandpa," she said.

"That would be my dad's parents. My parents and my maternal grandparents live in Florida. I've got lots and lots of family when you count up both sides." He set the beer on the bar and turned around to pick up a bottle of Jim Beam.

"Looks like you win the bet about this place being crowded tonight."

"Yep, it does," she agreed. "See any pretty bar bunnies you intend to sweet-talk out of their tight-fittin' jeans?"

"Been too busy to look," he said, "but when it clears out some, I'll peek at what's still left standing. Got to admit, that office is damn scary, and this floor looks pretty hard. I might just want to grab a shower and fall into bed. How about you? You going to celebrate our first night by picking out a cowboy and looking at the stars with him?"

"Only if he gives an amazing foot rub and doesn't even expect a kiss for it," she said. "My feet will be singin' the blues by two."

"Good luck with that." Cameron jerked the towel from his hip pocket and wiped down the top of the shiny wooden bar on his way to the other end to where two new women had sat down.

At midnight Chigger and Frankie waved goodbye to Cameron and Jorja. By one o'clock there were only a dozen folks left, and they were more interested in line dancing than in drinking or eating. Evidently, they knew exactly how to time the music because Alan Jackson's "Good Time" had just ended when the big clock on the wall above the door said it was 2:00 a.m.—closing time.

"Good times is right." Cameron followed the last of the customers to the door and locked it behind them. He went straight to the jukebox and plugged in a few coins. Then he rounded the end of the bar and held out a hand. "Miz Jorja, may I have this dance to celebrate our first night as partners?"

She put her hand in his and let him lead her out to the dance floor. Merle Haggard began to sing "Twinkle, Twinkle, Lucky Star" when Cameron drew her close to his chest.

Jorja laid her cheek against his chest and listened to the steady beat of his heart. The lyrics asked if the stars might send him love from where they were. After working together so smoothly for the last eight hours, she didn't want him to find love and ruin their partnership.

When the song ended, it started all over again. "This is one of my favorite songs," Cameron whispered. "My grand-dad used to play it all the time. He had it on vinyl and eight-track both, and he and my grandmother would dance around the kitchen as it played. If they were here tonight, they'd close down the place by playing it at least twice. Besides, he's the one who told me to follow my dream and move here."

"Your dream has been to own a bar?" she asked.

"Yep, and my own ranch. I reckon I can run both," he answered.

The song ended and she started to take a step back, but

he tipped up her chin with his fist and looked deep into her eyes. She barely had time to moisten her lips with the tip of her tongue before he brushed a sweet kiss across her mouth.

"What's that for?" she asked.

He pointed up at the mistletoe they were standing beneath. "Couldn't waste that after all the trouble it was to get it hung just right, and also because Grandpa always ends the second dance by giving Grammy a kiss." He grinned as he headed across the floor. "Let's do cleanup in the morning. We're both tired tonight."

"I want to tackle the office tomorrow." She yawned.

"We can do both." He turned out the lights and held the door into their apartment open for her. "But, honey, the desk in the office will take more than a day, so don't get discouraged."

She shook a finger at him. "I told you not to call me endearments."

"Well, *honey*…" He dragged out the word in a deep southern drawl. "After a sweet little good-night kiss like that, I thought it would be all right."

She tried to keep from giggling, but she lost the battle. "All right, but that's the only one and the only time."

"What if I kiss you again?" He raised an eyebrow and then winked.

She held up a palm. "I'm not having this conversation tonight. I get first dibs on the shower." She marched across the room and closed the bathroom door behind her. Any other time, she might have let the hot water beat down on her back for a half an hour, but not that night. She couldn't remember the last time she'd been awake past two o'clock in the morning and wondered if it was possible to fall asleep in the shower and drown.

When she'd finished getting the smell of grilled onions and grease from her body and hair, she dried off, got dressed in flannel pajama bottoms and a faded T-shirt, and opened the door.

"Your turn," she said as she started across the floor.

"Come look at this," Cameron said. "It's absolutely beautiful."

"What?" she asked.

In a couple of long strides, he went from the window to her side, took her hand in his, and turned out the lights in the apartment. "See what you missed by not going with that cowboy who wanted to take you out to see the stars?"

The thick grove of mesquite trees behind the Honky Tonk glistened with snow. Ice crystals reflected the light of a quarter moon in a sky of deep-blue velvet. A couple of owls were sitting side by side on a branch. One pair of doves and then those two crazy dogs was just happenstance, but now two owls? The whole scene took her breath away. No artist or photographer could capture such a gorgeous, peaceful picture.

"I didn't miss a single thing," she whispered. "That cowboy wouldn't have wanted to look at the stars as much as he'd have wanted to do other things, and if I'd gone with him, I wouldn't have seen those owls."

"Why are you whispering?" he asked.

"I don't want to scare them away until I have that scene memorized," she answered.

Cameron started humming the tune to "Twinkle, Twinkle, Lucky Star" as he drew her into his arms and two-stepped from the window all the way to her bed. "This cowboy just wanted to dance with you under the stars." He took a step back and brought her hand to his lips. "Sleep tight, partner."

Jorja sat down on the bed with a thud. Twenty-four hours ago, she hadn't even known her new co-owner was a guy, and he'd come close to sweeping her right off her feet in the last thirty minutes. She stood up and crawled beneath the covers. From her bed she had a clear picture out the window of twinkling stars dancing around the moon. She was humming the Merle Haggard tune as she drifted off to asleep.

Chapter 4

JORJA AWOKE ON TUESDAY MORNING TO THE SMELL OF coffee and the sound of sizzling bacon drifting across the room. She heard laughter and voices outside, and when she opened her eyes, she saw tree limbs sparkling with diamonds. She blinked a few times before she realized that she was looking out the window across the room at the sun shining on the bare branches of a big pecan tree covered in ice. She threw back the covers, sat up in bed, and stretched.

"Good mornin." Cameron crossed the room in a couple of long strides and offered her a mug full of steaming-hot coffee. "I tried to be quiet, but a couple of kids out there in the parking lot are building a snowman, and they don't understand that we didn't go to bed until after two o'clock."

She took the coffee from his hands. Two of everything—it had to be an omen. "I thought Mingus was a ghost town."

"Not quite. There's still a bank and a post office and even a church north of town. Didn't you do your research before you signed that deed?" He sat down on the end of the bed.

She shot a dirty look his way, but he didn't budge. "And all that means kids in the parking lot?"

"Yep, and it means folks can still get their mail. They have a bank for their business, and a church to pray for a crop failure, which they might need, thanks to us." He grinned.

She took a sip of the coffee, black as sin and strong enough to heat up Lucifer's pitchfork—just the way she liked it. "What do you mean by 'thanks to us'? We don't plant crops."

"No, but we provide the products for all the folks in this county and the one south of us that tend to make couples careless when they sow their wild oats on Saturday nights. They need a church to attend on Sunday so they can pray for a crop failure." He chuckled, but she still wasn't sure she understood.

"Where is this church?" she asked.

"North of town," he answered.

She giggled. "Sounds about right. They come 'down'"—she put air quotes around the last word—"here south of town to sow those wild oats and go up"—she pointed toward the ceiling—"to the church to do their praying. My mama and daddy would be so proud of me if I attended services on Sunday."

"You're funny"—he chuckled again—"but why would that make your parents proud of you? They do know you are now half owner of a bar, don't they?"

"Daddy is a preacher. Mama plays the piano for the services, and my sister, Abigail, teaches Sunday school." She set her coffee on the floor and kicked free of the covers. "And no, they don't know anything about the Honky Tonk. I'm not real sure how to tell them."

"Holy smokin' crap!" Cameron gasped. "Should I expect your dad to show up here with a shotgun?"

"I hope not." She stood up and headed toward the bathroom. "If he does, I bet I outrun you, but you don't have to worry for a little while. I have to tell them before Daddy's anger melts all the snow and ice from Hurricane Mills to here."

"I didn't think preachers had a temper." He stood up and headed back to the kitchen area. "I'm making breakfast burritos. Want one?"

"Nope," she said from the bathroom doorway. "I want two. I'm starving."

She washed her face, brushed her teeth, and stared at

her reflection in the mirror above the sink. Her curly hair was a fright. Every freckle seemed to shine, and her blue eyes looked as pale as her skin. Her mother, Paula, would be aghast at the very idea of Jorja letting anyone, including the stranger guy she was living with, see her looking like that. Not even Eli, the youth director she had been in a serious relationship with, had ever seen her looking so rugged.

"I said two burritos," she said. "Good God! What is the universe trying to tell me?" Again, she shrugged off the notion of omens and thought about Eli.

He had been a good man, but he believed too strongly that a woman's place was in the home and that the husband was the absolute head of the household. He had let her know that he might discuss things with his wife, but his decisions were final and not to be questioned. She kept hoping he would change and figured he was praying hard that she would see the light—his light of course. Neither happened so they'd split up, much to her parents' dismay.

"Now I have to tell them I'm living with a bartender and own half of the Honky Tonk," she muttered. "That ought to send them into shock. I just hope they don't bring Eli and Abigail out here to do an intervention."

"Breakfast is ready," Cameron called out.

She took a deep breath, swung the bathroom door open,

and crossed the floor to one of the chairs set at the small round table. "Thanks for cooking this morning. This looks good and smells even better."

"Peppers, onions, and a little salsa spice up the bacon and eggs. Just for the record, my parents are CEO Christians—that stands for Christmas and Easter Only—and they know that I'm the co-owner of this place. They were happy for me, but Dad still hopes that I'll get into ranchin' since that's what both sides of my family do." He sat down in the other chair and poured orange juice. "I'm glad Merle left the refrigerator and freezer in the bar stocked. We'll have to buy food sometime this week for in here, but for now, we can live on what we can scrounge up."

She'd taken the first bite of her food when her phone rang, and the ringtone told her that it was her sister, Abigail, calling. She chewed fast, swallowed on her way to the chest of drawers where the phone was, and answered it on the fourth ring.

"Good mornin', sis," she said but her voice sounded hollow in her own ears.

"Don't you good-mornin' me." Abigail lit into her in her best older-sister mode, and her voice oozed with self-righteousness. "I called Granny this morning to see how she was doing, and she told me what you've done and where you are. I expect that you aren't even coming home for the holidays, are you? You won't even be here to see your nieces and nephews playing parts in the Christmas play this year, and…"

Jorja butted in. "Do Mama and Daddy know?"

"No, and I'm not telling them either. That burden is on you, but you best let the cat out of the bag soon. They've invited Eli to Christmas dinner in hopes that y'all will get back together. Can't you bring your new co-owner of that horrible place home with you, even if it's just for a day? We'll do our best to make her real welcome." Abigail's voice turned as soft as butter, like it always did when she wanted something.

"Cameron is not a girl. Cameron is a guy," Jorja said.

"Lord have mercy!" The buttery voice turned hard as concrete. "Are you trying to kill Mama and Daddy both?"

"Nope. And right now, we're sharing an efficiency apartment in the back of the bar until we can figure out other living arrangements." Jorja knew Abigail could never keep all that juicy information to herself. "He just made breakfast and my food is getting cold. Maybe I can come home next summer for the family reunion."

Her sister hung up on her, and Jorja went back to the table.

"That sounded like an interesting conversation," Cameron grinned.

"Yep," Jorja agreed and ate faster than she ever had. She figured it would take ten minutes for Abigail to tell all the dirt on her sister and for the three of them to come up with a plan. They must've talked fast enough to fry the cell towers because her phone rang after only five minutes.

"Want me to leave the room?" Cameron asked.

"Nope," she said as she hit the Answer button. "Good mornin', Mama."

"Is what Abigail just told us a big joke, and are you on your way home for the holidays like always? If it is, I don't consider it a bit funny," Paula said in a stern tone.

"It's not a joke." Jorja was glad that the whole thing was out in the open.

"Then I'll have the Prayer Angels at church pray that you see the error in your decision and come home," Paula told her.

"To what? I've quit my job in Nashville." Jorja held the phone with one hand and carried her dirty plate to the sink with the other. The whole time she wondered if there were two Prayer Angels that would be praying for her.

"To Eli. Come home to Eli. He still loves you." Her mother sighed. "You just have to realize…"

"Mama, I don't love Eli, and what he loves is the idea he has in his head of what I would be if I changed everything about myself and became the woman he wants his wife to be. I'm not willing to do that." Jorja crossed the room and spread the bed up with her spare hand.

The phone went dead, and she held it out to look at the screen. "She's really pissed. She hung up on me."

"Eli didn't like your red hair?" Cameron asked. "I wasn't eavesdropping, but I couldn't help but hear what you said."

"Eli is the youth director at a big church in Nashville. He takes the scripture very literally and wants a submissive little wife who never questions his decisions. I'm not that woman," she answered. "It has nothing to do with my hair or my looks, and everything to do with my attitude."

"How long did y'all date?" Cameron drew his dark brows down.

"Almost a year." She refilled both their coffee cups.

"Is he slow-witted?" Cameron asked.

"No, he has a degree from seminary, and he's very smart." She popped her hands on her hips. "Do you think I can only go out with dumb guys?"

Cameron shrugged. "Evidently so. I knew you were full of spit and vinegar when I met you. Maybe you should've met *him* at the door with that pistol in your hands on your very first date. Eli must have rocks for brains if he thinks you'd let him have control over your life."

She tried to keep a poker face but couldn't hold back the grin. "You're absolutely right. Let's get these dishes done and go clean up the bar, and then we'll see what damage we can do to the office."

"I'll wash," he said. "You can dry."

"What if I want to wash?" She cut her eyes around at him.

He put up both palms defensively. "If you want to wash, then have at it. They can sit in the drainer for all I care. I'll go on out to the bar and start putting the chairs on the tables so we can mop the floor."

"Thank you." She nodded. "All I ask is to be given a choice."

"I'll remember that if you'll leave that gun in the drawer." He grinned at her again. "So, who's washing dishes?" He liked her sass and fire, and even though she was a newbie at the bar business, she'd taken to it like a cowboy to a rodeo.

"You can wash, and I'll dry. I like to have things put away," she said.

"Me too," he agreed.

She glanced over at his bed and nodded. "I can see that."

"Hey, come over here and look what those kids have done," he said.

She took a few steps forward so she could see out the small kitchen window. Standing so close to him that he could feel her body heat, and smelling like something akin to suntan lotion, sent sparks dancing all over the small apartment. A vision popped into his head of her in a bikini playing volleyball on the beach. In the visual, she wrapped one of those see-through scarf things around her waist and flirted with him when she came into his bar to order a margarita.

"That's amazing. Wonder where they got coal," she said.

He shook the vision from his head and said, "I think it's charred wood, probably from a fireplace, but it looks pretty real, and that's a nice-sized snowman. Look closer."

Jorja giggled when she realized they'd affixed a beer can to the branch that made Mr. Frosty's left arm. "I guess he's a lefty." She giggled.

"And he likes Bud Light." Cameron ran a sink full of water and began washing their plates, cups, and glasses.

"He's not from Texas, then, is he?" Jorja dried the dishes and put them away.

"Why would you say that?" Cameron finished up his job and dried his hands on the end of the towel she was using.

"From what I saw last night, most of these Texans like Coors," she answered.

"Yep, that and double shots of Jim Beam." He nodded.

"Look!" She pointed. "The owls are gone, but there's a couple of possums out there sniffin' around the snowman."

"They're probably trying to figure out why every other snowman in Mingus has a carrot for a nose, and this one doesn't." He chuckled. "You ready to tackle the bar and the office now?"

She hung her towel on the rack at the end of the cabinet. "Yep, let's do the bar first. I'll gladly sweep and mop if you'll take care of the chairs and the trash."

"Are you going like that?" His eyes started at her mismatched socks and traveled up the legs of her faded Rudolph pajama bottoms, and then took in her oversize T-shirt with its picture of Minnie Mouse wearing a Santa hat.

"Yes, I am." She started across the floor. "We're going to get sweaty and dirty, so why get cleaned up now and then again before we open the bar this evening? That don't make a bit of sense."

"I agree." He stopped long enough to put on his boots. They might look ridiculous with his baggy shorts, but there was no way he was going into that office in his socks—not when there could be spiders hiding in those piles of papers.

Jorja brought out a mop bucket and filled it with water, then stopped in her tracks, pulled out her phone, and took a picture of him setting chairs on the table.

"Why'd you do that?" he asked.

"If Abigail calls me again, I'm going to send the picture to her." She picked up the wide dust mop and began to sweep the floor.

"Why would you do that?" he asked.

"So that she'll know you're harmless." Jorja laughed.

"You could have given me a chance to pose," he teased.

Chapter 5

JORJA HEAVED A LONG SIGH AND THEN OPENED THE OFFICE door. Not one blessed thing had changed since she had found the checkbook to pay for the beer delivery. The place still looked like a tornado and a hurricane had had a fight in the middle of a post office.

"I'll get a big garbage bag." Cameron said.

He was so close to her that his warm breath caressed her neck and sent sweet little shivers down her spine. She dismissed the sparks by telling herself that she hadn't been out with a guy in over a year—not since she and Eli had broken up. Sure, Cameron was sexy, even in baggy shorts and cowboy boots, but he sure wasn't her type.

When she finally trusted herself to turn around, he was already on his way back to the office with the whole box of black bags. "Cleaning up that place will take more than one."

"Think it will all fit in the dumpster out back?" she asked.

He set the box down on top of the checkbook ledger, pulled one free and handed it to her. "If it doesn't, I'll find out where the dump is and take the rest off in my truck. Where do we start, and why did the last manager let things get this bad?"

Jorja shook the bag out, hung it over the back of a chair, and picked up part of a stack. "Maybe his or her job wasn't to take care of bills, and Merle didn't feel like messing with it. She must be eighty by now, because she's the same age as my granny." Items on the top of the precarious stack were dated three months earlier. As she worked her way down the mountain of mail, she sorted by putting the junk in the bag and organizing the rest into three different piles on a chair—unpaid bills, bills that were paid, and other things that had to be filed.

By noon, Cameron had hauled two bags out to the dumpster, and they could see one fourth of the desk. Cameron picked up a stack of paid bills, opened the file cabinet, and groaned. "You're not going to believe this." He pointed.

"I don't think anything would surprise me right now, unless it was a snake hiding in that drawer. If that's what you're looking at, then clear the way from here to Tennessee." She wiped sweat from her brow with the back of her hand. Thoughts of snakes and working with a sexy cowboy sure did heat up the room.

"No snakes, but if a spider comes up out of this drawer, I'm on my way to Florida," he declared. "The problem here is that not one of these files are labeled. How in the hell did Merle know what to take to her CPA for tax purposes?"

Jorja rounded the desk and stared into the open drawer. "Holy crap on a cracker," she moaned. "You do realize that since we took ownership before the first of the year, it's up to us to organize all this, and get it ready for the CPA in the next few weeks. What in the hell have we gotten ourselves into?"

"Key words there are 'in hell.'" He nodded.

"Amen, sweet Jesus." She sighed. "We'll put the stuff that should be filed in a box. When we get the desk cleaned off, we can start with one drawer at a time and get it all put to rights."

"And I thought I'd just walk into my own bar and start to work." Cameron groaned again. "Guess nothing comes for free."

"You got that right." Jorja took a step backward and stepped on a pencil, and her mind immediately told her it was a snake. She jumped as high as she could, but there was no way she was landing back on that evil monster. She wrapped her arms around Cameron's neck and both legs around his waist, and then hung on like he was a tree and she was a spider monkey.

"I murdered a spider for you, so you can kill that snake for me," she panted with her eyes tightly closed.

"I had a reason to do a stomp dance." He laughed. "But you're asking me to go to jail for murdering a pencil."

She opened one eye slightly and gave the yellow pencil a dirty look. Then she realized that Cameron had instinctively caught her by grabbing her butt with both hands. Her face heated up and she tried to wiggle free, but he tightened his grip.

"Let me go," she said.

"Not just yet." He took two steps back, rounded the end of the desk, and carried her all the way to their apartment.

"What are you doing?" she demanded.

He set her on a kitchen chair and said, "I need to borrow your pistol. Mine is out in my truck."

"What for?" she asked as she started for the chest of drawers. "You don't need a gun to kill a spider."

"Honey, there are two rattlesnakes, real ones, curled up together under the desk," he told her. "Thank God you didn't pull out the chair and sit down to work your way through those stacks of mail."

"You're teasing me, aren't you?" She drew her legs up and scanned the room. "Are you sure there's two?"

"Two heads, two tails. Is it all right if I get your pistol from the drawer, or should I go out to the truck for mine?" he asked again.

"Get mine and kill them. How did snakes get in the bar anyway?" she asked.

"I don't know, but I intend to check every crevice, crack, and corner in that office and the bar for unwelcome vermin. We need to be more careful until we get things in order." He took the gun from the drawer and started out of the room. "Stay right there until I get back."

"You'll get no argument out of me," she said.

———

He made sure the little thirty-eight revolver was loaded, and then he eased back into the office, tiptoed around the desk, and peeked under it. One critter was awake now and eyeing him. It would likely strike if Cameron tried to pull the office chair back. He took aim from halfway across the room and squeezed the trigger. The bullet went right through the snake's head and the back of the desk, and imbedded itself in the doorframe. He sucked in a lungful of air and let it out slowly, then aimed and fired again before he dragged the chair back out of the way.

Both snakes were dead, but Cameron had been around old barns enough to know that sometimes they brought more than one friend with them. He dragged the first carcass out with the broom handle, picked it up by the tail, and dropped it into the open garbage bag, and then did the same thing with the second one.

After that, he checked every crack, corner, and crevice in the whole room. When he was satisfied that the area was clear of both snakes and spiders, he carried the bag with the dead critters out to the dumpster. That's when it hit him that he and Jorja had been seeing everything in twos since they arrived at the Honky Tonk. Doves, dogs, owls, possums, snakes—surely that had a meaning of some kind.

He was back inside and headed toward the apartment when the adrenaline rush hit. Until then he'd been acting on impulse, killing something harmful, but now he thought about how far he and Jorja were from a doctor or hospital. He jogged the rest of the way, burst into the apartment, and stopped in the middle of the floor when he saw her sitting in the chair—which was on top of the table.

"Are they dead?" she whispered.

"Yes, ma'am, and in the dumpster, and I checked under and around everything to be sure he hadn't invited a friend to come in with him. All clear." He nodded. "I need a beer. How about you?"

"I need a double shot of Jack Daniel's. No ice." Her eyes were as big as saucers even yet. "Are you sure it's safe for me to go to the bar?"

Cameron crossed the room, scooped her up out of the chair like a bride, and carried her through the door. When she was settled on a barstool, he poured a triple shot of whiskey and handed it to her, then opened a beer for himself. He carried his beer around the end of the bar and sat down beside her. "I guess we've both eaten our bullfrog today."

"What does that mean?" she asked.

"My nanny used to say that if you get up and eat a bullfrog first thing every morning, nothing will faze you after that for the rest of the day. You've saved my life by killing a spider..."

She butted in before he could go on. "That little fuzzy black spider wouldn't have killed you, and you know it."

"Maybe not, but it could have caused me to fall, hit my head on the foot of my bed, and kill myself," he disagreed.

She took a sip of her whiskey. "On the other hand, that snake could've bitten me or you, and as big as he was, the venom..." She shivered and turned up her glass again.

Cameron laid a hand on her shoulder. "We've proven that we are survivors, no matter what anyone says."

"Are you really afraid of spiders?" She clamped a hand over his.

"Yep," he admitted. "When I was about five years old, I woke up one morning and this big-ass tarantula was sitting on my pillow, not three inches from my nose. I froze. Couldn't scream. Couldn't make a single peep until the sorry little sumbitch crawled over and put one of his hairy feet on my cheek. Been afraid of them things ever since. How about you and snakes?"

"Don't know that anything catastrophic like your spider thing ever happened, but I've always hated them. I shut my eyes if there's even one on television." She threw back the rest of her whiskey. "Should we go back in the office and do some more work?"

"Let's put it off until later. It's not like we have to have it all spick-and-span today," he said. "It's after three now. Let's have a burger and get cleaned up to face the crowd tonight. Think we should stay open on Christmas Eve or close up shop?"

"Why don't we ask Chigger and Frankie what they've done in the past? I can't imagine that we'll have much business." She removed her hand and wiggled free of his. "I'm going to have one more shot, and then we can make burgers."

"You can hold your liquor pretty good there," he said.

"Yep." She grinned. "You know what they say about preachers' daughters."

"That they're the wildest of the lot?" he answered.

"Oh, yeah." She giggled. "Except I was never really wild. I just happen to like whiskey like my granny Lila. She was an O'Malley before she got married and is second-generation Irish in this country. I inherited my red hair, my temper, and my ability to hold my liquor from her. She always thought it was a shame that her son, my father, decided to preach rather than to run a good old Irish pub like her grandfather did in County Cork."

"Must've skipped a generation," he said as he fired up the grill and started making burgers.

She hip bumped him as she turned the knob to start the deep fryer. "Does that mean my son will be a preacher?"

"If he grows up in the back room of the Honky Tonk, I kind of doubt that," Cameron answered.

"Would you raise a child in the back room?" she asked.

"Nice room back there, so I don't see why not, but I'd rather raise him on a ranch where he'd have plenty of runnin' room." He turned at the same time she did, and suddenly, their noses were just inches apart. Seemed like the only thing to do was lean in for a kiss. She moistened her lips with the tip of her tongue, and his mouth had barely touched hers when her phone rang. She jumped backward like a little girl who'd gotten caught messing around with her mother's makeup. She jerked the thing out of her pocket and said, "Hello, Abigail. Am I forgiven yet?"

Cameron could hear her sister's shrill voice even though he was two feet away.

"I will be there this weekend for an intervention so get ready for it, and I'm bringing you home with me. I will not take no for an answer, so have your things packed and ready to leave."

"Today Cameron killed two snakes." Ice hung on every word Jorja spoke. "I've faced off with the devil and lived through it, so I'm not afraid of you or your intervention bullshit. I'm not going anywhere with you or with anyone else, so bring an army or come by yourself. You are welcome to come see me, but you need to make reservations at a hotel, or else you'll be sleeping on the floor of the bar. Now I've got stuff to do, so goodbye."

She turned around, looped her arms around Cameron's neck, and tiptoed to kiss him. When their lips met, he felt a jolt of electricity like nothing he'd ever felt before. When the kiss ended, she took a step back and said, "Thank you for killing those vicious critters."

"I'll gladly kill another one for a kiss like that," he teased.

"I might bring one in the bar so you can shoot it," she shot back at him.

Jorja did not need an intervention, he thought. That red-headed ball of fire could take care of herself in any situation, and no one, not even the devil himself, could scare her—unless he brought a snake with him, and Cameron would take care of that for her.

Chapter 6

CHIGGER AND FRANKIE ASSURED THEM THAT IT WOULD be useless to open the bar on Christmas Eve. According to Chigger, the previous owners used to come back to Mingus on that night for a little homecoming celebration, but not anymore. Managers had come and gone so fast that they had almost worn out the hinges on the doors for the past five years. That's why Merle decided to give the bar away. According to what she'd told Chigger, she wanted to see the Honky Tonk loved and cherished, and not just from six in the evening until two in the morning by someone who got bored with it after a few months and moved on.

"That explains the office," Jorja said over breakfast on Christmas Eve morning.

"What does?" Cameron asked.

"Chigger said that lots of managers had come and gone through here. The place didn't belong to them, so they didn't care if the office was taken care of or not. I'm surprised the bar itself hasn't suffered from as much neglect." Jorja toyed with her empty coffee cup.

"You aren't thinking about the bar right now," Cameron said.

"You can't read my mind," she told him.

"No, but I know what's in my thoughts this morning, and I'd be willing to bet that yours aren't too different. You're thinking about your family and what you'd be doing if you were home, right?" he asked.

"I guess you *are* a mind reader." She managed a weak smile, but it wasn't heartfelt. If she was home, she and Abigail would be helping her mother make pecan pies for dinner the next day. Like they did every year, they would argue whether it was better to chop nuts or to leave them as halves, and they would wind up making one of each.

"Talk to me. What's your favorite part of Christmas Eve when you can go home?" Cameron got up from the table and refilled their coffee cups.

"Cookin' with Mama, and if we have snow, Abigail and I going to the church parking lot and building a snowman like we did when we were kids," she said. "We make cinnamon rolls for Christmas morning and get all the pies ready for Christmas dinner. We always open our presents on Christmas Eve—three presents for each of us because baby Jesus had three gifts, and Daddy reads the story of Jesus's birth from the Bible. Then the next morning, there will be one present under the tree for the grandkids from Santa, because he always stops at Granny and Poppa's house on his way back to the North Pole."

"You have nieces and nephews?" he asked.

"Just nieces. Two"—she hesitated and thought again of all the pairs or twos that kept sneaking into her life—"of them. They're ten and twelve now, but Mama says that when they say they don't believe in Santa, then he won't come around anymore. They're not stupid, so they'll never say that they don't believe." She laughed. "Abigail is six years older than me, and she married right out of college."

"So"—he chuckled—"Abigail has bossed you around forever, right?"

"You got it." She nodded. "What about you? What would you be doing?"

His expression changed from happy to sad in a split second. "I'd start off the day by going to the cemetery to tell my cousin Merry Christmas, and maybe I'd pour a can of Coors out at his tombstone. Jesse James Walsh. We called him JJ and he was my best friend. We were born three days apart and grew up together. He died in a motorcycle accident on Christmas Eve when we were nineteen. That would be twelve years ago now."

"I'm so sorry. As much as we disagree much of the time, I can't imagine losing Abigail. We argue and bicker, but to lose her, especially at Christmas..." Jorja shivered at the thought.

"This will be the first year I haven't gone to see him, and I miss that," Cameron said.

"Guess we've both given up family for this job. So, what do we do to get through Christmas Eve without letting it get us down?" She sighed.

"We don't have a churchyard, but we've got the Honky Tonk, and it has a parking lot, and about four inches of fresh snow fell last night, so we can make a snowman," he suggested.

"There's already one out there, and besides we need to bake something for dinner tomorrow. We should have something special to eat at least since it's Christmas," she told him.

"Our Honky Tonk snowman is lonely, so we should build him a girlfriend," Cameron insisted. "When we get done with that, we'll go to the grocery store and buy stuff to make a pie and whatever else we want. Then maybe we'll watch a Christmas movie before we go to sleep. We can't sit around and mope all day. JJ wouldn't like that, and neither would your folks." He finished off his coffee and put the cup in the sink.

"What kind of television reception do you think we get out here? I bet the cable has been turned off for years, and in this weather, we might not get much of anything without it." She pushed back her chair, crossed the room, and went to the closet. "I should probably wear my snow boots."

"Leave it to a woman to dress up to build a snowman, and, honey, it doesn't matter about the reception. I brought a DVD player and movies with me. JJ and I always watched *National Lampoon's Christmas Vacation*. I can do that this year even if I can't go visit him," he said.

"My sister and her girls always watch *A Smoky Mountain Christmas* with me." Jorja sat down on the edge of her bed and pulled on a pair of hot-pink rubber boots.

"I've got that one too. We're not used to getting to sleep before three in the morning, so we'll watch both of them." Cameron got his coat and cowboy hat from the closet.

Jorja stopped what she was doing and frowned. What in the hell would he be doing with a Dolly Parton chick flick? "You've got *A Smoky Mountain Christmas* with you?"

"Of course." He buttoned his fleece-lined denim jacket. "I've got nieces too."

"How many?" she asked.

"I have four brothers, all older than me and married, and six nephews and two nieces. The oldest niece and I always watch Miss Dolly sometime during the holidays," he told her.

"How does your family feel about you having a bar?" she asked.

"Happy for me now, but when I left college only one year away from getting my degree, they were all pretty pissed at me. They've mellowed a little, though, in the past ten years," he answered. "Let's go build a snowman."

She beat him to the door to the parking lot, rolled up a good, tight snowball, and pelted him in the chest with it the minute he walked out the back door. He ran across the parking lot, tackled her, and brought her down flat on her back in the snow. For a moment he lay on top of her, and her heart raced with a full head of steam. Her gaze went to his lips and then back up to sink into the depths of his dark-brown eyes. She was sure he was about to kiss her again, and she was disappointed when he rolled to the side to lie on his back and point to the gray skies.

"We'd better get busy if we're going to give old Frosty a drinkin' buddy. Looks like it could start snowing again or maybe sleeting," he said.

"I don't mind working in snow, but sleet's another matter." She popped up on her knees, patted a good-sized snowball together, and then began to roll it. That there would soon be two snowmen in the parking lot wasn't any surprise at all. She started humming "Let It Snow" as she worked, just like she had done the last time she and her sister and her nieces had made a snowman in Hurricane Mills. She hadn't figured on missing them all so damn much this year. She thought she'd go to Mingus and be so busy she wouldn't have time to even think about the holiday season.

Thoughts get you in trouble. You thought Cameron was a girl. Her grandmother's voice giggled inside her head.

You didn't tell me he was a damn fine sexy cowboy, Jorja argued. She stole a sideways look at him halfway across the parking lot. Tight jeans, cowboy boots, and a black hat all caked with snow—her type or not, he looked pretty damn fine.

"You make the middle, and I'll work on the bottom," Cameron said and then began to sing the song she was humming.

His deep voice rang out across the area and was right on key.

"Have you ever done any professional singing?" she asked.

"Only if the shower is considered professional," he answered. "When me and JJ were little guys, we each got a guitar for Christmas and fancied ourselves country singers. We entertained the cows out in Grandpa's pasture, but they usually ran the other way when we hit the first chords."

Jorja heard what he was saying, but her mind strayed from his singing to something deeper. She'd known this cowboy for only a few days, and she already felt more comfortable with him than she ever had with Eli—even after she'd dated him for a year. That seemed crazy, but it was the truth.

"No comment?" Cameron asked.

"About what?" Jorja stopped and sat down beside the middle part of the snowman.

"About what I just said," he answered.

"Oh, that." She smiled up at him. "That's just plain old unadulterated bullshit. You could put most country artists to shame."

He tipped his hat toward her. "Well, thank you, ma'am. I'm sure if JJ heard that, he'd tell you that he was even better than me."

"I'd have to hear him sing before I'd believe him," she argued. "Right now, I guess we'd better lift this big belly up on that bottom you've got made and then make a head for this old boy."

"Boy," Cameron said and wiggled his eyebrows. "So, it's a drinkin' buddy and not a girlfriend?"

"Yep, Frosty doesn't need a girlfriend. He needs a buddy to have a beer with for Christmas. He's lonely."

Cameron lifted the huge ball of snow up onto the bottom layer without even huffing or groaning, proving that he had been picking up more than bottles of beer and double shots of whiskey for a while now. Then she watched as he quickly rolled up a head and set it in place, making the whole creation even taller than himself.

"Wait right here," Cameron said and jogged through the snow back to the bar. When he returned, he brought a fistful of beer bottle caps and used them for the eyes and the mouth.

"Got a carrot for his nose?" she asked.

"This is a Honky Tonk snowman," he grinned as he took the top of a Coors bottle out of his pocket. "I found this in the trash can. It's about the size of a carrot nose." He set the bottle top in place, then stepped back, folded his arms over his chest, and frowned.

"Never thought we'd have a use for the neck of a busted beer bottle," Jorja said. She had tossed one toward the trash the night before and the top had broken off smooth.

"Me neither, but it works for our drinkin' buddy here," Cameron insisted, "but he still needs something."

"Use the rest of those beer caps for buttons on his chest. He does need something." Jorja stood back and studied their creation. "A scarf. That's what he needs."

She raced into the house and grabbed the red-and-green-plaid scarf that Abigail had given her for Christmas a few years back. When she returned, Cameron had found branches for the new fellow's arms and he had a can of Coors in his hand.

"I really don't think Frank James can drink that," she joked as she tiptoed and whipped the scarf around the snowman's neck.

"Who?" Cameron asked as he opened the can of beer and poured it on the ground. "This is for you, JJ. Remembering all the good times, the bad times, and all the ones in between." His voice was just a raspy whisper.

Jorja slipped an arm around his waist, and together they stood there in silence for several moments. She couldn't fathom building a snowman like this one with her sister, and yet the thing looked just right sitting there in the parking lot of the Honky Tonk.

"Cowboys don't cry." He wiped away a single tear from his cheek.

"Good men do when they remember a lost best friend," she said past the lump in her own throat.

"Thank you for that." He managed a weak smile. "Why did you name him Frank James?"

"He's named for Jesse's real brother. I thought it would be confusing to call him Cameron since some folks might think he was a girl." She bumped him with her hip and then stepped back to eye their snowman with the beer puddling around his base.

"Great name for our snowman." Cameron removed a knife from his pocket and poked a hole in the beer can and stuck it on the left tree branch that served as an arm.

"Why'd you put it on the left side? Was Frank a leftie?" she asked.

"Have no idea, but JJ was," he grinned. "Now, let's go to the grocery store before it closes, and we get all depressed again. This is supposed to be a cheerful day, not a sad one. We've been given a bar to run, and we've each made a brand-new friend because of it."

"So, you think I'm your friend?" Jorja flirted.

"I damn sure hope so, since we're going to be working together for a long, long time"—he wiggled his eyebrows—"unless you're so homesick that you want to sell me your half of this place and go home. You could be there in time for Santa Claus presents tomorrow morning if you leave right now."

"Not in your wildest dreams, cowboy." She gathered up a fistful of snow, threw it at him, and then ran as fast as she could back toward the bar.

She would have made it if she had been wearing anything but rubber boots.

Cameron tackled her for the second time and brought them both down to the ground with her on top of him this time. She started to roll to the side, but he held on to her, and suddenly, everything around them ceased to exist. She felt as if she was drowning in his dark-brown eyes. One of his hands went to the back of her head to gently pull her lips toward his, and then her heart began to race.

When their lips met, the temperature seemed to jack up at least twenty degrees, and her whole body melted into his as each kiss deepened. He sat up, keeping her in his lap, and moved his hands to her waist. If they didn't stop soon, they would be undressing each other right out there in the open and having wild sex in the snow.

She pushed away from him and shifted her weight to the side so that she was sitting beside him instead of in his lap. "That certainly made me forget all about homesickness," she said, panting.

"Me too." He grinned as he got to his feet and extended a hand to help her up. "We should lock the door and go to the store."

"In rubber boots?" She took his hand and let him help her to her feet. "Shouldn't we change into something more appropriate?"

"After those scaldin'-hot kisses, I'm not sure we would be safe being that close to the beds in our apartment," he said. "I'll start the truck if you'll lock the door."

"I'll grab my purse while I'm in there," she said, "and I'll also change my boots."

"Women!" He chuckled.

"Aren't we amazing?" She let go of his hand and dashed in the back door. She took time to change her boots and peek into the mirror above her chest of drawers. Her cheeks were bright red. Her lips were bee-stung and her eyes were still glazed over. Sweet Jesus! She'd only known the man a few days, and she'd almost been ready to drag him into the apartment and spend the rest of the day with him on a twin bed.

"Merry Christmas to me if I had." She touched her lips to see if they were as hot as they felt, but surprisingly enough, they were cool.

You are going to be the death of your family for thinking like that. Abigail's voice popped into Jorja's head.

Take off your holier-than-thou britches, Jorja argued. *Thinking something doesn't mean I'm going to act on it.*

Chapter 7

WHEN JORJA GOT INTO THE TRUCK AND FASTENED THE seat belt, Cameron was still smoldering hot from that make-out session, but he turned the heater on low for her benefit. She now wore a pair of red cowboy boots, but that was all that had been changed. Tight jeans hugged every curve, and her cheeks were flushed from the cold—or maybe from all that kissing. Had it heated her up as much as it had him, he wondered?

Think about cooking or something, anything but the way she felt in your arms, he told himself as he turned on the windshield wipers and drove away from the parking lot. "North or south?" he asked.

"Why?" she asked.

"Distance is a little over thirty miles either way," he answered.

"Is Gordon that far? I got the idea from Frankie that it wasn't but a few miles," she said.

"We need a supermarket, not a convenience store. Mineral Wells is to the northeast. South is Stephenville. Both have a Walmart and several grocery stores," he explained. "I looked it all up before I moved from Florida, so I'd know what to expect. If one of us needs a hospital, we'd probably go to one of those towns too," he answered.

"Either one is fine with me, then," she answered. "Just how much food are we buying today?"

"Let's try for two weeks' worth. I'm ready for something more than burgers and fries." Talking about food almost took his mind off her lips and the way he felt with her lying on top of his body.

"Me, too. I've been starving for fried chicken," she said.

"We could go to KFC while we're out and about," he offered.

"Why don't we start our own tradition?" She would make a lousy poker player, because her face lit up and her eyes started to twinkle. "Since we can't go home for the holidays, let's do it our way. We'll have fried chicken, mashed potatoes and gravy, hot biscuits, and corn on the cob for our Christmas dinner. What's your very favorite kind of pie?"

"Cherry cobbler with ice cream on top," he answered.

"And you're making me hungry talking about a dinner like that."

"Then we'll have cobbler for dessert," she said. "We can get ice cream at the Mingus convenience store on the way back home. That way it won't melt." She took a deep breath and went on. "But for today, let's go have something like Mexican or Italian."

"Sounds good to me." Cameron was glad the highway had been cleaned off and that the traffic was light that day.

He was humming a new country song by Jason Isbell titled "Cover Me Up" and planning to ask the jukebox guy to include it the next time he came by when he noticed movement out of his peripheral vision. He stomped the brakes, hit a patch of ice, and slid to a stop as a buck and a doe crossed the road in front of them.

"Two again," he said.

"What was that?" she asked.

"Seems like everywhere I look there's two of everything, beginning with those two doves that we hung above the bar," he answered.

"So you noticed that too," she said. "Think it means anything?"

"I don't believe in signs, magic, and miracles." He chuckled.

The trip took a little longer than what the map app on his

phone said, but they were in Mineral Wells before noon. He noticed a sign for a barbecue place a mile up the road and pointed it out to Jorja.

"How about some brisket?" he asked.

"Yes!" She clapped her hands. "And I hope they have good beans. Mama makes the best baked beans in the whole world."

"I'd have to argue with you there," Cameron said. "My nana wears that crown, and if you don't believe me, you'll have to go to Sunday dinner with me sometime over at her house."

"I'd have to taste them before I'd agree with you, and I got to tell you, my mother's will be a hard act to follow."

She was definitely flirting with him, and suddenly he got cold feet. There were at least a hundred reasons why he should shut this down, and number one was that they were partners. They had come pretty damn close to going inside and having sex that morning. Thank God she had the good sense to stop it, and they could think about things before they dived into that passion pool.

What if they did get physically involved, and then it fizzled? They'd still be partners and things would get awkward in a hurry, but what if it didn't burn out after the first few weeks and turned into a serious relationship? Could they take it to that plane and still work together?

"You sure got quiet," she commented when he pulled his truck into the parking lot of the barbecue place.

"Thinkin' about those baked beans." JJ would have called that a half lie, and those didn't matter since they weren't one hundred percent fibs. Cameron had been thinking about food earlier, so it was not a full-fledged lie.

"You must be hungry," she said as she unfastened her seat belt and got out of the truck before he could rush around and open the door for her.

"Look!" She pointed at two cardinals, a bright-red male and his lady friend, sitting on the bench outside the door. "Still think it's not a sign of some kind?"

"Coincidence," he muttered as he held the door for her.

The restaurant was nearly empty, which did not bode well for its reputation in Cameron's opinion, but the waitress told them to sit anywhere they wanted and was quick to bring them a menu once they'd chosen a table. "We're only going to be open for another hour, so y'all just got here in time. We are out of smoked chicken, but we've still got almost everything else."

"I'll have a pulled-pork sandwich, baked beans, coleslaw and potato salad, and a glass of sweet tea," Jorja said.

"That was quick," Cameron said.

"I don't want to spend my whole hour looking at the

menu," she told him. "I want to take time to enjoy every bite of my food."

"I'll have the dinner plate with everything she said, except I want half a rack of ribs." He handed the lady the menus and turned his attention back to Jorja. "I'll share my ribs if you'll give me half your sandwich. Both sounded good."

"Are you sure about that? Adam sure got in trouble when God took one of his ribs to make a woman," Jorja teased.

"I'll take my chances." He chuckled.

She unwrapped the napkin from around her silverware and picked up the fork. "If you're that brave, then yes, I will share with you, but I'm warnin' you, I do not share my fried chicken legs with anyone." She accentuated every single word with a jab of her fork.

"No worries, darlin'." He grinned. "These folks are out of chicken—and I'm a breast man so I'm not interested in legs anyway."

Jorja could feel the heat rising on her neck. There was no way she could prevent it from reaching her face, but she'd be damned if she let Cameron get ahead of her. "You're a lucky man since a chicken has two breasts."

"I've always been a lucky cowboy." He winked.

"Always might fail you in the future." She fluffed out the oversize red napkin and put it in her lap.

"I hope not." A wide grin covered his face.

The waitress brought their tea and a basket of hot rolls and set them down on the table. "Be right back with your food."

"See how lucky I am," Cameron teased. "We don't even have to wait an hour to be served."

"That's not luck, cowboy," Jorja argued. "That's just because everyone else is home with their families today, and we're probably going to get the last of what's in the pots, and it won't be worth eating."

"The last is always the best," he said.

"Are we still talking about food?" she asked.

"Of course." He looked as innocent as a little boy in Sunday school class.

Jorja made a vow never to play poker with him. If he could use his expressions to lie like that, he'd win all her money, or her clothes if they were playing that kind of poker.

The waitress brought their food, and Jorja cut her sandwich in half. She put one part on his plate, forked over two ribs onto her own plate, and then began to eat. "Good ribs and great beans."

"Oh, yeah," he agreed between bites. "We'll have to come back here again."

They finished their food, which was exceptionally good,

bypassed dessert, and headed straight to Walmart to get their groceries. That took two hours, and half of that time was spent standing in line to check out. All those folks that weren't at the barbecue place were evidently in Walmart buying food for the next day.

"I'm glad we shopped for two weeks," she said as they loaded the bags into the back seat of his truck. "I'd hate to do this every single week. It would blow a whole day to drive up here, shop, and then get home in time to open the bar at six."

"Yep," he agreed.

The roads had been clear on the way to Mineral Wells, but by the time they started home, they were slick with sleet and ice. Cameron had slowed down to thirty miles an hour when she saw the bull and cow right across a barbed wire fence.

"You've got to start believing in signs," she told him.

"Why?" He kept his hands on the wheel and his eyes straight ahead.

"Take a look to your right," she answered him. "And they've even got bells around their necks. Dogs with antlers and now cattle with bells."

"It's Christmas," he said. "Folks do silly things during this season."

"Possums?" she asked.

"Looking for carrots," he answered.

Thank God they were in a heavy truck with four-wheel drive, or the thirty-minute trip would have taken a lot longer than an hour and a half. She didn't realize she was gripping the handrest on the inside of the door so hard until they came to a long greasy sliding stop in the parking lot of the Honky Tonk.

"Don't hit Frank James," she squealed.

"Doin' my best not to," Cameron said through clenched teeth, and then let out a loud whoosh of pent-up breath when the truck finally stopped a few feet from the two snowmen. "That was too close for comfort."

"Amen. Who'd have thought the weather would get so bad so quickly?" Jorja opened the door and stepped out, only to slip and fall square on her butt.

She started to grab the tire and work her way back up when Cameron scooped her up and started for the back door with her in his strong arms. "Are you hurt?" he asked.

"Just my pride," she answered. "I should have kept my rubber boots on."

"Honey, as slick as this damn parking lot is, we need ice skates to get around." He set her down on the back stoop and unlocked the door. "I'll bring in the groceries if you'll put them away."

"You'll get no argument from me on that deal." She headed

down the short hall to the doorway leading into their living quarters. Never had a little efficiency apartment looked so good as this one did after what seemed like a sled ride home.

"Home," she muttered as she pulled off her coat and stocking hat, then kicked off her boots.

Nashville had not been home even though she'd lived there for years. She'd always thought of her place as "the apartment." Home was Hurricane Mills, where she'd grown up. How could home suddenly be an old honky tonk in a town thirty miles from a Walmart and a doctor's office?

Sometimes Santa Claus brings you a present you didn't even ask for. Her grandmother's voice was back in her head. *Last spring you told me you were ready to get serious and settle down, but there were no good men left in the world. Then you said that you would love to be your own boss. Merry Christmas, darlin' girl.*

Jorja remembered that conversation as if it had happened only yesterday, and then her mother's words from years ago came back to haunt her. *Be careful what you wish for. You just might get it and not know what to do with it.*

Cameron brought in two fists full of plastic bags and set them on the table. "Got about that many more. We forgot to stop and get ice cream for tomorrow. I'll drive back to the convenience store and get it when I get done unloading."

"You will not!" she exclaimed. "We slipped and slid on the ice so much that we barely got stopped once. No sense in testing fate a second time, no matter how lucky you think you are. We'll get some whipped cream from the bar and use it on our cobbler."

He held up his palms defensively. "Hey, with that tone, I won't even think of arguing with you. I like whipped cream on my pie as well as ice cream anyway...and if we're discussing whipped cream..." He grinned.

She pointed a finger at him. "Don't go there." She'd blushed more in the past twenty-four hours than she had in her entire life.

And you felt more alive in that time than you ever did before. Her grandmother was back again.

"Go where?" he asked, and there was that innocent look again.

"I bet you could sweet-talk a nun into falling into bed with you," she smarted off.

"Never tried, and quite frankly, I'd be kind of afraid of that. I'm fast, but, honey, lightning is faster than I could ever be." He chuckled as he went back out for the rest of the groceries.

She found herself humming "Twinkle, Twinkle Lucky Star" as she put the food away.

Then suddenly, the song filled the whole apartment and Cameron brought in the last of the groceries. "I stopped by the jukebox to play a little music while we make some popcorn and hot chocolate and get ready for our movies. I only plugged in three songs. If we need more, I can go back and put more money in." He put the bags on the table and held out his arms. "May I have this dance?"

She set down two cans of green beans and walked into his embrace. He two-stepped with her around the apartment, between the beds, and then out into the bar where there was more room. To her surprise, he'd not only put money in the jukebox, but he'd turned on the Christmas tree lights. She glanced out the window as he danced her around the tables with chairs sitting on top of them to Merle singing about a lucky star, and there were two raccoons staring right at her. They had their little paws on the outside windowsill, and she could've sworn they were smiling.

The sky was gray with heavy clouds, so there were no stars shining that night, but the one on the Christmas tree was glowing all pretty and bright. When she was in a position to see out the window again, the raccoons were gone, but she had no doubt now that the universe really was sending her signs right and left. Everything, including the warm fuzzy feeling in her heart, said that the past had faded like the sky, and her future was that lucky star sitting on top of a thirty-year-old Christmas tree.

"It's an omen," she whispered.

"What is?" he asked.

"All this." The song ended and Mary Chapin Carpenter started singing "I Feel Lucky." Cameron spun her around in a swing dance. Both of them were laughing when he brought her back to his chest.

"What about all this? How can it be an omen?" he asked.

She laughed and looked up into his twinkling eyes. "Both songs talk about us being lucky, and everywhere we look there's two of something. I just know it means something."

"Maybe it means that it's great to have a partner," he said.

"Don't you get the feeling we were meant to be right here at Christmas?" she asked.

Life in Mingus, Texas, was going to be just fine. She'd found one of the last good men in the world, and their journey together might not be what she expected when she made that wish last spring, but it would be their story no matter where it led.

He brushed a soft kiss across her lips. "I wouldn't want to be anywhere else."

Chapter 8

JORJA HUMMED SONGS ABOUT FEELING LUCKY WHILE SHE watched the bag of popcorn in the microwave. A scraping noise behind her made her whip around to see Cameron moving his bed across the floor. If he thought a few kisses gave him permission to turn two beds into one, he had rocks or cow patties for brains. She opened her mouth to say something and then realized that he had made an L-shape out of the beds.

"Now we've got a sectional to use to watch our movies," he said. "We won't have to strain our necks trying to see the television. I don't know why the folks who put it in hung the damned thing on the wall."

"Probably because they didn't have room for an entertainment unit or even a stand to put it on." Couldn't he see how small the place they shared really was?

"Maybe so." He put the first movie in the player, which was sitting on a chair from the bar, and picked up the remote. "Need some help over there?"

"I got it under control, but I'm wondering what we're going to use for a coffee table or end table to set our mugs on." She poured two big cups full of hot chocolate and added a fistful of miniature marshmallows to each of them.

"How about another chair? We can put it right here where the beds meet up." He headed out to the bar before she could answer.

She poured the popcorn into a bowl and carried it over to the new sectional. The part that faced the television was his bed, so she set it somewhere close to the middle and went back for the hot chocolate. By the time she'd carried that from the kitchen area, he had set the chair where it was needed and had flopped down on the bed with the remote in his hand. She sat down on the other side of the popcorn bowl and drew her legs up under her to sit cross-legged.

"Are we ready?" He pointed the remote toward the television like it was a gun.

"Nope, we have to dim the lights." She hopped up and flipped the light switch next to the back door. "Did you ever realize that if we came home drunk some night, we might get confused and try to open the wrong back door?"

"Honey, if we come home drunk, we'll just stagger in here from the bar." He laughed. "I guess the original Honky Tonk always had the front door and back door, but when they built on this apartment, they decided to make it accessible through the parking lot. Now are we ready?"

She sat back down and nodded. "*Laissez les bon temps rouler.*"

"Let the good times roll." He interpreted what she'd said.

She had her hand in the popcorn bowl when *Home Alone* started instead of one of the two that they'd talked about. "I love this, but…"

He covered her hand with his. "I figured we were starting our own traditions. Besides, if we watch what we used to see with our families, we'll get homesick. This one will make us laugh. We will watch it every Christmas and remember what a good time we had on our first Christmas together."

"So, you think we'll be together for years on down the road?" She slid her hand out from under his and filled her mouth with popcorn.

"Yep, I do." He picked up a few kernels and popped them into his mouth.

"We should take pictures of Frank James and our tree and decorations in the bar and even our apartment," she said. "I'll make a scrapbook to keep them all in…" She stopped and stared at the television. "This is my favorite part. Someday I'm going to have a son like Kevin."

"Are you going to forget him when you fly to Paris?" Cameron teased.

"Hell, no! To begin with, I'll have a bar to run, so I won't even be flying to Paris, Texas, much less to the one across the big pond," she answered as she fluffed up his pillow and leaned an elbow on it.

"What about all the other kids? Are you going to let them call him FedEx?" Cameron chuckled.

"Nope, and what makes you think there's going to be other children?" she asked.

"A boy needs siblings," Cameron said. "Someone to fight with and stand up with when someone else picks a fight."

"That's something to think about later. Right now, I don't want to miss a minute of this movie," she told him.

———————

Cameron awoke to nothing but a blank television screen staring at him. *Home Alone 2* had ended, the credits had rolled, and the digital clock on the DVD player told him that it was three thirty in the morning. He was stretched out on the front side of the bed. Jorja was spooned right up to his back and had one leg thrown over him. Her arm was tucked tightly around his chest as if she was afraid that she would fall off the back side of the bed. He wished he had a picture of the two of them to put in her scrapbook, but there was no way he could reach his phone without waking her. He managed to pick up the remote and turn off the television, and then he closed his hand around hers and went back to sleep.

He was awakened again at ten o'clock in the morning when she gasped and jumped off the bed. He rolled to the wrong side and wound up on the floor about the same time that a spider rappelled down from the ceiling and hung suspended about six inches above his nose. Then another one swung down right beside it, so now there were two of the monsters staring at him as if he was going to be their supper.

"Jorja, a little help here," he whispered.

"Help nothing!" she said loudly. "I'm making sure I've still got all my clothes on the right way. We didn't…" She leaned over and stared right past the evil creatures dancing the mambo right above his head. "Did we?"

"We slept together." He was surprised that he could move his lips to speak. "We didn't do any more than that. Would you please kill these two varmints so I can see if I broke any bones when I fell off the bed?"

"What are you talking about? Is there a snake?" She headed in the direction of her chest of drawers to get her gun.

"No snake," he whispered. "It's damn spiders. Please don't try to kill them with a bullet. You might miss and hit me."

"Well, why didn't you say so?" she asked as she leaned over the bed, grabbed both webs, and brought the dangling devils her way. Once she cleared the bed, she lowered the things to the floor and stomped on them. "Two of them. Do you believe what I've been telling you about signs now?"

"I'm a believer." He sat up. "Evidently even spiders and snakes need partners."

"You can check for broken bones. Do I need to take you to the hospital?" she asked. "I'm not good at driving on slick roads, but I'll do my best."

He sat up and shook his head. "Everything seems fine, but we're damn sure having this place exterminated as soon as we can get a man out here to do it."

She sat down on the edge of his bed. "Let's don't make this a part of our Christmas tradition."

"What? Falling asleep together or the spiders?" he asked as he got up and moved his bed back to its usual place.

She opened her mouth to say something but abruptly whipped around and went to the stove. "I'm making cinnamon rolls for breakfast. They won't be the fancy kind like

Mama makes in Hurricane Mills, but they'll be what we have on Christmas morning."

"What can I do to help?" he asked. "And, honey, I didn't mean to embarrass you. Who knows where we'll be next year at Christmas, but I really think it would be all right if we made it a tradition of falling asleep together. I liked the feeling of waking up in the middle of the night with you keeping me warm."

"You can get out the brown sugar, butter, and cinnamon. I'm just going to roll out some biscuits from a can." She tried to sidestep replying to what he had said, but it didn't work. "And I had a wonderful Christmas Eve. Thank you for making me laugh, for dancing with me, taking me out to eat, and for"—she stopped and looked up into his eyes—"and for just sleeping with me."

"What does that mean?" He brought out the ingredients she'd asked for.

"It means, 'Thank you for being a gentleman,' she answered.

"Like I said before, I'm not afraid of snakes, bullies, or redheaded women, but I am afraid of spiders and my mama, even though I'm thirty-one years old. I'm glad you're here to kill the spiders for me, but, honey, not even you with your cute little pistol could protect me from my mama if I was anything less than a gentleman. And just for the record, I'm more afraid of her than I would be of any tarantula," he said.

Her smile turned into a giggle. That soon became laughter, and then they were both guffawing. Cameron grabbed up a dish towel and dried her eyes with it and then his own. "You might think I'm kiddin', but that, darlin', is the gospel truth."

"I would like your mama," Jorja said.

"You'll have to meet her someday." He moved to the other end of the short cabinet and put on a pot of coffee. His mother would love to see her baby boy settled down, and there was no doubt that she would adore Jorja's sass.

Holy smokin' hell! What was the matter with him? He'd been runnin' from commitment and serious relationships since he was a teenager. He'd known Jorja less than a week, and he didn't even stumble or stutter when he thought about "settling down."

Chapter 9

"I was right, wasn't I?" Chigger grinned as she leaned in between two cowboys on barstools and ordered a pitcher of beer. "Christmas is over, and folks are ready to get out of the house. They're tired of turkey and fixin's, and they're probably like me and just want some good old greasy burgers and fries."

"Christmas isn't over until midnight." Jorja set two burger baskets in front of the guys at the bar. "But you were sure enough right. Did you have a good Christmas?"

Chigger flashed a diamond ring at her. "Frankie and I are engaged. I said yes, but the wedding ain't happenin' for a long time."

"Why's that?" Cameron handed her the pitcher of beer.

"It took five years for me to say yes to the ring. I'm in no hurry to say yes to the wedding cake or the dress either one." Chigger grinned. "Did y'all have a good Christmas?"

"The best," Jorja answered and went back to work on the next order.

"Really?" Cameron asked. "We didn't even have presents."

"Yes, we did," she protested with a bump of her hip against his. "I killed spiders on Christmas morning for you, and you made me laugh. Those things are more important than material things."

"Does that mean we're not giving gifts next year?" he asked.

"Hell, no! I still believe in Santa, so he'd better bring me something next year, and I do like my Santa in a Stetson," she flirted.

He chuckled. "What do you think you'll give Santa next year?"

"A can of bug spray to start with," she answered, "and a flyswatter."

"Sounds good to me." He set two shot glasses on the bar and poured them full of Jack Daniel's.

"I'll be your Santa, darlin'." One of the cowboys winked and tipped his black cowboy hat toward Jorja. "I've got the hat, and I'll get you a big beautiful present."

"That's so sweet, but from that ring on your finger, darlin',

I'd say you better be saving all your pennies to get your wife something big and beautiful," she told him.

"Busted!" The cowboy laughed.

"Good catch," Cameron whispered.

Jorja had settled into her new job so effortlessly that she wondered if she hadn't owned a bar in a past life—if reincarnation even existed. She felt like she'd been right there, working beside Cameron for months, not days. There had to be a logical explanation for it, but she was too busy to give it much thought. She finished up the order she was working on, put it on a tray, and took it out to a table with four young women. They were all dressed in what looked like brand-new blinged-out jeans, cowgirl boots, and western shirts. Their Santa Claus had certainly been good to them that year, and before the night was over, they just might have a little more luck in their lives.

The idea of luck brought Haggard's song back to her mind, and as fate would have it, someone played it on the jukebox. Jorja had to weave in and out among the people on the crowded dance floor to get back to the bar. Folks must really like that song, she thought. Everyone was dancing except for one blonde who was sitting on a stool with her back turned. She looked vaguely familiar, which meant that she'd probably been in the Honky Tonk earlier in the week. Someday Jorja would be able to put names with faces.

She rounded the end of the bar and turned around. "What can I get you?" she asked without really looking at the woman.

"A suitcase to pack your things in," Abigail said.

Jorja jerked her head up to see her sister glaring right at her. "Merry Christmas to you too."

"I'm in no mood for your sass. Mama sent me to bring you home. I got an Uber from the airport and it was a horrible trip, so come out from there, and let's start packing. I'll be riding with you in your car on the way back." Abigail's mouth was set in a thin line that said she wasn't taking no for an answer.

Jorja flipped two meat patties onto the grill and filled the deep fry basket with onion rings. "You must be hungry."

"I am starving, but you won't change my mind with a burger basket. I'm not going home without you," Abigail declared.

Jorja wouldn't argue with her sister right there in her place of business, but she wasn't going anywhere—most of all not back to Hurricane Mills.

She motioned for Cameron to come to her end of the bar. "Need some help?" he called out over the top of the noise.

"Yes, I do." Jorja tried to let him know with her expression that he was walking into something worse than a whole nest of spiders.

"What can I do?" He stopped right in front of her.

"You can meet my sister, Abigail, who for some crazy reason thinks I'm going to let her drive my car back to Tennessee," she answered.

"Pleased to meet you." Cameron nodded toward Abigail and then turned his focus back to Jorja. "Honey, if she needs your car, we've still got my pickup. We'll be fine with one vehicle."

"She thinks I'm going to be in the car with her, daw…lin.'" Jorja dragged out the endearment like a native of southern Louisiana.

"Oh, well now, that poses a real problem." Cameron chuckled. "I can't run this place by myself. You have super-powers and protect me from spiders and make me believe in signs, miracles, and magic."

"I don't know what you're talking about, but Jorja is not going to disgrace the family by owning or working in a place like this. Call it an intervention or a kidnapping or whatever you want, but if I have to hog-tie you and strap you to the top of your car, I *will* take you home." Abigail shot daggers by turn at each of them.

Jorja finished making the food and set it in front of Abigail. "Eat this and then go through that door right there and take a nap on my bed. You'll know which one it is by the look of it. We'll talk at two o'clock when Cameron and I close up the place and, honey, the universe has spoken to me. Who am I to refuse to listen when something that big and important tells me this is where I belong."

"I'm not going anywhere," Abigail bit into a hot onion ring. "I don't trust you not to go somewhere and hide, and what do you mean, I'll know your bed? Are you sleeping in the same room with this man?"

"Yes, ma'am, I am, and I think I remember telling you that already," Jorja answered.

Chigger sat down on the stool right beside Abigail and nudged her with her shoulder. "I'm Chigger and, honey, if she wasn't sharing the Honky Tonk apartment with Cameron, I'd give my brand-new engagement ring back to Frankie and offer to share more than a room with him. Jorja, darlin', would you get me and Frankie an order of fries? We done worked up an appetite out there on the dance floor."

The grease sizzled when Jorja sank the basket of frozen fries into it, but it couldn't possibly sizzle as much as the temper she was holding inside of her. How dare her sister show up and think she could control her life! Jorja was almost thirty years old, by damn, and she'd lived on her own for more than a decade. No one had come to Nashville and tried to force her to go back to Hurricane Mills when she took the job with an obscure country music label.

"What are you going to do?" Cameron whispered as he got two longneck Coors from the refrigerator.

"My job," Jorja answered, "and ignore my sister. If she wants to get blisters on her butt sitting there, then she can live with the pain of them all the way back to Tennessee. Maybe enough drunk cowboys will hit on her that she'll give up and go take a nap."

Nothing or no one could have convinced Jorja more quickly that she was right where she needed to be, and where she intended to stay, than Abigail showing up and making her demands. Jorja liked working with Cameron, loved living with him, and really liked the way his kisses jacked up her pulse. The devil himself, wearing a black Stetson and tight blue jeans, and riding a big white horse would have a fight on his hands if he even thought he could drag Jorja back to Tennessee.

Jorja and Cameron were swamped for the next four hours. She didn't have time to talk to Abigail, and her sister didn't budge off the stool—not even to make a trip to the ladies' room. Only a few die-hards were still at the bar when Cameron pointed at the clock.

"Time to close, guys. Wishing all y'all one more Merry Christmas," Cameron said.

They stumbled to the coatrack beside the door and

retrieved their jackets. Cameron locked the door behind them and then sank down in a chair as far away from the bar as possible.

Traitor, Jorja thought, *you could come on over here and give me some support.*

"Why don't y'all get something cold to drink, and we'll visit?" he said.

Abigail's high heels sounded like pops from a .22 rifle as she made her way across the wooden floor. Jorja grabbed a diet root beer and two bottles of Coors from the refrigerator and carried them to the table.

"I'm not leaving." Jorja set the drinks down and pulled a chair over closer to Cameron.

"I hate to admit it, but I understand." Abigail sighed.

"Are you drunk or sleep-deprived?" Jorja asked.

"No, I just got my eyes opened tonight." Abigail got up and hugged her sister. "Cameron, would you mind if Jorja and I talked privately?"

"Not one bit." He picked up one of the beers. "I'll go get my shower while you ladies visit, and I'll be glad to sleep on the sofa in the office if Abigail wants to spend the night."

"Thank you." Abigail nodded.

Jorja waited until he was out of the room before she glared at her sister. "What did you and Mama think gave you the right to do something like this? I'm a grown woman, and I can make my own decisions."

"We love you, and this seemed so"—Abigail struggled with the right word—"so crazy. Hanging out in a bar in the middle of nowhere in Texas with a man you'd never met before, and that's before we even knew y'all were living together. What would you have done if you had a daughter and she was doing this?"

"I hope I would trust her enough to make her own decisions and support her in them." Jorja twisted the cap off her beer and took a long drink.

"Well, I hope one of my girls never puts me to this test." Abigail eyed the beer, but finally took a sip of her root beer. "I'm not staying here tonight. I'm going back to Fort Worth as soon as I finish this root beer and use the ladies' room."

"Why? What changed your mind?" Jorja asked.

"You'll think I'm crazy if I tell you." Abigail's cheeks turned slightly red.

"Probably, but I already think you're insane for flying out here on Christmas with the intention of kidnapping me, so spit it out," Jorja said.

"It's the way that Cameron looks at you," Abigail said. "Daddy still looks at Mama like that, and the second thing is that you are happy. I can see it in your face when you're working, and I heard you humming a couple of times."

"I had to hum to calm myself down. I wanted to climb on top of the bar and kick you off that barstool." Jorja was pretty sure that her sister was creating an excuse to tell their mother so she wouldn't be in trouble for not bringing her errant younger sister back with her. "You are right on one count. I am happy. I don't have to worry about deadlines or what people think of my work. I just have to show up, draw beer, and man the grill. Cameron and I get along famously well, and we like each other a lot."

"I can see that, and I believe he's a good man. If he's not, I trust you to take care of things." Abigail finished off her root beer. "I'm going home. I've already called, and an Uber will be here in ten minutes to take me back to the airport. I can get an early-morning flight out of Fort Worth and be home in time to have leftovers for lunch. I'll pave the way for when you bring Cameron home to ask Daddy for your hand in marriage."

"Hey, now!" Jorja threw up both palms. "Let's don't get ahead of ourselves."

"Just callin' it like I see it and, honey, don't worry. Cameron don't even know it yet either. If someone had told me I'd sit in an old dive bar for four hours and leave without you, I would have had them committed, but I feel in my heart that you are right where you belong and with who you belong with." She pushed her chair back and bent to give

Jorja a hug. "Merry Christmas and promise me you'll try to get away to come visit us soon. I don't think I'll be able to drag Mama and Daddy to a place like this, and they really want to see you."

"Miracles really do happen at Christmas." Jorja grinned.

———————

Cameron took a quick shower, pulled on a pair of pajama pants that his mother had given him last Christmas and a T-shirt, and then began to pace the floor. If Abigail talked Jorja into going back to Tennessee, he'd have to find someone to help run the bar. He and Jorja had fallen into the partnership so easily that it was like they could read each other's minds from the beginning. Cameron didn't believe in love at first sight, and his disbelief was compounded by the fact that Jorja had a gun pointed at him the first time he laid eyes on her. That disbelief aside, he couldn't explain in any other way this thing that was obviously developing between them.

Finally, after several trips from the wall where the television hung to the kitchen sink and back again, he heard a vehicle start up. He rushed to the window, cupped his hands around his eyes, and looked out, but he couldn't see a blessed thing. Was one person or two in the car? He couldn't tell, but lo and behold, there were two squirrels playing chase up and down Mr. Frank James Snowman. A bit of tinsel sparkled on one of their tails.

"I'll be damned." He chuckled. "Jorja is right. Fate or the universe or the magic of Christmas is trying to tell us something. Squirrels don't even come out to play at night, and yet there they are. I can't deny all the signs any longer now."

The door from the bar into the apartment swung open, and Jorja headed toward the bathroom. He was almost afraid to turn around. Now that he had admitted that they belonged together as more than just partners, he didn't want her to leave. Should he beg her to stay? He finally whipped around and locked eyes with her.

"Are you leaving or staying?" He couldn't tell from her expression. Maybe her intention was to get her Christmas shower curtain and pack it with the rest of her stuff.

Jorja yawned. "I'm not going anywhere, and Abigail is on her way back to Fort Worth to the airport. She says there's an early-morning flight to Nashville, and she'll be on it."

"Thank God." He heaved a big sigh of relief.

"Are you glad she's going so you don't have to sleep on that lumpy sofa in the office, or because I'm staying and you can get a decent night's rest in your own bed?" she asked.

He took a couple of long steps toward her, wrapped her

in his arms, and swung her around. "I'd sleep on the floor if I had to, darlin'. I'm just glad you are stayin'. We make a good couple, and I didn't want you to leave."

"As in partners, or…"

He answered her question when his lips came down on hers in a long, passionate kiss. When it ended, he led her to the table and pulled a chair out for her. "As in everything, Jorja Jenks. I don't know what the future holds, but right now, no matter what it is, I want us to be together in all of it."

"I don't take risks," she whispered. "I usually calculate every single move I make. Signing the papers to take over this bar with you was the most impulsive thing I have ever done. After watching my sister glare at me for the past four hours, it seems like the smartest move I've ever made." She stopped and took a deep breath. "And no matter what the future holds, we can face it together. After all, you are the snake slayer and I'm the spider killer. We make an excellent couple." She took him by the hand, stood up, and led him out into the bar.

The place was a total mess with bottles, mugs, and pitchers on the tables, and chairs strewn about everywhere, but that didn't matter. All the decorations were still lit up and sparkling.

"Look," Jorja pointed to the window. "The sky has cleared, and the stars are dancing around the moon."

"What are we doing in here?" he asked. "If we're going to have a midnight snack, I'd rather have a chunk of that cobbler you made for our dinner."

"Later," she told him as she plugged coins into the jukebox, took him by the hand, and pulled him toward the door.

When they were on the porch, she wrapped her arms around his neck and pressed her body close to his, then pointed at the porch rail where a pair of robins were roosting. "Robins are a harbinger of spring. They're telling us that we belong together every season in the year, not just at Christmas," he said.

"I believe it," she said. "This is our song, and I wanted to have this dance with you out here under the real lucky stars."

"Yes, ma'am," Cameron two-stepped with her on the porch for the first verse and then danced her back into the bar for the rest of the song. "Well freeze if we stay out there any longer," he said.

"Not when I'm in your arms," she whispered. "We should close out Christmas this way from now on."

"I love that idea. Merry Christmas to us," he agreed and brushed a soft kiss across her lips.

Summertime
on the
RANCH

Chapter 1

BECCA SCOLDED HERSELF FOR LEAVING THE DOOR OPEN.

Now Dalton's pesky dog had snuck into the watermelon wine shed. If he scratched off a hair and it landed in one of the containers of juice, she intended to strangle the shaggy critter and hang him out on the barbed wire fence to show all the other ugly mutts in southern Oklahoma what happens when a dog hair got into her wine.

She crammed the air lock down on the bottle, wiped the outside, and hurried over to the door. "Get out of here!" she yelled as she pointed outside. Austin had trusted her with the wine shed for a whole week, and she was not going to let her boss and best friend down.

Tuff rolled over on his back and looked up at her with big brown eyes. "I said, 'Go!'" She stomped her foot, but the dog just wagged his tail. "Who names a raggedy-ass mutt Tuff, anyway?" She grabbed a broom, and his tail flipped back and forth so fast that it was a blur.

"He ain't afraid of a broom." Dalton's deep Texas drawl startled her. "I use one just like that to scratch his tummy out in the barn, and he's named after Tuff Hydeman, who is a world champion professional bull rider." He gave a shrill whistle, and Tuff jumped up from the floor and stood at attention. "Come on, boy. We won't stay where we're not wanted."

"Shaggy from the old Scooby-Doo shows fits him better," Becca said.

"Now, you're just hurting the poor little fella's feelings," Dalton said. "Don't pay no attention to what she says, Tuff. She don't know jack squat about a good rodeo dog like you."

Becca popped her hands on her hips. "I've been to rodeos, and I grew up on a ranch. Don't tell me that I don't know nothing about cattle dogs."

Dalton Wilson's confidence oozed out of him, but then there wasn't a woman in the whole universe who wouldn't jump at the chance to walk down the aisle with him. Sweet Lord, the cowboy looked like sex on a stick.

Dalton flashed a brilliant smile that softened his square jaw. "You should never judge a book by its cover." He gave another shrill whistle, and Tuff pranced toward the door, head and tail held high as if he was marching up to the judge's stand to receive the biggest trophy in a prestigious dog show.

In Becca's opinion, he was still as ugly as sin on Sunday morning.

Together, Dalton and Tuff strutted out of the shed. One sexy cowboy that Becca was determined not to let get under her skin or in her heart, and a wiry dog that shared DNA with steel wool.

"Dammit!" Becca swore under her breath. "I've probably joined all the women in the universe in admiring him, but the difference is that I'm stronger than they are, and I can damn well fight off his charms."

Becca McKay lived up to her Irish heritage with her flaming-red hair and mossy-green eyes. She loved Irish coffee and Irish food and had a little of the Irish accent, just like her daddy who'd been born in County Cork. When it came to music and the southern accent in her voice, she was her mama's daughter, and she was country through and through.

Becca had covered songs by Tanya Tucker, Reba McEntire, Dolly Parton, and a whole host of other female country artists from the time she could hold a microphone at county fairs, family reunions, or anywhere anyone would let her sing. With stars in her eyes, she'd gone to Nashville right out of high school, intent on making a career as a country music recording artist. By Christmas, she figured she would have a contract, and all the folks back home in Ringgold, Texas, would be listening to her sing on the radio.

Yeah, right.

At Christmas, she was working for one of the dinner theaters in the evenings and singing on street corners just to make rent for the one-bedroom apartment she shared with four other girls. Ten years later, she was working at Tootsie's Orchid Lounge as a bartender at night, in a winery during the day, and living in the same walk-up apartment. At least by that time, she was sharing the place with only one other girl, who was just as desperate as she was to get a toe in the door as a country singer.

The previous December, she had been on her way home from Tootsie's sometime after two in the morning when the high heel of her boot stabbed a piece of paper. No matter how hard she shook her foot, it wouldn't let go. Finally, she leaned against the brick wall of a building and removed it with her fingers.

The streetlight illuminated the paper enough that she could identify it as the last page of a contract that had no signature. The next morning, her grandmother, who lived just over the Red River from Texas in Terral, Oklahoma, called to tell her that she had fallen and twisted her ankle. Could Becca come home for a few weeks to help her out? Everything seemed like an omen—the contract with no name on it suggested that she would never sign with a record company, and her grandmother, who never asked for help from anyone, seemed to say that Nashville would never really be her home.

Becca gave notice at both her jobs, handed her set of apartment keys to her roommate, and drove west, watching her hopes and dreams fade away in the rearview mirror. Grammie McKay, Irish to the bone and with a thick Irish accent, got her the job with Austin O'Donnell's wine business. Grammie's ankle healed, and she was getting around really well these days. Becca enjoyed her work, but Terral, population less than four hundred, sure didn't provide many opportunities for her to sing.

"Maybe that's a good thing," she muttered as she closed the door to the wine shed and went back to squeezing the juice from the first watermelons of the season.

The door hinges squeaked, and Becca flipped around, ready to yell at Tuff if he'd figured out a way to get inside again. She might not like Dalton's dog, but her pulse jacked up a few notches at the thought of seeing Dalton a second time that morning. She was already visualizing him in those faded tight-fitting jeans, scuffed-up cowboy boots, and his dusty old straw hat, as she turned away from the watermelon she was cutting into chunks. In her mind's eye, she could see his dark hair curling on his chambray shirt collar, and his bright blue eyes twinkling as he teased her about his worthless dog.

"Rodeo dog, my butt," she muttered.

"You callin' me a dog, darlin' girl, or have you given up singin' and gone to ridin' bulls?" Grammie McKay's accent jerked the picture of Dalton right out of Becca's head.

"No, ma'am," she answered. "I was fussin' to myself about that mutt of Dalton Wilson's. Seems like every time it gets a chance, it comes lookin' for me."

Grammie sat down in a lawn chair. This morning she wore a bright-green sweat suit that brought out the glimmer in eyes that were almost the same color as Becca's. Her red hair, now sprinkled with gray, was twisted up in a knot on the top of her head. "There'd be something wrong with a lassie who doesn't like a dog, so maybe you better examine yourself instead of poor old Tuff. Pooch can't help the way God made him any more than you can help the way the good Lord made you. What's really eatin' on your heart this mornin'? Are you afraid you can't run this wine-makin' business for a spell all by yourself?"

"Nothing like that, and Lord knows Austin and Rye and

those precious children of theirs need a vacation. I'm glad Austin trusted me enough to leave me to do the job for a week." Becca admitted that much, but she sure didn't want to talk about the way the cowboy who lived across the dirt road affected her. Dalton Wilson was known all over southern Oklahoma and north Texas for his bad boy reputation, and Becca sure didn't need that in her life.

"Then is it Dalton and not his poor old ugly dog that's gotten your knickers in a twist?" Grammie asked.

Becca dragged a lawn chair across the room and sat down beside her grandmother. "I don't have time for a one-night-stand kind of guy. Dalton is a love-'em-and-leave-'em cowboy, and I refuse to be just another notch on his bedpost."

"Ahhh, darlin' girl." Grammie smiled. "That does bring back memories. That's exactly what my mama told me about your grandpapa. She said, 'Greta, that boy will break your heart, and you'll be nothing but a notch on his bedpost.' It takes a brave and determined woman to tame a wild boy, but once you get the job done, they make mighty fine husbands, fathers, and lovers," she said with a sly wink. "And I'd be living testimony of that. I tamed Seamus McKay. Not to say it didn't take a while, but by the time we had your daddy, he had come through the fire and was pure gold until the day he died."

"Fire?" Becca asked.

"Do you think that tamin' him was easy? I had to light a few blazes under him before the job was finished. Dalton might be wild as a March hare right now, but maybe he hasn't met the right Irish woman, someone willin' to strike the match like I was with my Seamus."

"Well, I hope he meets her soon and quits crossing the road to this part of the O'Donnell property," Becca smarted off.

"Better think hard about what you ask for, Miss Greta Rebecca McKay." Grammie used her full name, which meant she was dead serious.

———

Dalton gave his best cowboy boots one more swipe with the brush, settled his good straw hat on his head, and headed for the door that Saturday evening. Tuff whined and thumped his tail against the wooden floor. Dalton stooped down to scratch the dog's ears and whisper, "If I get lucky, I'll be back right after breakfast. If I don't, I'll see you before dawn. Hold down the fort. I left the cartoon channel on for you." He lowered his voice to a whisper. "And thanks for this morning, ole boy. You done good, sneaking into the wine shed so I could see Becca. That woman has gotten under my skin, and I'm running out of excuses to go over there and talk to her." He patted the dog on the head one more time. "You're a good wingman, Tuff, but the Broken Bit don't let us cowboys bring our four-legged buddies with us."

Dalton was whistling as he got into his truck and drove west through the tiny town of Terral. He'd grown up in Bowie, Texas. Strangely enough, Becca had lived in Ringgold, just twenty minutes up Highway 81, and he'd never met her until she came to work for Austin last December.

Dalton had known from the time he could take his first steps that he wanted to be a rancher. By the time he was a freshman in high school, he was on the payroll at his grandfather's ranch a few miles south of Bowie in Fruitland. When he graduated, he went to work full time for his grandfather, and then two years ago, he met Rye at a rodeo. Rye was looking for a foreman. Dalton was wanting to spread his wings, so he took the job in Terral, Oklahoma, when Rye offered it to him. The only bad thing about jumping over the Red River to live in Terral was that Dalton sure had to endure a lot of teasing during the Texas-Oklahoma football weekend. Dalton was a die-hard Texas fan, and there was no way he'd ever turn his back on the Longhorns.

He had turned on the radio even before he adjusted the air conditioner. Good country music would get him in the mood for some two-stepping and beer drinking that evening, and maybe, like he'd told Tuff, he would even get lucky and not be home until after breakfast.

There's not a woman in the world who can satisfy that itch you've got for Becca. His father's voice popped into his head just as Blake Shelton began to sing "Honey Bee" on the radio.

He ignored his late father's advice and sang along with Blake. Dalton had always thought love at first sight was a bunch of overfried bologna. Rye had told him all about how he'd been downright love drunk when he first met Austin, and Dalton had thought he was crazy. Now, he wasn't so sure, because he was feeling what Rye described for Becca.

"And she's not even my type," he muttered when he turned south. "She's too tall. She's a redhead and everyone knows they've got a temper. To top it all off, she's got those green eyes that I could drown in."

A mile down the highway, he glanced over at the new casino that had gone up three years ago. Sitting right on the edge of the Red River, it drew people in from all over north Texas and provided a few jobs for the folks around the little town of Terral. He almost stopped there to have a drink or two and blow a twenty-dollar bill at the slots, but that would put him late getting to the Broken Bit, which would mean all the ladies would already be taken. Besides, he wanted to flirt with a cute little brunette and maybe get lucky enough to get Becca off his mind.

He crossed the river bridge into Texas and drove another

five miles to Ringgold. There he made a right-hand turn on Highway 82 and headed toward Henrietta. In another ten minutes, he pulled into the Broken Bit's dimly lit parking lot. Judging by all the pickups and cars and the loud music that seemed to be raising the roof a few inches, the place was booming—just the way he liked it. He got out of the truck, locked it, and shoved the keys into his pocket.

"Hey, Dalton," a feminine voice called out behind him.

He turned around to see Lacy Ruiz not ten feet away. "Hey, girl. You just now getting here?"

"Yep," she answered. "You want to save me the last dance?"

A broad grin covered his face. Lacy was his kind of woman—short, brunette, a good dancer, and he had spent enough nights with her to know that she made a mean western omelet the next morning.

"We'll have to see about that," he said as he pulled a ten-dollar bill from his pocket and gave it to the man at the door for both their cover charges. "Never know what might happen between now and closin' time."

"Ain't that the truth, but we could be each other's backup plan," she suggested.

"Sounds good to me."

She disappeared into the crowd of folks doing a line dance. The female vocalist was doing a credible job of the band's rendition of "Any Man of Mine" by Shania Twain. Dalton followed Lacy inside, slid onto the last empty barstool, and ordered a longneck Coors.

"How about you, Dalton?" Tessa, the bartender, grinned. "You goin' to ever walk the line like the song says, or are you going to go to your grave still chasin' women?"

"Haven't decided," Dalton answered. "All the good ones like you are done taken."

"Honey, I'm old enough to be your mama," Tessa told him. "And there's plenty of good ones still out there. I just doubt you'll ever find the one for you in a place like this."

"You're here," he said.

"Yeah, but my husband and I met at a church social. It wasn't until we'd been married twenty years that we bought this place, and for your information, we'll both be in church tomorrow morning," she told him.

"So will I," Dalton said.

"Sure, you will," Tessa giggled.

"What's that supposed to mean?" Dalton asked.

"You'll sow wild oats tonight. Tomorrow mornin', you'll be sittin' on the back pew praying for a crop failure. You can't fool me, cowboy," she said. "I hear that Austin and Rye are off on a vacation and have left you and Becca McKay in charge of the place for the next week. You might want to put those wild oats on the back burner tonight and be a responsible foreman."

"You givin' me advice now, Miz Tessa?" he asked.

"Yep, I surely am." Tessa headed off to the other end of the bar.

The lady singer stepped back from the microphone and took her place behind a keyboard, and the male singer started singing Travis Tritt's "T.R.O.U.B.L.E." The lyrics had just said something about looking at what just walked through the door when Dalton caught sight of a tall woman with flaming-red hair in his peripheral vision. He turned to look and almost dropped his beer when he saw Becca coming straight toward the bar.

"You are a genius, Travis," Dalton murmured.

Becca crossed the room, weaving her way among the line dancers, and sat down on the barstool right next to him. He waited until she ordered a beer and then tossed a bill on the counter when Tessa brought it to her.

"I'll buy your first drink tonight in exchange for the last dance of the evening," Dalton said.

"Good God!" Becca exclaimed. "Where did you come from?"

"Been right here the whole time." He grinned.

"I'll pay for my own beer," she said.

"Too late." Tessa pocketed the bill. "Don't forget that you owe him the last dance."

"I never force a woman to dance with me." Dalton turned around to face Becca. Damn, but she was beautiful in her tight jeans, that cute little dark-blue lace shirt with the pearl snaps, and those fancy cowgirl boots. Her red hair floated on her shoulders, framing her face like a halo, and even in the dim light, her green eyes glimmered.

"I pay my debts, cowboy." Becca took a long drink of the beer and then held it up toward him. "Thanks for this."

"You are so welcome. Want to pay for it right now? I can teach you to two-step." He arched an eyebrow.

"Darlin', I've been in Nashville for the past ten years, and besides I was two-steppin' when I still had a pacifier in my mouth." She took another drink of her beer and motioned for Tessa. "Set this back until I finish showing this smart-ass how to dance."

"You might ought to let me just dump it and start all over with a cold one," Tessa teased. "It might get warm before you get him taught."

"You got a point there." Becca slid off the barstool and headed to the dance floor.

Dalton finished off his beer and set the empty bottle on the bar. This was his lucky night even if he had to make his own breakfast in the morning. Tessa could be wrong about meeting the right girl in a bar, he was thinking.

You met her five months ago, the pesky voice in his head reminded him.

He didn't even bother to argue but simply held out his hand toward Becca. He'd wondered what it would be like to hold her in his arms, and he was not one bit disappointed when she moved in close to him.

"Lesson number one," she said, "is not to hold a woman too closely on the first dance."

"Darlin', I know how to two-step," he whispered into her ear.

"But do you know how to dance with a woman who's almost as tall as you are?" she asked. "I hear that you prefer short little gals with dark hair."

"So, you've been asking questions about me?" He avoided answering her question. Truth was, he had not danced with many tall women, but oh, sweet Jesus, he did like the way Becca fit into his arms. He was tempted to tip up her chin and kiss her when the male vocalist in the band started singing "Tennessee Whiskey," but he didn't dare push his luck.

"Don't have to ask questions about a rounder like you, Dalton," she answered. "The news just floats around this part of the world like dandelion fluff in the springtime. Everyone knows who and what you are."

"And that is?" Dalton asked.

"They'd call you a player in the big cities, but in this part of the world, I think you're just referred to as a bad boy," she told him.

"Do you like bad boys?" he asked.

"Only on Saturday night when I'm in the mood to dance, and, honey, I might dance the last two-step with you to pay for that first drink, but when this place closes down, I will be going home alone, so let's get that straight right now," she told him.

"I bet you can't cook up a decent breakfast for a hungry old cowboy anyway," he teased.

"You won't be finding that out in the morning." She smiled up at him.

His heart melted. His pulse raced. She didn't say that he'd *never* find out, but she said *in the morning*. Someday, he hoped, this woman would make his breakfast every single morning—or maybe he'd make the morning meal for her. He'd sure be willing to do that if it meant he would get to wake up with her in his arms.

Chapter 2

"You do not come into my kitchen with that grumpy face," Grammie said on Sunday morning. "This is the Lord's day, and He expects us to be happy."

If Becca had still been in Nashville, she wouldn't even have been up that early on Sunday morning. She would have worked a double at Tootsie's on Saturday, gone home long after two o'clock when the place was cleaned up, and fallen into bed to sleep until sometime in the afternoon. The old cuckoo clock in the foyer had struck twice, telling everyone in Jefferson County that it was two thirty, when she had taken a quick shower and tried to go to sleep, but the sun was peeking over the far horizon when she finally drifted off.

Becca groaned as she threw her legs over the side of the

bed and padded barefoot to the kitchen. "I've had less than three hours' sleep."

"And that, darlin' girl, would be your own fault, not our Lord and Savior's, so get a cup of my good, strong black coffee and wake yourself up." Grammie pointed toward the half-full pot on the countertop.

Becca yawned and poured a full cup of the thick black stuff her grandmother called coffee. Without a little cream and sugar, it was strong enough to melt the silver plating off the spoon, but that morning, she needed an extra boost, so she took it straight up.

"Muffins are on the table, and we'll be heading to church soon. Jesus, Mary, and Joseph! You can't be goin' to church wired to the moon," Grammie said as she slathered butter on a blueberry muffin and handed it to Becca.

Poppa McKay had died when Becca was eight years old, and Grammie had left Ireland to live closer to her only son who lived in Ringgold, Texas. In the past twenty years, she'd left some of her Irish slang behind, but when she blasphemed, she did it with the whole family, and *wired to the moon* was another way of saying that Becca was hungover.

"I only had three beers all night," Becca argued and then bit into the muffin.

"Your eyes are tellin' me a different story, but I'm not

fussin' at you. I remember when I was a young woman and spent my Saturday nights at the local pub." Grammie's eyes went slightly dreamy. "I met my Seamus at that pub, and we had fifty good years together." She blinked and sat down at the table. "My mam didn't let me miss church just because I was still sleepy. No, ma'am. Not one single time. So, eat your breakfast and get all prettied up. We'll sit on the front pew, so you won't be fallin' asleep."

"Grammie!" Becca gasped.

Greta giggled. "I'm just funnin' you. We'll sit on our regular pew about halfway back in the church. I figure that's a safe place for you. The devil can't drag you through the back door with all those folks around you."

Becca reached for a second muffin. "What makes you think the devil even wants me?"

"Honey, he wants all of us. We just got to outsmart him, kind of like I did my Seamus back in the day." Greta stood up and headed out of the kitchen. "I'll be waitin' by the door with my purse and Bible in my hand at a quarter of eleven."

"Yes, ma'am, but that's two hours from now," Becca said.

Greta stopped in the doorway. "Us older ladies take a little longer to get beautified than you young'uns. What gravity ain't got a hold of, wrinkles have. Finish your coffee and then go make yourself pretty for that cowboy you been runnin' from since Christmas. If you run hard enough, you'll catch him." She giggled as she disappeared down the hallway toward her bedroom.

"I'm not sure I want to catch him," Becca muttered as she finished off the last of her coffee and then pushed back her chair. She put the dirty plates and cups in the dishwasher and went to her room. Six outfits later, she finally decided on a sundress the color of her eyes and a pair of strappy high heels that matched it. She was sitting on a ladder-back chair in the foyer when her grandmother appeared with her white patent-leather purse slung over her arm.

Greta pointed at Becca's feet. "I'm pea green with jealousy over those shoes, darlin' girl. You might be named after me, but you got those long legs from your mama. I bet Dalton's old heart throws in an extra beat this morning when he sees you walk past him."

Becca stood up and slung an arm around her grandmother's shoulders and tried to veer her away from Dalton. "Grammie, I've seen pictures of you when you were my age. You were stunning."

"Don't you be tryin' to butter me up so I won't talk about Dalton Wilson." Greta shook a finger toward her. "I might be old, but I ain't stupid."

The old folks around town kept saying that they were

in for one hot summer, and Becca believed every word of it when she opened the door and a blast of hot air rushed across the porch to meet them. Hot summer. Hot cowboy. Hot everything—or so it seemed.

Nothing in Terral was more than ten minutes away, not even the new casino that had been built out at the edge of the Red River. To go from the ranch and watermelon farm to the only restaurant on Main Street, the churches, or the convenience store up on the corner of Apache Avenue—the street most folks called Main—and Highway 81 took half that time. Driving the four blocks from her grandmother's place to the church took about three minutes. Becca's little compact car wasn't even cooled down when she turned into the gravel parking lot. That old saying that if you blinked while driving through the two blocks that were downtown, you'd miss it was the unadulterated, guaranteed truth.

As luck would have it, Dalton arrived at the same time as Becca and her grandmother, and he rushed over to be the perfect gentleman and help Greta out of the car. Becca opened her door, slung her long legs out, and turned to look over the top of the car—and locked eyes with Dalton.

"I just asked this handsome young man to sit with us," Greta said.

He arched an eyebrow toward Becca.

"And what did he say?" Becca's eyes didn't leave his.

"That he'd be glad to attend church with us this mornin'." Greta flashed her brightest grin, deepening the wrinkles around her mouth. "If you two kids are real nice and sing pretty, maybe he can even go home with us for Sunday dinner. I put a pot roast in the oven, and it will be done by the time services are over."

"I can be the best cowboy in the whole state for a Sunday dinner like that." Dalton grinned. "Here, Miz Greta, take my arm. Those steps going up to the church are pretty steep."

You can worm your way into my grandmother's heart, cowboy, Becca thought as she followed them into the sanctuary. *You can dance with me, and even have dinner at Grammie's house, but I refuse to be another conquest in your line of one-night stands.* She felt like a little puppy trailing along after her two masters as the three of them made their way into the church and down the center aisle.

"This is where I like to sit." Greta stopped in her tracks about the middle of the church.

"Yes, ma'am." Dalton stood to one side.

Becca bit back a groan when she realized she would be sitting between her grandmother and Dalton. Three of Greta's friends had already sat down on the other end of the pew, and like always, there was only room for two more people to sit comfortably. Adding a big strapping cowboy like Dalton would squeeze them together, but there was nothing she could do but sit down.

Dalton wedged himself into the space that remained, but with the end of the pew on one side and Becca's body on the other, there was very little room for him.

"There's no sense in you two bein' crowded up like this," Greta whispered. "Go on and find yourselves a seat up closer to the front."

"I'm fine." Becca's voice sounded a little high in her own ears, but then her heart was thumping and her pulse racing. Dalton looked like the cover model for a western romance novel in his tight jeans, plaid shirt, and polished boots. She took a deep breath, hoping to put out all the sparks dancing around them, but whatever shaving lotion he had used that morning sent her senses reeling.

"No problem here." Dalton smiled.

"No leaning on each other and falling asleep," Greta warned with a shake of her finger. "Or yawning, and if you snore, there will be no Sunday dinner."

"Yes, ma'am," Becca and Dalton said in unison.

The congregation sang two songs, and since there was only one hymnbook available, Becca had to share with Dalton. Their fingertips touched, and the contact sent unholy pictures flashing through her mind of him in tangled sheets. She checked out the window on the south side to be sure there were no black clouds shooting lightning streaks toward the church.

The preacher took his place, adjusted the microphone, and said, "It's been laid upon my heart to preach from Corinthians about love."

Sweet Jesus! Becca rolled her eyes toward the ceiling.

Greta elbowed her in the ribs and whispered, "Pay attention and stop checkin' to see if there's cobwebs on the ceiling fan."

Somewhere between the parts about love being kind and not seeking its own way, Becca's eyes got heavy. She leaned on what she thought was the arm of the pew and planned to rest her eyes for a minute, but a movement startled her. Several folks around her chuckled, and for a split second she wondered if she had, indeed, snored. She jerked her arm away to find that she had really propped it on Dalton's shoulder. Then she felt a weight in her lap and looked down to find Tuff had stretched his wiry body out across both Dalton's and her laps. The dog had slipped into the church through the open doors and made himself comfortable.

"I guess we have a four-legged visitor." The preacher laughed with the rest of the congregation. "I suppose if God knows the very hairs on our head and when every sparrow drops, then He surely won't mind if Dalton's dog attends the rest of the service—as long as he doesn't snore."

A few more chuckles echoed through the building. Becca was wide awake by then with a dog's head planted in her lap. Tuff's big brown eyes were looking right at her face, and damned if it didn't look like he was smiling.

━━━━━━━━━

Dalton was always welcome to Sunday dinner at his grandpa's place in Fruitland. Nana Wilson usually fried up a mean batch of chicken after church, and her biscuits were the best in the whole world. He had a standing invitation, and if he wasn't there by noon, Nana put a plate back for him. Very seldom did he miss at least running by to say hello to them on Sunday. He figured they would understand his absence if it had to do with him going to church and dinner with a woman, but he still planned to give them a quick call on his way to Greta's place. They'd be elated, since they had gone past throwing out hints and were making serious comments about how it was time for him to hang up his wild ways and settle down. They wanted to see a few great-grandchildren before the end of their time, and since Dalton was their only grandchild, that responsibility fell on him.

The preacher finally asked Eli White to deliver the benediction. Mr. Eli stood to his feet, bowed his head, and began to thank God for everything from the good watermelon crop that was coming in to the ladies who cleaned the church. He spoke slowly in a monotone, and if it hadn't been for Dalton's growling stomach, he might have really snored by the time Eli finally said, "Amen."

"Thank God that's over," Greta muttered as she stood to her feet. "Another minute on this hard pew and my hips and knees would have rebelled."

"I'd carry you out to the car if that happened." Dalton grinned.

Tuff must have realized the service was over, because he jumped down and meandered down the center aisle toward the door.

"Poor thing must've been worn out," Greta said. "It's four miles out to the ranch, and that's a long way for him to walk just to get to church. He's a good dog to feel his need to be here."

Dalton didn't tell them that Tuff had hitched a ride in the back of his truck like he did every Sunday morning. Lots of times, he just curled up and took an hour-long nap, or else ran around the town, checking out the female mutts and hiking his leg on every bush he could find.

"His fur is kind of soft. I figured it would feel like steel wool," Becca admitted as she got to her feet. "You're not going to make him walk all the way back to the ranch, are you?"

"Naw," Dalton drawled. "I'll park under that big old pecan tree in Miss Greta's yard, and he can sleep in the truck bed. I thought you hated him."

"I don't hate Tuff," Becca protested. "I just don't want any of his hair to get loose and taint my wine."

Greta hung back and talked to her friends. Dalton ushered Becca outside with a hand on the small of her back. She could feel the burn all the way through her body, and her palms were sweaty when it was her turn to shake with the preacher.

"I'm glad to see y'all sitting together this mornin'," the preacher said and then dropped her hand. "And Tuff was such a good boy. You can tell him he's welcome at services anytime. I shook hands with him a few minutes ago, and I believe he's headed out to your truck."

"I'll tell him." Dalton stuck out his hand next. "Good sermon this morning."

"It's that time of year when young folks are planning summer weddings, so they need to think about what it truly means to be in love." The preacher winked.

"Yes, sir." Dalton nodded. "See you next week."

"Did you really listen to the sermon?" Becca asked. "Or were you just saying something nice?"

"It was all about what it's like to fall in love, right?" Dalton stopped beside her car and opened the door for her.

"So, Dalton Wilson, how many times have you been in love?" She slid behind the wheel.

"I might have to take my boots off to count that far," he answered.

"I mean in real love, not lust," she said.

"Well, in that case…" He closed his eyes as if trying to count. "That would be one time." No way was he admitting that the time was right now. The woman was Becca, and it had been love at first sight. "How about you? Give me a number."

"Lust a few times. Love, never. I was too busy concentrating on getting a music contract to let a man into my heart and life," she said.

"You going back to that anytime soon?" he asked.

"No." She shook her head. "I gave it my best for ten years, and it didn't work. It's time to leave that dream behind and move on."

"To what?" he asked.

"Right now, making wine. I'm enjoying the work, and

I've even entertained notions of putting in a vineyard of my own," she answered.

"There's lots of good sandy land to do that around here," he suggested.

"Hey, are you two about starved?" Greta yelled as she started down the stairs.

In a few long strides, Dalton was beside her and had looped her arm in his. "Here, Miz Greta, let me help you, and yes, I'm starving. I didn't have time to eat breakfast, so I might be just about to embarrass Becca."

"I love a man with a good appetite." Greta smiled up at him.

"That's great, because I *love* good home cookin'," he told her.

When Greta was settled and her seat belt fastened, Dalton went to his truck and followed them to the house. After he'd first met her at the watermelon farm, he'd driven around town until he spotted Becca's little dark-blue car with its Tennessee license plate. That was another thing he'd never admit because it made him sound like a stalker.

Greta was out of the car and headed toward the porch by the time he got parked. He saw her lips moving, but he couldn't tell what she was saying. From Becca's expression and the way she rolled those big beautiful green eyes, it was something that she didn't really agree with.

"Hey," Becca waved. "I'm supposed to tell you that it's too

hot for Tuff to spend the afternoon in the back of the truck, and you're supposed to bring him inside. I hope he's housebroken."

"Of course he is, and he appreciates the offer." Dalton gave a shrill whistle, and Tuff bounded out of the back of the truck. Tail wagging and head held up, he marched right up on the porch and lay down in the shade. "He says that if he could have a bowl of water, he'd be right comfortable out here."

"I believe we can manage that," Becca said. "Come on in."

The redbrick house had a wide-enough front porch to support a swing at one end. A white chaise lounge with bright-green pillows sat on the other end. A gentle summer breeze spread the scent of the red roses that grew across the front of the place.

Dalton followed Becca inside, removed his hat, and hung it on a hall tree right inside the door. "Nice place," he said.

"We like it just fine. Daddy wanted Grammie to buy property down in Ringgold, but she checked the property taxes, and they were cheaper in Oklahoma." Becca kicked her high heels off and slid them up under a ladder-back chair. "It's only a five-minute drive down to Daddy's ranch, so it's not that big a deal unless it floods and they close the river bridge."

"Becca, darlin' girl, you can come on in here and make the salad," Greta called out.

"I'm glad to help out." Dalton followed her into the kitchen.

"Where's Tuff?" Greta asked.

"He opted to protect the house from the front porch," Dalton answered as he rolled up his sleeves.

"Good dog, that one," Greta said. "Never know when we might get one of them salesmen or Bible-thumpin' folks knockin' on the door. Tuff has my permission to bite either of them on the arse."

"If you will point me in the right direction, I'll set the table." Dalton rolled up his sleeves. "Been pettin' Tuff, so I'll need to wash up. All right if I do that in the sink?"

"Sure thing," Greta said. "My Seamus always got cleaned up in the kitchen sink. Brings back good memories."

Dalton washed his hands all the way to the elbows and then turned to look for a towel. Becca was standing right behind him, towel in hand. He took it from her and started drying the water from his arms.

"My turn." She hip butted him to one side. "Can't be tearin' up the lettuce with the smell of dog on me either. Plates are right there. We'll need salad bowls too, and you might as well get dessert dishes down. Grammie made a pecan pie for dessert."

"I've died and gone to heaven," Dalton groaned. "Pecan pie is my favorite, right next to apple, cherry, and peach cobbler, and banana cream."

"In other words, you like pie?" Becca finished washing her hands.

Dalton gave her the towel and took down the plates. Thank God Nana had raised him by the goose and gander law. She always said what was good for the goose was good for the gander, and insisted he learn a little about cooking and keeping house as well as how to work cattle and build a barn. "I love pie of any kind, cake of any kind, and ice cream and homemade fudge, and I could go on and on. I have a sweet tooth that is never satisfied."

Becca giggled. "That sounds like a pickup line."

Greta laughed with her. "And the next thing you should say is, 'And you're the sweetest thing I've ever seen,' right?"

"I'll have to remember that." Dalton grinned as he set plates and cutlery in the proper places.

When everything was ready, Greta told Dalton to sit at the head of the table, and she sat to his left, leaving the place to his right for Becca. "I'll say grace," she said, and gave a twenty-second grace for the food. "Eli already blessed everything in the whole bloody county, so that's enough even if it is Sunday." She passed the platter with the pot roast, potatoes, and carrots over to Dalton.

"This is one fine meal," he said as he heaped his plate and handed the platter to Becca. "Thank you so much for inviting me."

"You're very welcome. It's nice to have a man at the table." Greta took out a good portion of meat and vegetables when Becca was finished. "Us McKays are not a bit bashful when it comes to eating. We like our food, and we're not ashamed to take seconds, so don't hold back, Dalton, but do remember that we have pecan pie for dessert."

"Yes, ma'am." He tried to eat slowly so he could spend more time with Becca, but he was so danged hungry that he finished off his plate in record time.

"After dinner, me and my friends are going down to the casino to see if we can turn twenty dollars into a hundred," Greta said as she reached for a second helping. "There's movies in the entertainment center. You kids can pick out one and watch it while I'm gone, unless you've got somewhere you need to be, Dalton."

"No, ma'am." He grinned and picked up a second hot roll. "I'd love to settle in and watch a movie with Becca."

"Just don't fall asleep." Greta grinned. "My granddaughter can be a real practical joker."

"Oh, really?" He arched an eyebrow toward Becca.

She shrugged. "Fall asleep and find out."

Chapter 3

GRAMMIE WAS A SNEAKY ONE.

Becca was *not* going to watch a movie with Dalton that afternoon. She intended to curl up on the porch swing and read one of the romance novels her mother had given her last weekend. Or she might go down to Ringgold, saddle up her horse, and go for a ride across her folks' ranch. She had fended off all the real cowboys, wannabe cowboys, and cowboy singers in Nashville, but she had to admit she was attracted to Dalton. The chemistry between them was way too strong to spend a whole afternoon alone with him.

Or is it? She pondered.

Dalton Wilson could be like chocolate. If she had too much of it and got downright sick of the taste, she might not want to ever look at it again. If she spent some time with the man, she might possibly find all kinds of things about him that she didn't like.

Grammie was also more than a little controlling.

"I've got the perfect movie for y'all to watch this afternoon," Grammie said as she rifled through the drawers in her entertainment center. "Here it is. It's an old one, probably popular when y'all were just kids."

"What's the title?" Becca set a glass of sweet tea on the end table and then plopped down on the sofa.

"It's got Patrick Dempsey in it, and it's"—she held up the movie to show them that it was *Lucky 7*—"and Kimberly Williams, and it's all about a girl who thinks…" She stopped and smiled. "Y'all just watch it. I'll be back in a couple of hours. It won't take us long to lose twenty bucks at the casino." She picked up her purse from the coffee table and left the house when the sound of a car horn blasted out in the front yard.

"You ever watched this?" Dalton sat down on the other end of the sofa.

"Nope." Becca said. "Grammie loves chick flick movies, so you can bet your bottom dollar this is not an action film. You can sneak away if you want to."

"Naw," Dalton grinned and put the disk she handed him into the player. "I don't reckon one love movie will hurt me."

Becca picked up the remote, hit the Play button, and then

read the back of the container that held the movie. Oh, yes, sir, Grammie was playing matchmaker for sure.

"Mind if I take off my boots?" Dalton asked.

"Not one bit." Becca propped her bare feet up on the coffee table. "Grammie says this is what a coffee table should be for, not for doilies and fancy flower arrangements."

"Smart woman." Dalton removed his boots, set them to the side, and stretched his long legs out. "What do you like, Becca? Do you prefer fancy fixin's, or do you follow after Greta?"

"A little of both," she answered and focused on the movie, which showed a bagel shop right close to the beginning. She missed grabbing a bagel on the way to work each morning the way she had done in Nashville. She hadn't even minded driving a little bit out of the way over to Abbot Martin Road to get a fresh one.

"So, this girl is going to be waiting for her seventh boyfriend to really fall in love, right?" Dalton asked after the very first flashback scene to where a young girl was visiting with her dying mother. "Tell me that your mother is alive and well, and that you aren't waiting for number seven."

"My mama is Trudy McKay, and she is very much alive," Becca answered. "I'm not waiting for any particular number."

Dalton wiped his forehead in a fake dramatic gesture.

"Whew! I was afraid I'd have a long wait if I had to go on home and wait until you went through six boyfriends."

She started to smart off with a quick comeback, but a scratching noise distracted her. She stood up, crossed the room, and found Tuff with what looked like a big gray rat in his mouth. The ugly critter was wagging his tail like he expected praise for bringing the dead varmint to her. She quickly closed her eyes so she wouldn't have to look at it anymore, slammed the door, and yelled, "Dalton!"

In what seemed like the blink of an eye, he was right beside her. "Are you all right? What happened? You're as pale as a ghost."

"I hate rats," she said.

"Where is it?" Dalton looked around the foyer. "Which way did it run? I'll catch it and get rid of it for you."

She pointed. "Tuff has it on the porch."

Dalton opened the door just enough to peek outside. "Tuff has brought you a present, but it's not a rat. Come on over here and take a look. He was raised with cats, and he loves kittens."

Becca eased across the room, and sure enough, there was a little gray kitten fighting with Tuff's tail as it swished back and forth on the porch. "Ohhh, isn't it the cutest thing? Where do you think he stole it from?"

"I'm sure he filled out all the adoption papers and everything is legal." Dalton slung open the door and picked the gray ball of fur up by the scruff of the neck. Tuff ran into the house, stopped, and looked back over his shoulder. He whined and the kitten let out a pitiful meow.

"Is it going to try to scratch my eyes out?" Becca reached her hands out.

"Don't know, but evidently, he didn't want this one to be raised as an only child." Dalton pointed to a yellow-colored kitten just about the same size as the gray one sitting on the porch. "Or else he thought you and Greta each needed your own pet." He opened the door again.

Becca picked the kitten up as it entered the house like it owned the place. It flopped over in her arms like a baby and started purring. "These have to belong to someone. We can't keep them. We'll get attached and then have to give them back."

"Tell you what." Dalton put the gray kitten in her arms with the yellow one. "Tuff and I are going to take a little walk around the block. I bet we find the owner, and I'll ask if they want them back. How's that?"

"Thank you," Becca answered, but it was too late. She'd already lost her heart to the two little critters.

———————

Dalton whistled and Tuff came out of the living room with his head hanging and tail wagging. "You did good, ole boy, but we've got to be sure that the owners of those two babies don't want them back. We need to go for a little walk and find out where they came from."

Tuff barked once and followed Dalton back to the sofa. Dalton jerked his boots on and nodded toward Becca. "Don't name 'em until I get back."

Tuff ran on ahead of Dalton when they stepped off the porch. Two houses down the street, he stopped, sniffed the air, hiked his leg on a bush, and then sat down.

"This isn't going to work," Dalton told him. "You know very well where you stole those kittens. What if there's a third one, and we want to take it home with us?"

The dog stood up and slowly made his way to the end of the block. He sat down at the end of the porch steps of the last house on the block and yipped twice.

"Is this the place?" Dalton walked up to the door and knocked.

"Hey, Dalton, what's up?" Frankie, one of his hired hands, asked as he rounded the side of the house.

"You got some kittens around this place?" Dalton asked. "Tuff has dragged a couple down to Greta McKay's house."

"Had five out in the storage shed. Gave three away last

week and been tryin' to get rid of the other two ever since. Their mama got killed on the road. If Miz Greta don't want them, I was goin' to ask you if you'd like to have them for barn cats. Their mama was a real good mouser," Frankie said. "Come on inside. Want a beer?"

"Thanks. A cold one sounds good, but I'd better get on back to Miz Greta's. Becca and I've got a movie on pause. I just didn't want her to get attached to a couple of kittens if you weren't giving them away," Dalton said. "See you at the ranch in the morning."

"I'll be there bright and early," Frankie said. "Hey, have you heard from Austin and Rye? Are they havin' a good time?"

"Haven't talked to them, but Rye said he'd call in this evening to check on things," Dalton said.

Frankie waved and went on inside. Dalton turned around and headed back down the block with Tuff right at his heels. "You done good, boy, but next time scratch on the door and ask if you can take another man's property."

Tuff barked a couple of times and tore off down the road like the devil was chasing him. When Dalton reached the house, the dog was sleeping under the porch swing. "I guess you figure you've done your good deed for the week, right?"

The dog didn't open his eyes, but his tail thumped a few

times. Dalton raised his hand to knock, but Becca threw the door open with the kittens still in her arms.

"What did you find out?"

"Frankie says he's glad to get rid of them," Dalton answered. "Do you think you should ask Miz Greta about them before…?"

Becca butted in before he could finish his sentence. "I already did. She said she and her friends were going down to Bowie for ice cream. She's going to pick up kitten food and litter while she's there."

"If you love cats so much, why haven't you had one before now?" He followed her into the living room, kicked off his boots for the second time, and sat down on the end of the sofa.

"I lived in an apartment in Nashville that didn't allow any pets, not even a goldfish. With four of us in a small apartment and all of us scrambling for jobs and hoping for a contract, we didn't have time for pets anyway, and then my last roommate was allergic to everything that had fur." She handed the gray kitten to him. "Meet George and this right here is Dolly. Grammie and I already named them."

He took the kitten from her. "Hello, George. I betcha you got your name from those two singing 'The Blues Man.'"

"How'd you know about that song?" Becca asked.

"My grandpa loves anything by George, and Nana is real partial to Dolly Parton." He laid the cat up on his shoulder.

———————

A big old sexy cowboy holding a kitten that wasn't as big as one of his rough hands melted Becca's heart. She kept stealing glances over at him. Could it be that beneath bad boy exterior there was a man who wanted to settle down someday? Grammie had said that when she met *her Seamus*, as she always referred to him, he'd been a player too. The only time Becca had gotten to spend a month with them in Ireland, he'd been such a loving husband to her grammie that Becca couldn't imagine him ever even looking sideways at another woman.

"I wonder how they got so tame." Becca was talking about the cats, but her mind was still on her grandfather and Dalton and the business of taming them.

"Frankie and his wife have a bunch of grandkids that are always popping in and out of their house. I imagine they played with them and got them ready to give away to good homes." Dalton leaned his head back on the sofa and closed his eyes.

He and the kitten both were sleeping soundly within a few seconds. Dolly curled up in Becca's lap and put a paw over her little nose. For several minutes Becca looked her fill of Dalton. Women were already falling at his feet so rapidly that it was a wonder he didn't have one of those take-a-number-and-wait machines attached to his porch post. If those ladies could see him now with a kitten on his shoulder, the poor old Terral police would be having to break up catfights.

She only meant to rest her eyes for a second, but in minutes she was sound asleep. She didn't even hear the front door open or Greta fussing about having to haul in supplies. She did wake up when Tuff licked her, starting at her chin, going up across her cheek, and not stopping until he reached her hairline. Becca came up off the sofa wiping at her mouth, then stopped dead in her tracks and looked around to see if she'd thrown the new baby kitten off on to the floor.

Tuff made a hasty retreat to hide behind Grammie's recliner when he got a taste of hair spray. Dalton opened his eyes slowly to find that both cats were now on his shoulder and tangled up together.

"Awww, look at the wee babies asleep with Dalton. It's a good man, yes, it is, that animals love," Greta said in a high baby-talking voice. "I've been thinkin' about gettin' us some kittens for a while now." She reached out and picked up the gray one. "Come with Grammie, darlin' kit-tee, and I'll show you the new litter box and fix you a bowl of kit-tee food."

Her accent got thicker with every word. "It's been a while since I've had babies in the house. We're all going to have a good time, aren't we?" She kissed the little gray kitten right on the nose. "Not to worry, Dolly, I'll be right back to get you, darlin' baby."

"Well, that worked out well. Do I dare put my boots on, or have you played some kind of practical joke on me?" Dalton asked.

"I slept as long as you did, and we never did get back to the movie," she said. "We could finish it now since Grammie is taking care of the babies."

"Yes, I am, and what's this about not watching the movie?" Greta plucked the yellow kitten from Dalton's shoulder.

"We got so involved with the kittens that we forgot to watch the rest of it," Becca admitted.

"Well, that's for another day," Greta told her. "The girls are coming over to play cards this evening, so you can't watch it now. We set up our table in here."

"I should be getting home." Dalton pulled on his boots again. "Rye and I just keep a skeleton crew on weekends, so I should help with the evening chores. If you're not playing cards, you could come drive the truck for me."

Listen to four old women drink wine and argue over gin rummy, or go with Dalton? She chose the lesser of the two evils and smiled at him. "If you'll give me five minutes to change into jeans, I'll go drive for you."

He nodded. "Take ten, and after we get the chores done, we'll drive down to Bowie for some ice cream."

Was ice cream a date? Becca wondered as she hurried to her bedroom and changed into jeans and a T-shirt. Would he expect more than a friendly handshake or a kiss on the cheek when he brought her home? Or worse yet, would she be disappointed if he didn't kiss her good night? She ran a brush through her long hair and reapplied a little lipstick.

"It's not a date," she muttered as she headed down the hall.

Grammie was sitting in her recliner when she reached the living room. Both kittens were in her lap, and she was singing to them. She stopped when Becca entered the room and winked. "They're good kit-tees. They both used the litter box and ate some of their special food, and now they're sleeping. The girls are going to love them, but Dolly and George are going to love me more than anyone."

"Why haven't you gotten a pet before?" Dalton stood up and rolled the kinks out of his neck.

"I don't know," Greta answered. "I guess it's because I had to leave my old mama cat behind with my best friend in Ireland when I moved to the States. I missed her real bad, but I felt like I would be dishonoring all the years she caught mice for me if I brought in another cat. But Tuff brought these to me, so in a way, it makes it all right."

"I'm glad," Dalton said. "I'll tell him you said thank you."

"And the next time I make a ham, I'll save him the bone," Greta said. "Now, you kids get on out of here. You've got chores to do and ice cream to buy. I won't wait up for you, Becca." She threw a sly wink her way.

"We won't be that late," Becca said. "I've got to be up early in the morning to get some more watermelons squeezed and ready to start into wine."

"You could bring home a bottle of that so we can celebrate our new babies," Greta suggested with a raised eyebrow.

"I'll see what I can do." Becca smiled.

"We could bring a bottle by on our way to Bowie for the ladies who are playing cards with you," Dalton offered.

"You are such a sweetheart." Greta flashed her brightest smile at him.

"You are spoiling her," Becca whispered as they left the house.

"She spoiled me with a good dinner and a great nap. Do you realize that I haven't even kissed you, and we already slept together?" he teased.

"We slept, as in close our eyes and snore. We did not have sex," she told him.

"Don't know about you, but we did in my dreams." He chuckled as she opened the truck door for her.

She'd heard of hot flashes in older women, but Jesus, Mary, and Joseph, they couldn't be as hot as the heat filling her body as she watched him strut around the front end of the truck. She might need enough ice cream to fill a bathtub just to cool down after the pictures his comment painted in her mind.

Chapter 4

TO GET TO KNOW SOMEONE REALLY WELL, SPEND SOME TIME working beside them.

That's what Grammie had told Becca more times than she could remember. Seeing Dalton's gentle nature with the cattle as he fed them that evening just added to the feeling that she'd had when she watched him sleep with a kitten on his shoulder. He had a soft heart, and for crying out loud, he'd even named some of the bulls.

"Hey, that does it for this job." He crawled into the passenger seat of the ranch work truck. "You about ready for ice cream?"

"What I'd rather have is a big juicy bacon cheeseburger," she answered.

"A woman after my own heart," he grinned. "Got a particular place in mind?"

"Dairy Queen in Nocona," she answered.

"Then drive us back to my truck, and we can be there in twenty minutes," he told her.

"Fifteen if I drive." She smiled.

"A cowboy always drives his lady wherever she wants to go," he said.

"Oh, so I'm your lady?" She shifted the truck into reverse and turned it around in the pasture.

"You could be," he answered.

"Why not your woman? Or your one-night stand? Or the redhead that you got lucky with?" she asked.

"A cowboy's lady is so much more than any of those things you just said," he answered.

"How so?" she asked.

"I respect all women. That's the way I was raised, and it's the cowboy code. But a cowboy's lady goes way beyond plain old respect. She's put on a pedestal," he answered.

Put that in your corncob pipe and smoke it, Grammie's voice popped into her head.

Becca ignored the comment and asked, "And how does a lady feel about her cowboy?"

"One hundred percent the same as he feels about her," Dalton answered. "Just park right beside my truck, and we'll make the switch and go to Nocona."

Becca didn't have a corncob pipe and she didn't smoke, but she sure thought a lot about what he'd said. That was exactly the example she had seen in her grandparents, both maternal and paternal, and in her own parents.

She put the truck in Park, turned off the engine, and was about to open the door when it swung open. Dalton held out his hand to help her out of the truck, and she slipped her hand into his outstretched one. Men had opened vehicle doors for her since her first date when she was sixteen, but in that moment, even though she was wearing jeans, she felt as if she had a crown on her head and was truly royalty. Not a single man she'd ever known had made her feel so special.

"Aren't you the perfect gentleman?" she said.

"Honey, I'm thirty years old, but my mama and my grandmother both would take a switch to me if I didn't treat a woman right." He kept her hand in his all the way to his truck where he helped get her settled into the passenger seat.

Her phone rang as she was buckling her seat belt and trying to watch him walk around the front of the truck to get behind the wheel. "Hello, Grammie," she answered.

"Are y'all done with chores?" she asked.

"Yes, ma'am. Do you need me to come on home?" Becca crossed her fingers like a little child, hoping that the answer would be no. She really was looking forward to that cheeseburger.

"Lands, no, child," Greta said. "If y'all are still going to Bowie for ice cream, I want you to go to Walmart and get me a couple of baby blankets and some cat toys."

"We're going to Nocona for cheeseburgers," Becca said.

"Then go to the Dollar General there. I'm sure they'll have what I want. Go on and get half a dozen blankets so we can keep the babies with a fresh one every day. One more thing, I checked these babies. George is a girl so her new name is Loretta, so buy pink blankets," Greta said. "Is this a date?"

"I have no idea, but probably not." Becca smiled at Dalton as he started the engine.

"If he kisses you good night, it's a date. See you later, and I *will* wait up for you," Greta said.

"Greta need something?" he asked.

"George is a girl and has been renamed Loretta. She wants us to bring pink baby blankets and some cat toys," Becca answered.

"Didn't even think to see if we had boys or girls." He chuckled. "If we can't find what she wants in Nocona, we'll drive down to Walmart in Bowie. Who would have thought she'd fall in love with those kittens? Tuff did a good thing when he pilfered them from Frankie."

"Looks like he did," Becca agreed. "I thought one of them might belong to me, but I'm beginning to doubt it."

"When and if you ever get a place of your own, I'll have a visit with Tuff and tell him to bring you a kitten of your very own," Dalton said as he backed the truck out of the drive and headed west toward town. "Got a particular color in mind?"

"I don't think Tuff is that good." Becca laughed.

"Never underestimate the powers of a dog trying to please a lady."

There was that word again—*lady*. For some crazy reason, the old animated movie *Lady and the Tramp* came to Becca's mind. She stole a glance over at Dalton and decided in a split second that he definitely didn't look like the dog in the movie, but Tuff dang sure did. A picture of her and Dalton sharing a plate of spaghetti like on the movie poster flashed in her head. Thank goodness they were having cheeseburgers, or she'd never get the blush off her cheeks. No amount of blinking seemed to make it disappear.

"I'm not sure I want a kitten when I get my own place. I might want a puppy," she said.

"What kind? A Pomeranian that you can carry in your purse?" he teased.

"Nope, I was thinking about a cocker spaniel," she said.

"Good dogs." He nodded. "They make excellent pets and they're easy to train."

Maybe Tuff will fall in love with Lady, which is what I'll name my dog, and then we'll have our own real-life movie right here in Terral, Becca thought with a big smile.

Don't you ever accuse me of matchmaking when you're thinking like that, Grammie's voice was back in her head.

"You were smiling one minute and then frowning the next," Dalton said. "Who are you fighting with?"

"Grammie," she answered honestly.

"About what?"

"My dog that I haven't even gotten," she said. "When I get one, I want a female."

———————

Dalton was already trying to figure out where he might buy her a cocker spaniel for Christmas if things worked out between them. Suddenly, that old movie he had seen as a kid popped into his mind. "*Lady and the Tramp.*" He said aloud and snapped his fingers.

"What?" she asked.

"I was thinking about the old movie *Lady and the Tramp.* Did you see it when you were a kid?" he asked.

"Of course," she smiled. "Mama has every Disney movie

ever made. She bought them when I was a little girl and says she's saving them for her grandkids."

"Did you know they made a new one of those a couple of years ago? We should rent it or buy it and watch it some evening."

"I didn't know, but I'd love to see the new one. Do you realize how much Tuff looks like the Tramp?" she asked.

"Not until you mentioned a cocker spaniel, and that movie popped into my mind because that's what breed Lady was. Don't go tellin' Tuff that he looks like a movie star, or he'll want to go to Hollywood, and he's a damn good cow dog," Dalton told her.

"You should never stand in the way of his dream," Becca scolded, but couldn't keep the grin off her face.

"He told me he knew he wanted to work on a ranch when he was just a puppy," Dalton protested.

She shook her finger at him. "I'm living proof that a person, or a dog in this case, can change their dreams."

Dalton loved bantering with Becca. Women who he picked up at the Broken Bit on the nights he was lucky didn't want to do much talking. They were more interested in shedding clothing, starting at the front door and leaving a trail all the way to the bedroom or the living room sofa, or once even on the credenza right there in the foyer. Not that he didn't have a good time with each of them… Hell, it was more than just good; it was almost always a great night.

This thing with Becca went way beyond that, though. Who would ever have thought that Dalton Wilson would be having a wonderful time flirting with no thought of getting lucky that night? Maybe his nana was right about him settling down. He glanced over at Becca, and yep, whether he believed it or not, he'd fallen in love with her at first sight. With his past and with her dream of a recording career just shattered, though, he would have to take things slow. Dalton was a patient man. He could take his time and follow the rainbow to its end when he knew there was a pot of gold waiting on him.

Only a few vehicles were parked in the Dairy Queen lot when they arrived, so he snagged a spot close to the front door. The stars had begun to pop out in the sky by the time they were inside and had ordered. Since there were few other customers, the waitress brought their order pretty quickly, and Becca dived right into the double-meat-and-cheese bacon burger.

"This is one thing I missed in Nashville," she said between bites.

"They don't have Dairy Queen in Tennessee?" Dalton asked.

"Yes, they do, and their burgers are good, but not as good as these. Maybe it's because I'm home when I have one here," she answered.

"You weren't home out there?"

"Home isn't a place. It's a feeling," she told him. "I was always scrambling out there. Here I'm just Becca McKay, someone who sings sometimes at church and entertains sometimes at a Watermelon Festival, but I'm not doing it to follow a dream of being a famous singer. I'm singing for fun."

"Well, I for one am glad that you feel at home in this part of the world. Austin says that you're the best help she's ever had in the wine shed, and she hopes you don't get the itch to go back to Nashville." Dalton ate slowly so that they could spend more time together.

"I love working there. One of my part-time jobs in Nashville was working in a winery," she told him. "Like I told you before, I wouldn't mind having a vineyard of my own and trying my hand at creating my own label someday."

"What would it be named?" he asked.

"I haven't gotten that far," she answered.

"I've got a name for you." He grinned.

"Spit it out," she told him.

"Southern Lady. That sounds classy like you." His grin got bigger.

"Thank you, and I do like that for a label," she said and then pointed at the huge Coca-Cola clock hanging on the wall of the burger joint. "The Dollar General closes at eight. That means we've only got thirty minutes to round up the stuff for the kittens."

"Then we'd better get going." He slid out of the booth and waited for her, then ushered her to the door with his hand on her back. Walking beside a woman like that wasn't anything new to him, but the heat radiating through his hand damn sure was. This must be an extension of that love-at-first-sight thing Rye kept telling him about.

The Dollar General was right next door to the Dairy Queen, so it only took a couple of minutes to walk over to it. When they were inside, Becca latched onto a cart and pushed it right back to the baby section. Dalton followed behind her and located a rack with packages of three baby blankets in each.

"Pink," she reminded him when he picked up the first one and it had a blue striped one in it.

He hung it back and riffled through the rest of the packages until he found two that had all pink ones. "Will this do? Some are striped and some are plaid."

"If it's got pink on it, Grammie will be fine with them," she answered.

"Well, well, well!" Lacy Ruiz came around the end of the aisle with a cartload of merchandise. "So, this is why you…"

"We're buying these for…" Dalton started to try to explain, but then he figured that telling his old standby with the credenza in her living room that they were buying blankets for cats would sound totally crazy. "A gift for a couple of new babies."

"Yeah, right." Lacy started at Becca's toes and slowly let her eyes travel up to the top of her red hair. "I guess I'll lose my five dollars."

"I'm Becca McKay," she introduced herself. "How are you going to lose five dollars because we're buying blankets for new babies?"

"Lacy Ruiz," she nodded. "We've got a pot goin' at the Broken Bit about what kind of woman will finally rope Dalton, and I sure didn't bet on it being a tall redhead. I guess there's more than one way to get a cowboy to the altar." Her eyes shifted from Becca's stomach to the blankets in the cart. "I've got several things to get before the store closes." She paused and patted Dalton on the cheek. "I just can't see you as a daddy. I guess this will keep you away from the Broken Bit, but if it goes south, darlin', you know where I live."

"Sweet Lord!" Becca gasped when the woman had gone.

"I expect they'll all be disappointed in nine months." Dalton shrugged. "Let's go find the cat toys now."

"Why didn't you tell her we were buying these for kittens?" Becca asked.

"You think she would have believed me? That sounds like a lame excuse," Dalton said.

Becca giggled. "It does, doesn't it? I guess I'd better tell Grammie about this as soon as I get home. I bet that hussy is calling everyone she knows on her cell phone right now, and I sure don't want to have Grammie yelling at me because she heard it first from one of her friends."

"So…" Dalton dragged out the word. "Are you going to marry me and make a decent man of me?"

"Nope." She shook her head slowly as she tossed half a dozen cat toys into the cart. "I'd never rope a guy in by getting pregnant. Marriage should be for love, not necessity, and there should never be regrets."

"How did you get so smart?" he asked.

"It's the Irish in me." She started toward the checkout counter. "Grammie says we're born smart."

"I believe it." Dalton's eyes glanced at Becca's flat stomach behind the waistband of her jeans, and he wondered what she'd look like pregnant. If they ever did establish a permanent relationship, their children would be tall for sure. With him standing at six foot two inches and Becca almost kissing six feet, there was no way they'd be short. Would they have dark hair like his or red like hers? Would their eyes be blue or green, or maybe even brown like his maternal grandfather's?

"Earth to Dalton." She poked him on the arm.

"Sorry, I was off in another world," he said.

"What world would that be?" she asked.

"I've got to deliver some rodeo bulls down to a ranch rodeo in Haskell, Texas, on Friday." He said the first thing that came to his mind. "Want to ride along with me? We'll be back by suppertime."

"Depends on what's going on in the wine shed," she answered.

At least she didn't say no, he thought as he pushed the empty cart away from the counter for her.

The trip back to Terral seemed to go by in a flash, and suddenly, they were parked outside Greta's house. There wasn't a full lover's moon hanging in the sky, but it was a three-quarter one with stars dancing around it. He could think of all kinds of come-on lines, but not a single one of them seemed appropriate for a woman like his Becca.

My Becca, he thought. *Someday, maybe—if I'm as lucky as Rye was when he fell for Austin at first sight.*

He got out of the truck, helped her out, and carried the

bag of their purchases to the door for her. "I had a great time today, and thanks for helping me with chores."

"Thanks for supper." She locked eyes with him.

He dropped the bag on the porch and tipped up her chin with his fist. Her eyes fluttered shut, and her thick lashes fanned out on her cheek. He wanted to kiss her eyes, but that could come later. Right then, he craved the taste of her full lips.

When the kiss ended, he politely picked up the bag and put it in her hands. "Good night, Becca." His voice sounded strange in his own ears.

"Good night, Dalton," she whispered.

"I'll call you tomorrow," he said.

"Okay," she said.

———

"I guess it was a date," she muttered as she took the blankets and toys into the house.

"So?" Greta raised an eyebrow.

Becca held up the bag. "Six pink blankets and toys. Where's Loretta and Dolly?"

"I made them a special bed out of a laundry basket, and they're sleeping soundly in my room," she answered. "I'm not talking about the baby stuff. I got a phone call from Mavis a while ago. She says that you're pregnant. Am I going to be a great-grandmother, and is Dalton the daddy?"

"Gossip travels faster than the speed of sound." Becca plopped down on the sofa, removed her boots, and propped her feet on the coffee table. "We were buying baby blankets when Lacy Ruiz came into the store… No, that's not right." She drew her brows down and then snapped her fingers. "Lacy Ruiz…that's her name. Do you know her?"

"Oh, yes," Greta nodded.

"She got the wrong impression, and did you know there's a bet about what kind of woman Dalton will finally wind up with?" Becca asked.

"I'm not surprised. That boy has a reputation like my Seamus had before he fell in love with me," Greta said. "So, you were buying baby blankets and Lacy got the wrong idea. Did you tell her it was for our new kittens?"

"Think about it, Grammie," Becca said. "Would you have believed a story like that?"

Greta's giggle even had an Irish accent. "I don't guess I would. It does sound a bit like bull coodle. I guess when you don't swell up like you've swallowed watermelon seeds, they'll realize that Lacy's full of…"

"You're in America, Grammie," Becca told her. "You can say *bullshit*."

That made Greta laugh even harder. "The one way you could get around this mess is to marry the boy, you know, and let him make an honest woman of you."

"We've only been out on one date, and it could hardly be considered a date," Becca gasped.

"Then he did kiss you good night," Greta raised an eyebrow. "Did it send a shot of heat all the way to your toenails?"

"I don't kiss and tell," Becca answered.

Chapter 5

MONDAY WAS A LONG DAY FOR BECCA. THE HARVESTERS brought a pickup load of melons to the shed, and she spent the whole day squeezing the juice from them. She wanted to get all of them ready for the next step, so she didn't go home until after eight that evening. Dalton called and said that he and the hired hands had been hauling hay all day, and since it was supposed to rain the next day, they'd be working by the headlights of the trucks until the job was done.

"Watermelons and hay," she said.

"We must love it, or we wouldn't stay with it, right?" he asked.

"Ain't it the truth," she sighed.

"I'm at the barn with this load, so good night. Maybe I'll have time to come by the wine shed tomorrow," he said.

"Good night." She looked forward to seeing him. Lord only knew how often she'd thought of him that day, but maybe it was better if they both had a little space after that steaming-hot kiss they had shared the night before.

His voice sounded almost as tired as she felt that evening. She was glad to see a note from Greta saying that she'd gone to the movies with her friends and wouldn't be home until late. The kittens came tumbling out of the living room, purring and rubbing around Becca's ankles as she made her way to the bathroom and ran water in the old claw-foot tub.

"Sorry, Loretta and Dolly," she said as she slipped out of her clothing and sank down into the warm water. "Cats don't like baths, so you have to just sit there and talk to me. So, how was your day?"

Loretta meowed pitifully.

Dolly gave Becca a dirty look, picked up a pair of socks in her mouth, and carried them out into the hallway.

"Well, my day was crazy. I juiced a whole truckload of melons, checked the progress of all the wine in the place, and loaded the rinds in the back of the work truck to take to the chickens over on the ranch. I saw Dalton from a distance once and got a hot flash just looking at him with no shirt on out there in the hayfield. I'm glad you can't talk, because I have no doubt you'd go tell Grammie what I just said," she told the kittens.

Tuesday morning went just fine except that it poured down rain most of the time. Becca stopped working long enough at noon to prop her feet up and eat a sandwich she'd brought from home. She had tossed the plastic baggie and the napkin in the trash and was headed back across the room to begin scooping out more melons to juice when she heard the first bump against the wooden door.

Her heart skipped a beat and then raced ahead with a full head of steam. Dalton had arrived, and she hadn't seen him up close since he had kissed her good night on Sunday. Would things be awkward between them?

The second bump was followed by a bellow, and the walls of the metal shed rattled. That wasn't a cowboy—it was a bull! If he knocked the door down, the old saying about a bull in a china shop wouldn't begin to describe the damage he could do. Becca grabbed her cell phone and called Dalton.

"Do you have a bull out of the pasture? I've got one trying to get into the wine shed," she said.

The noise of another loud bellow echoed through the roar of the rain beating down on the metal roof, and then a big horn poked right through the wooden door.

"That sounds like Big John," Dalton said.

"Well, you'd best come get him or he's going to be Dead John," Becca said. "I keep a five-shot thirty-eight in my purse, and if another horn comes through the door, I'm going to start shooting until it's empty. Then I'll reload and keep it up until he's ready to go to the dog-meat factory."

"Don't shoot," Dalton said. "I'm on my way. The crazy bull loves watermelon. He was probably headed to the field and caught a whiff of what's in the shed."

The call ended and the horn disappeared from the door. Becca picked up a butcher knife and deftly halved a melon, scooped out a little of the middle, and then stuck it up to the hole in the door. "I'm willing to share if you'll back away from the door and let me open it."

Her original plan was to toss the melon out into the yard and then slam the door, but when she peeked out, the bull took a step forward. "Oh, no! You will not come inside, and you aren't eating this on this side of the road."

The animal lowered his head and rolled his eyes. She stomped her foot, glared at him, and took the first step out of the shed. She held the melon out so he could smell it, and then jerked it back. "You can follow me to your pasture, or I'll take it back inside and you can do without."

She had dealt with cattle all her life, and Big John didn't

scare her one bit. If he turned malicious and came at her, she could always throw the melon down and run like hell. Rain soaked her to the skin, and her long red hair was hanging limp before she had taken half a dozen steps, but the bull followed behind her like a lost puppy.

Dalton drove up in the ranch work truck about the time she made it to the middle of the dirt road. He rolled down the window a few inches and yelled, "Are you crazy? Big John is the meanest bull at the rodeos. He could kill you in a split second."

"Not as long as I've got a watermelon in my hands. Turn the truck around and show me which pasture to put him in." She took another step, and her foot sank down in mud that came up over the top of her shoes. Not even the rain could mask the sucking noise when she pulled the shoe out and kept walking. There was no way she could go across the cattle guard with the bull, but she saw where he had broken down the fence on his way to the watermelon field.

"Okay, Big John," she told him. "We're going in the same way you came out. If you rip up a leg on the barbed wire, I'm not going to feel a bit sorry for you."

The bull threw back his head and bellowed louder than ever before.

"If you want this watermelon, then you can quit your

belly-achin' and get over one little strand of barbed wire," she told him.

Dalton drove across the cattle guard and headed toward the gate into the pasture nearest the gap in the fence. He stopped the truck and Becca saw a flash of yellow. She cradled the chunk of melon like a baby and wiped the rain from her eyes. "You've got a rain slicker and I'm wet to the hide," she grumbled. "Thank God you don't have a camera."

Dalton opened a gate and she carried the watermelon through it with Big John right behind her. When she was twenty feet into the pasture, she set the watermelon down on the ground and slowly backed out through the gate. Big John lowered his head, and Becca could have sworn the bull sighed.

Dalton slammed the gate shut and started to take off his slicker.

She shook her head. "No sense in both of us being soaked."

"At least, come up to my house with me and let me throw your things in the washer and dryer," he said.

"All right." She wiped water from her eyes and glanced at the house, a good twenty yards away. "But I'm not getting in your truck. It's only a little way, so I'll walk. I'm not ruining the seats."

"They're well-worn leather. I can dry them with a towel with no problem," he argued. "And it's warmer in there. If you get a cold from enticing my prize rodeo bull home, Greta will kill me and never ask me to Sunday dinner again."

Becca walked through mud puddles over to his truck and climbed inside when he swung the door open for her. Water dripped from her hair, her clothing, and her body, and saturated the seat while he drove up to his small house. She left a puddle behind when she stepped out into the still pouring rain. A quick glance at the driver's seat told her that it didn't look a bit better than hers.

"You're going to need a lot of towels to clean that up," she said as she headed toward the porch.

Tuff came out from under a lawn chair and shook from head to toe. Any other time she might have fussed about the spray, but what were a few more drops when she was already saturated?

Dalton rushed up the steps, slung open the door for her, and apologized for Tuff. "I would have brought him along to help corral Big John, but the bull hates him. He's the only critter on the ranch that Tuff doesn't have his bluff in on. Let me show you to the bathroom."

Becca dripped water on the hardwood floor all the way from the living room down the short hall. The place was even cleaner than Grammie's house, and that woman had never met a speck of dust that she couldn't conquer. The aroma of his woodsy shaving lotion lingered in the bathroom. She was surprised to see a big claw-foot tub on one side of the tiny space and a walk-in shower on the other.

He pointed to a hook on the wall. "You can use my robe until we get your clothes washed and dried. Toss them out in the hallway, and I'll put them in the washing machine. In an hour, you'll be all dry and ready to go back to the watermelon shed."

"You don't have to wash my things. I can do that," she said.

"I don't mind. I'll put on a pot of coffee. You could use something warm to take the chill off. Crazy, isn't it, how that even in the summer, the rain can feel cold?"

"Yep," she agreed.

"Big John doesn't like most people. I'm surprised he didn't just run you down and take that melon away from you," Dalton said.

"Maybe I'm a bull whisperer," Becca suggested.

"I can believe it after what just happened," Dalton nodded. "Just follow your nose to the kitchen when you've taken a shower." He finally closed the door and left her alone.

The air conditioner kicked on, and cold air flowing down from a vent in the ceiling sent shivers up and down Becca's body. She turned on the water in the shower and quickly slipped out of her clothing.

"Of all the days for me to wear faded blue cotton underpants," she groaned as she peeled them down from her hips. When she was completely naked, she threw her jeans, socks, shirt, and underwear out into the hallway and fought the urge to cuss when the panties landed a foot from the rest of her things.

She stepped into the shower and was surprised to find a bottle of lavender-scented shampoo and matching conditioner. "Well, that proves he keeps things ready for the women he brings home with him," she muttered as she worked some of the shampoo into her hair.

When she'd finished, she slid back the glass door, stepped out of the shower, and wrapped a towel around her long hair and used a second one to dry her body. Then she slipped on the white terry robe and wondered how many other women had worn it while they had breakfast with him. Just as he'd suggested, she followed the smell of coffee down the hall and into the kitchen.

"Have a seat." Dalton motioned toward the wooden table with four chairs around it. "Have a cookie while I pour coffee. Cream and sugar?"

"Nope, just black, and thank you." She felt very vulnerable wearing nothing but a robe that could be opened with only a tug on its belt.

"Your stuff is all in the washer. The cycle will be done in a few minutes, and we'll throw them into the dryer. I'm not sure what to do about your sneakers. I sprayed them off in the sink, but…"

"I've gone barefoot before." She pulled out a chair and sat down.

He brought two mugs of coffee to the table and sat down across from her. "Me too, but that was when I was a kid. If your feet weren't so small, you could wear my rubber boots."

"Only little part of my whole body. I've been told lots of times that someone who's six feet tall shouldn't wear a size six shoe." She picked up a cookie and bit into it. "Are these homemade?"

"My nana believed that a boy should be just as at home in the kitchen as the barn. If I'd had a sister, she would have made her haul hay and work cattle, but I'm an only child," he answered. "When I can't sleep, I bake."

"So do I." She took a sip of her coffee and then set the mug back on the table. "I like to cook, but I really love baking."

"We should have a cookie evening," he suggested. "How about tonight?"

"I've got plans for the next couple of nights," she answered, "but Thursday is free. My place or yours?"

"Mine," he replied. "I'll have everything ready. You bring

a bottle of wine, and we'll make sugar cookies. According to Austin and Rye, they go really good with watermelon wine."

"Grammie has an amazing recipe for sugar cookies. I'll bring a copy with me," she said.

What am I doing? she scolded herself. A week ago, she wouldn't have given Dalton the time of day, and she really didn't like Tuff. How could things have changed so fast?

"I've got one question before we do this," she said.

"Shoot." He grinned. "But I assure you, I keep a full pantry, so when I'm in the mood to cook, I've got what I need."

"How many women have worn this robe?"

"One, and that's you. I don't share my toys with others very well," he answered.

"Then why is there lavender-scented shampoo in your shower?" she asked.

"My mama likes it, and last week she was down here helping me get my spring cleaning done," he answered. "I don't bring women to the ranch, Becca. I'm not a saint, and probably seventy percent of what you've heard about me is pure truth, but when I spend the night with a woman, it's not at my place."

"Why?" she asked.

"Because someday I will settle down, and this will be my home until I can have enough saved for my own ranch.

I wouldn't want my wife to feel the ghosts of girlfriends past every time she turned a corner," he answered.

"That's pretty nice of you," she said and picked up a second cookie.

———————

Dalton grinned as he pushed back his chair and stood up. "I'm just a nice cowboy. The washer just quit. I'll throw your things over into the dryer."

He had just gotten her stuff into the dryer when his phone rang. He slipped it out of the hip pocket of his jeans, saw that it was Rye, and answered on the second ring.

"Hey, how's things in Florida?"

"Hot and humid and the kids are loving every minute," Rye answered.

Dalton leaned his back against the washer. "How about you?"

"I'd rather be ranching"—Rye chuckled—"but it's not too bad. I love seeing the expressions on Austin and the kids' faces, and the food is really good. Everything under control there?"

"Yep, and you'll never guess what happened today. Big John broke through the fence…" He went on to tell Rye the whole story, ending with "And I couldn't believe that Becca did that. She's sitting in my kitchen now while her clothes are drying."

"You've got a woman in your house?" Rye asked.

"I told you before you left that it was love at first sight," Dalton said.

"I didn't believe you," Rye said. "I remember that feeling. I'll just hope that you can convince her you're ready to settle down. I can't wait to tell Austin. Believe me, she'll do all she can do to help you out. She and Becca have become good friends these past months."

"Thanks," Dalton told him. "Anything you want me to do more than what we're doing?"

"Just be sure the rodeo stock gets down to Haskell on Friday. I'll be home Sunday evening, so I'll go pick them up on Monday," Rye said.

"I might take Becca with me to control Big John," Dalton said, chuckling.

"Tell her to take a couple of watermelons along." Rye laughed. "It's our turn to line up for a ride. Talk to you later. Austin says to tell Becca hello."

The call ended, and Dalton headed back to the kitchen. "Austin says to tell you hello."

"Are they having a good time?" Becca smiled up at him.

He refilled their coffee mugs and sat down. "Yep, but Rye says he'd rather be ranchin'."

"I can understand that for sure," Becca said. "Amusement

parks are not my idea of a fun week. I'd rather stay home and make wine, or maybe go to a nice quiet beach and listen to the ocean waves coming in and going out."

Damn! This girl was really after his heart in every way. "Me too, or maybe take a trip up into the mountains when there's snow on the ground, build a roaring blaze in a fireplace, and just sit in front of it with a good cold beer."

"That sounds pretty amazing too," she agreed. "Put on some good slow country music in either one of those places, and I'd love it."

He made a mental note to have music playing while they made cookies on Thursday evening. "Was it a cultural shock to come home after spending ten years in Nashville?"

"Not as much as it was going to Nashville after being raised in Ringgold," she answered. "I got used to it after a while, and coming home, well…it's home." She raised a shoulder in half a shrug.

"Reckon you'll sing at local events?" he asked.

"Maybe," she answered. "Making the decision to give up on my dream wasn't easy, but as time goes by, it's becoming something of the past. Does that make sense?"

"More than you'll ever know." He nodded in agreement.

"What makes you say that?" she asked.

"I wanted to be a champion bull rider as well as a rancher.

It took about eight years and a few broken bones for me to realize that I'm just not that good," he said. "Not that I'm sayin' you're not good enough to make it in country music, but when I finally figured out that I wasn't cut out to ride bulls, I put that dream behind me and put my all into ranchin.'"

"And chasin' women?" She raised an eyebrow.

"Bull ridin' gets more ladies than plain old ranchin,'" he replied. "I've sown my wild oats in both arenas—ranchin' and rodeoin'. I'm lucky that I didn't have to reap a harvest from that, but I'm thirty years old now, and I'm finding that all that glitters is not gold."

"Seems like there was an old song that said that same thing," she said.

Dalton nodded again. "Yep, and every word of it is true. The dryer just dinged."

"I'll get my things and get dressed." She pushed back her chair and headed out of the kitchen.

His robe only came to her knees, and her hips curved out from her small waist where she'd roped the belt tightly. She whipped the towel from her hair, and just looking at her long legs, her bare feet, and all that tangled, damp hair made his heart throw in an extra beat. He'd love to untie that robe, watch it fall into a puddle at her feet, and then scoop her up in his arms and carry her to his bed.

If he was lucky, maybe that would happen someday.

She carried her clothes straight to the bathroom and emerged five minutes later, fully dressed except for shoes. Her long hair had been brushed and drawn up into a still damp ponytail. She reminded him of one of those Greek goddesses that had stepped forward in time to the twenty-first century. He might not be able to untie the belt or slip the robe off her shoulders at the moment, but the muddy yard gave him every excuse to carry her to the truck.

The rain had finally stopped. They stepped out onto the porch, and without asking permission, he took a step forward, picked her up like a new bride, and said, "No need for you to get your feet muddy."

"I don't think I've ever been..." she gasped.

"Then, darlin', you've must have been dating the wrong guys."

Chapter 6

On Tuesday Becca hit the ground running and didn't stop until it was almost dark. She was dragging by the time she made it back home. She plopped down on the sofa the minute she got into the living room. Both kittens climbed the arm of the sofa like it was a tree and walked across the back until they reached her. Then they used her ponytail for a batting toy.

"Did you see Dalton today?" Greta asked.

"Nope," she answered. "He's been in the hayfield all day. They got a second cutting on one of the big pastures. He texted me a few times. Grammie, I like him a lot, but…"

"Honey, you listen to your heart. If it tells you to walk away, then do it. If your heart tells you to stick with it, then do that. Ain't a one of us old ladies or any of your young friends can give you solid advice on love. I like the cowboy. He's got a helluva bad reputation when it comes to lovin' and leavin', but…" Greta shrugged.

"But what?" Becca pushed for more.

"But he looks at you like my Seamus looked at me. It might sound crazy to you, but it means something to me. Now, get on in there and dip you up a plate full of corned beef and cabbage. You look like you're on your last leg. A little nourishment will be good for you." Greta pointed toward the kitchen.

"Yes, ma'am." Both kittens had already climbed to Becca's shoulder and were curling up to take a nap. She set them on the floor and headed toward the kitchen. "Hey, did I tell you that Dalton can cook, and that he makes great cookies?"

"My Seamus liked to help me in the kitchen. His meat pies were the best in the world. I never have been able to make pie crust as good as his." Greta raised her voice.

Becca dipped up a bowl full of food and carried it to the living room. "We're making cookies on Thursday night."

"That's a good thing," Greta said. "You need to spend time with him, so your old heart knows what to tell you to do. How would it know whether this is a real thing or just a passin' fancy if you avoid him like you've done since you got here?"

"I needed time to figure out whether I was going to go back to Nashville to give it one more year," she answered. "Besides, I'd heard that all he was interested in was a good time."

"You still yearnin' after that dream of singin'?" Greta asked.

"No, I'm pretty content now where I am," Becca said. "Why? Are you wantin' me to get out of your house so you can flirt with some old guy?"

"Bloody hell, no!" Greta gasped. "I love havin' you here, and I gave my Seamus my whole heart. Ain't nothin' left to give another man."

Becca wanted that kind of thing for her own—someday. She wasn't in a hurry to find it by any means, but she didn't intend to settle down to a permanent relationship with anything less than what Grammie had had with *her Seamus*.

———

Wednesday crawled by like a snail in a foot of snow on the way to a funeral. Every time Dalton looked at the clock, only thirty seconds had passed. Thursday was even worse. He helped the hired hands repair fence all day, and yet time seemed to stand still.

Finally, the day ground to an end. He rushed home, took

a quick shower, shaved, and then got into his truck and drove into town to pick up Becca. Without a doubt, he'd just spent the longest three days of his life, and if he could avoid it, he'd never go that long without seeing Becca again. He'd proven that *out of sight, out of mind* was a crock of bullshit.

She was sitting on the porch when he arrived. She was wearing a cute little dress with strings for straps, and a pair of sandals. Strands of her hair had escaped the messy knot on top of her head. Just looking at her made his mouth go as dry as if he'd just bitten down on a green persimmon. She picked up her purse and a paper bag and started toward the truck. He jumped out of the truck and rushed around to open the door for her. A whiff of her perfume—something with a hint of vanilla—sent his senses reeling.

"You sure are gorgeous tonight. Maybe we should forget all about cooking and go out to dinner at a fancy restaurant," he suggested.

She handed the paper bag to him. "I'm cooking tonight, and then we're making cookies. My mouth has been watering for sugar cookies all day."

"What are you cooking?" He set the bag in the back seat.

"Chicken Alfredo. And I'm making a salad, and I've got a loaf of Grammie's homemade bread to go with it," she said.

"And the wine?" he asked.

"It's in my purse. Two bottles. One for supper. One for dessert." She smiled.

"I always wondered why women liked big purses." He shut her door and rounded the front of the truck. When he was behind the wheel, he adjusted the AC and shifted the gear into reverse.

"The bigger the purse, the more wine we can bring home," she teased.

"You think two bottles is enough?" he asked.

"Depends on how much you drink. I'm Irish. I can hold my liquor, wine, or even good beer. How about you?" she threw back at him.

"Is that a challenge?" he asked. "Because if it is, honey, I've got about five kinds of whiskey, a bottle of coconut rum, one of tequila, and two of vodka, and a six-pack of cold beer in the refrigerator. We can do shots, or even make a vodka watermelon if we run out of wine."

"Oh, I do love a booze melon," she said. "It's crazy that I was raised right here in watermelon country and never had a vodka melon until I went to Nashville. Let's stop by the watermelon field where the sugar baby melons are grown. They're the best ones for wine and for vodka melons."

"What's the prize for the one who's still sober enough to drive you home at the end of the evening?" he asked.

"A kiss good night." She was definitely flirting.

"I don't shave for a second time in a day for less than at least a thirty-minute make-out session if I'm the winner," he shot back at her.

She stuck her hand across the console. "If I'm the winner, I get to name the time and place for that make-out session."

———————

Becca knew she was playing with fire, but Grammie had advised her to get to know him. What could be better than making out for thirty minutes? Besides, she'd missed him the past three days, and she'd never felt like that about any man in her past. With her work, time for dates was scarce, and there had only been one relationship—if six dates, one weekend in bed, and a couple of quick lunches could qualify as such.

They stopped by the watermelon field closest to the wine shed on the way back to the ranch, and Dalton insisted that he knew the difference between a sugar baby and the other types of melons. "You sit right there, and I'll put a couple in the back of the truck. You can decide which one you want to juice up with vodka."

"Thank you," she said.

He thumped around on a few melons. Each time he

cocked his ear to listen for a hollow sound. When he was satisfied that a couple of smaller ones would be perfect, he cut the vine with his pocketknife, tucked each one under an arm, and carried them out of the field. He gently laid them in the back of the truck and then crawled in behind the wheel. "Those should do the trick. After a bottle of wine, I bet we'll be loosened up enough to dance."

"We're not going to the Broken Bit, are we?" she asked.

"No, darlin.'" He reached across the console and laid a hand on her shoulder. "We can dance in the living room and not have to bump into anyone else."

That fire she'd thought about earlier seemed to be getting hotter and hotter. He drove across the road, parked the truck, and helped her out of the passenger seat. Then he picked up the bag of groceries in one hand and one of the melons in the other. "I guess you'll have to open the door for me this time, but you've got to promise not to tell my mama or my nana. They'd tack my hide to the smokehouse door if they found out I wasn't a gentleman."

"My lips are sealed," she said as she threw the door open and then followed him inside. She set her purse on the kitchen table and unloaded the things she needed to make supper from the bag. "I should have asked you whether you even like Alfredo."

"Love it." He uncapped a bottle of vodka, set the lid on the side of the watermelon, and used it as a pattern to draw a circle. Then he carefully cut a plug from the melon and inverted the bottle into the hole without spilling a single drop. A few air bubbles floated up to the top of the bottle and the vodka began to slowly seep into the meat of the melon.

"This is not your first rodeo, is it?" she asked.

"Nope, and I really like for the vodka to infuse into the melon for twelve to twenty-four hours. If we decide the wine is enough for our bet, then we can have this tomorrow night." He raised an eyebrow and grinned, "Or maybe for breakfast in the morning?"

"I don't think I'll be around at breakfast, but you think there's going to be a tomorrow night?" she asked.

"I can always hope," he answered. "Now, what can I do to help with supper? I'm starving."

"You can make a salad and slice the bread while I put the Alfredo together. The wine is chilled, and I see you've already set the table," she replied.

"Did that when I came in for a lunch break," he admitted. "Today was the slowest day in history. I began to think it was like the preacher said about a thousand years being as one day."

She found a large cast-iron skillet under the cabinet and

dumped the chicken she'd cooked the night before into it. "I agree. Do you know what *wait* is?"

"It's misery," he said.

"No, it's a four-letter word." She giggled.

"Amen to that, and Nana would wash my mouth out with soap for saying those kinds of words." He finished making salads in two small bowls and put them on the table. Then he got out a sharp knife and sliced half the loaf of bread.

When he reached for two wineglasses, his hip bumped against hers. "Sorry about that."

"I'm not," she muttered as she whipped around and laced her arms around his neck. "Did you feel some electricity between us?"

"Honey, I feel the chemistry between us every time we're in the same room," he admitted as his lips found hers in a long, steamy kiss. "I've dreamed about kissing you all day," he whispered when the kiss ended.

"Did it live up to your expectations?" she asked.

"One hundred and fifty percent." He gave her a quick peck on the forehead, picked up the glasses, and took them to the table.

Every nerve ending in her whole body hummed with desire. Good old common sense told her that more than sharing a few kisses was out of the question. That didn't mean she didn't want to forget about wine, vodka-infused watermelon, and even supper and slowly undress him on the way to the bedroom.

The noodles took longer to cook than the sauce, but the Alfredo was ready in fifteen minutes. She carried the skillet to the table and set it on a hot pad. A fancy bowl would have gone better with the pretty table Dalton had set, but the cast-iron would keep the food hot longer.

He pulled out a chair for her and then poured the wine. "Are you going to say grace, or am I?"

"It's your house, so it's your call," she told him. "Do you always pray?"

"Yep," he answered as he took her hand in his. "I grew up in a household that said grace before every meal, and it just don't seem right not to give thanks."

"Me too." She bowed her head.

He said a simple prayer and then held up his wineglass. "To us."

She picked up her glass and touched his. "To us."

By the time supper was over, they'd finished the first bottle of wine. As Becca had bragged earlier, she could hold her liquor as well as any good Irishwoman, but she'd never had good aged watermelon wine. When she got up to help clear the table, the room did a couple of spins. She finally got it under control by holding on to the counter for just a minute.

"All right," Dalton said when he put the last plate in the dishwasher. "Great supper. Good wine. Amazing company. Now let's make cookies and pop open that second bottle of wine. I've got a confession. I thought wine was for sissies until Rye introduced me to watermelon wine. I liked it from the beginning, but I like this stuff even better." He thumped the watermelon on the counter, removed the empty vodka bottle, and put the plug he had cut out of the melon back in place. "And one more confession…I talk a lot when I get a good buzz going."

The door is open. Don't lose the opportunity. Grammie's voice was loud and clear in Becca's mind even if she did have a little buzz going on in her own head. *If he's got a mind to talk, then ask questions.*

"So, you are a happy drunk, not a mean one?" she asked.

He chuckled as he got out the ingredients to make sugar cookies. "I usually stop drinking after a little buzz. I don't like to be drunk, and I hate hangovers." He laid his phone on the counter and touched the screen. "A little music," he said as Garth Brooks sang "The River."

The lyrics said something about standing on the shoreline and letting the waters run by. Becca nodded in agreement when Garth sang about rough waters. "What made you choose this song?"

"I like that line that says, 'I'll never reach my destination if I don't try,'" he said. "I like you, Becca McKay." He leaned over the container of flour and kissed her on the tip of the nose. "I have to try to make you like me back, even if I have to do what the song says and sail my vessel until the river runs dry."

"I don't think you'll have to try until the *Red River* is completely dry," she whispered.

"Good." He grinned. "I was worried about that."

"You are a charmer," she said.

"Nana told me when I was just a little boy that good looks would take me far in life, but charm would get me whatever I wanted," he told her.

"And has it?" She measured out the flour and then cut a stick of butter into it.

"Until you came into my life," he said. "I thought you were immune to my sweet-talkin'."

"I had to get the past out of my system before I could…" She paused and locked eyes with him. "Are you just tryin' to get me into bed, or are you serious about a long-term relationship?"

"Darlin', I'm as serious as a cowboy tryin' to hang on to a buckin' bull for eight seconds," he said.

That might not sound like a declaration to some women, but Becca sure understood what he was saying.

"Okay, then," she said. "I believe you."

"Thank you for that. I don't lie, Becca. I will tell you the truth, even if it hurts me to do it," he said as he put the first pan of cookies into the oven.

She refilled their wineglasses and took a sip. "I'm pretty much the same. That might have been part of my problem in Nashville. I wasn't willing to do anything for a contract. If I couldn't get one with my singing, I damn sure didn't want one if it meant I had to fall on my back or drop down on my knees."

Dalton chuckled. "You are pretty straightforward, aren't you?"

"Yep, it's the only way to be," she said. "And speaking of that, I'm tellin' you right now, this is some damn fine wine, and it's hittin' me harder than whiskey usually does."

"This must be Austin's good stuff. Did you get it from the top shelf?" he asked.

"Yes, I did. I wanted to bring the best," she answered.

He removed the pan of cookies and slid the second batch into the oven. "Like 'em warm?"

"Honey, I like 'em hot," she said, giggling.

"Let's take them to the living room." He lifted twenty

cookies off the pan with a spatula and put them onto a plate. "You carry the wine, and I'll bring this."

"Don't you dare drop them on the floor," Becca cautioned. "I've looked forward to warm cookies and cold wine all day."

"If I do, we'll just sit down on the floor and eat them. You don't have to worry. My floors are just that clean," he told her.

"Did you see that episode of *Friends* when Joey and Rachel and Chandler eat cheesecake off the floor? This reminds me of that night, only they were stone-cold sober." She picked up the wine and took short steps all the way to the living room where she set the glasses on the coffee table and then sank down into the sofa.

"And we are not." Dalton sat down beside her and draped an arm around her shoulders. "I'm not sure if it's the wine or if I'm slap happy because you're here. After almost six months of wanting this to happen, now it is, and I could be drunk on that and not the wine."

"You are a charmer for sure." Becca reached for a cookie, took a bite, and then sipped the wine. "Very good together. Do we really have to wait until tomorrow night to get into our vodka melon?"

"It takes at least twelve hours for it to infuse, but if you want to have it earlier, you are welcome to spend the night," he told her.

Before she could answer, someone knocked on the door and then came right in without being invited. Becca hoped like hell it wasn't his mother or his grandmother. Either of them seeing her half-lit would not bode well.

"Well, well, well? So, it's true. You're not pregnant. If you were, you wouldn't be drinking wine." Lacy stopped inside the door and popped her hands on her hips.

"What the hell are you doing here?" Dalton asked.

"I came to tell you that you were having twins, only not by the same mama, but I guess you'll only be getting one little dark-haired baby in about seven months." She pointed down at her flat belly.

"Oh, no!" he said loudly. "If you're pregnant, it's not mine. I haven't been with you since before Christmas."

"Are you sure?" She raised both eyebrows. "Run along home, Becca McKay. He lives by the cowboy code, and he'll marry me because it's the right thing to do."

"She's lying," Dalton whispered. "She's trying to cause trouble. I swear to God, I haven't been with her since right after Thanksgiving."

Becca shook off his arm and stood up. "You clean up this mess before you text or call me again."

"You're too drunk to drive," he said.

"I don't plan on getting behind the wheel. I'll sleep it off in the watermelon shed," she told him as she went to the kitchen, picked up her purse, and headed toward the door. "Forget about me going with you to deliver the rodeo animals tomorrow."

"I'll swear on a Bible, take a DNA test, whatever it takes, Becca. Trust me," he said.

With tears running down her cheeks, she staggered down the lane and across the dirt road. She was almost to the watermelon shed when she heard a vehicle. Her hands knotted into fists. If it was Lacy, she might drown the bitch in a five-gallon bucket of watermelon juice and swear to God that she had nothing to do with it. The truck came to a stop and Dalton got out and tried to take her hands in his, but she wasn't having any of it. She might be able to forget the past and her dreams, but evidently his wild oats were going to follow him around forever.

"I'm so sorry, but I mean it. If she is pregnant, it's not my baby," he said.

"We both need to sober up before we talk," she said. "Go home, Dalton. You shouldn't even be behind the wheel."

"Can I call you tomorrow?" he asked.

"I suppose." She nodded. "But not until you get back from Texas."

Chapter 7

GRETA CAME THROUGH THE DOOR LIKE A CATEGORY 5 tornado. "Get your drunk arse up and go get in the car. You're comin' home with me right now, girl. There ain't no way you are sleeping in a lawn chair all night."

"I'm not drunk. I'm barely buzzed, and I'm perfectly fine sleeping right here," Becca argued.

Greta pointed toward the door. The expression on her face said that she wasn't about to repeat herself and she wasn't taking no for an answer. Becca slowly got to her feet and stumbled that way. She didn't have the energy to fight with her grandmother, especially when the odds were against her. Not once in all of her twenty-eight years had she won an argument with her grandmother.

When they were in the car and on the way home, Greta glanced over at her and said, "What in the hell happened?"

"Nothing," Becca growled. "And I'm going home with you, so you win."

"Don't you sass me, Rebecca McKay," Greta told her. "I told you that spending time with that cowboy would prove if you should be with him or not, one way or the other. Evidently, it's not."

"Yep," Becca agreed.

"If he can't trust you, then you don't have a foundation to build on anyway, so it's best to end it before it even gets started," Greta said as she parked in front of her house.

"Yep," Becca said a second time. "Whoa! Wait a minute. Him trust *me*? Evidently, he called you because you came to get me, but it wasn't *me* who's…" She paused and glared at her grandmother.

"I know what I said, and it's exactly what I meant. You should have stood up for him when Lacy came bursting in accusing him of something that he says couldn't be true. Bloody hell, Becca. That woman's like a doorknob on a public loo. Everyone has given it a turn with her, and if he said he hasn't been with her in more than six months, then why didn't you believe him?"

Greta parked in the drive, got out of the car and marched up to the porch. She didn't even turn around to see if Becca was all right. Becca sat there a couple of minutes; then she slung the door open, got out, slammed it shut, and stomped to the porch, carrying guilt on her shoulders like a heavy blanket in the middle of a July heat wave. She went straight to the bathroom, brushed her teeth, and met Greta in the hallway when she came out.

"You can be mad at me, but that don't make me wrong." Greta picked up the kittens and carried them to her bedroom.

"No, but I don't have to like it." Becca muttered as she closed her bedroom door. She dropped her dress and underwear on the floor, kicked off her sandals, realized that her feet were dirty, and padded back to the bathroom.

She stood under the warm shower for several minutes, letting the spray beat down on her back. Her grandmother was right. Becca should have popped up on her feet, glared down at Lacy, and then showed her to the door. "Hindsight, and all that shit," she said as she stepped out and picked up a towel.

When she got back to her bedroom, she pulled on a pair of underpants and her lucky sleep shirt, fell into bed, and practically passed out. When she opened her eyes, the sun coming through her window was attempting to burn holes in them. With a moan, she buried her face in the pillow. Her head felt like rock music was blasting away with the bass turned all the way up. She couldn't remember the last time she'd had a hangover and vowed never to touch watermelon wine again if this was the price she had to pay for it.

She crawled out of bed, dressed in jeans and a T-shirt, and stumbled into the kitchen with her hand over her forehead.

Greta poured her a cup of hot tea and set it before her. "Drink this while I make you a good Irish breakfast to cure that wine hangover."

"I couldn't eat a bite of food," Becca groaned. "I don't get drunk. I don't have hangovers. And on wine, Grammie? Have I lost my Irish wings?"

"No, darlin', not until you have a morning like this after good Irish whiskey. Austin has figured out a few secrets, like how to make her top-shelf wine more potent. Did y'all drink a whole bottle?" Greta asked.

Becca held up two fingers.

"Bloody hell, Becca. No wonder you were *fluthered*! Me and the girls share a bottle and all four of us get downright giggly." Greta set about making breakfast for two. "'Tis a good Irish breakfast you need, and another cup of tea, and then you'll be ready to go to work."

"Grammie!" Becca groaned. "Not a full Irish breakfast. I'm just two steps away from heading for the bathroom right now."

"When you eat every bite of what I'm making, you will

be cured. The black pudding, beans, and fried tomatoes are already done. Do you know how much trouble it is to get good black pudding in this part of the world? I have to go all the way to Saint Jo to get it, so you won't be wastin' a bite of it. Do you hear me?" Greta shook an egg turner at Becca.

"Yes, ma'am," Becca groaned.

"I just need to finish up the bacon, sausage, and eggs. Then I'll pop the toast in the machine, and you can begin to eat," Greta said. "Besides, I've been starving for a breakfast like this. I love it even when I don't have a watermelon wine hangover."

Becca sipped her tea and hoped that she would be able to get a few bites down. Black pudding wasn't something she enjoyed even when she was sober, but if Grammie said it would cure her aching head, she would force it down.

"Have you thought about what an opportunity you missed last night?" Greta asked as she put half a dozen pieces of bacon into the skillet.

"I can't think at all," Becca answered. "My head hurts too bad."

"Then drink some more tea," Greta told her.

"Why would Lacy do that?" Becca whispered.

"Because Dalton is showing signs of being ready to settle down, and she wants him." Greta turned the bacon and cracked two eggs into another skillet. "He'd be a good catch, and besides all that, she's probably got a bet going about how long it will take her to get him in front of the preacher. She'll make some money and have a good husband too."

"That's just wrong!" Becca narrowed her eyes and set her jaw.

"Sin is sin. One ain't no more wrong than the other. You not letting him explain or believe him was just as wrong as what she is doing." Greta finished making two plates and carried them to the table. "Eat and then you'll feel all better."

"Do you think she's really pregnant?" Becca cut up her eggs, dipped a corner of a piece of toast in the yellow, and put it in her mouth.

"Maybe she is, but if she is, then it's not Dalton's. Think about it: Why would he get careless after all these years? He said he hasn't been with her in six months, and I believe him," Greta cut off a piece of the black pudding. "Cowboys have a code. If she is pregnant and the baby is his, he will marry her, but if it's not, then…" Greta shrugged. "Y'all need to talk."

———

Those last four words were still rattling around in Becca's mind when she reached the wine shed that morning. Just like Greta had promised, the tea and all that breakfast did make her feel much better. Her head still felt slightly like one of the round watermelons she sliced open to juice, but that was minor compared to the way she had felt when she first woke up.

She gave the bottles of wine on the top shelf of the winery a dirty look as she flipped the strap of a bibbed apron over her head. The hired hands had already unloaded a pickup load of melons into the shed, and there would be at least that many more arriving after lunch. If she'd gone with Dalton on his stock delivery, she would have been working long hours over the weekend to catch up.

She figured more watermelons were coming in when she heard the hinges on the door squeak. "Just stack them over against the wall."

"Hey," Dalton said.

His deep Texas drawl made her drop the butcher knife on the floor.

"Hey." Her eyes locked with his across the room.

"You ready to talk?" he asked, but he didn't take a step forward.

"How did you get back from Haskell so quick?" she asked.

"I didn't go," he answered. "Didn't plan to take the bulls myself from the beginning. I just thought it would be a good little trip for the two of us, but…" He blinked and took a deep breath. "Need some help?"

"Doin' what? Apologizing for not trusting you, or juicing melons?" she asked.

"I was thinkin' of melons," he said. "Are we going to talk about last night or pretend it didn't happen?"

"I think we'd better talk about it." She picked up the knife and carried it over to the sink. "I'm not a big believer in sweeping things under the rug." She motioned to a couple of green lawn chairs over in the corner.

He waited for her to sit down, and then he eased down in the chair beside her. "I visited with Lacy this morning on the phone. I didn't go to her place or invite her to come to mine. Everyone in town knows that I live out here on the ranch in the original old house, but until last night she'd never been in my place."

"I believe you," Becca said. "I shouldn't have reacted the way I did."

"Actually, you had every right to react that way. I also talked to my grandpa and my dad this morning. They both reminded me that I was just reaping what I'd sown. I've chased women since I was a teenager, and they told me time after time that the day would come when I would have regrets about being so wild," he confessed.

"Grammie read me the riot act too, only she said that we shouldn't even consider having a few dates because I didn't trust you," Becca told him. "In her opinion I should have kicked Lacy's arse out of the house when you told her that the baby couldn't be yours."

"She's not pregnant," Dalton said. "She got angry when she saw us buying baby blankets, and she wanted to break us up."

"What a bitch!" Becca said.

"She might be, but it worked for her last night anyway," Dalton said. "Now what do we do?"

"I'm sorry for the way I acted," Becca said. "Everyone has a past, no matter how good or bad it is. The important thing is to leave all that where it belongs and go forward."

"Is there a forward for us?" he asked.

She had loved being with him on Sunday and then again last night. She had swallowed her pride and apologized.

"I sense by your hesitation that you don't know," he said. "Anything I can do to change your mind?"

"You could ask me out on a date that doesn't involve wine, and we could take it one step at a time, if you're willing to do that," she said.

"Becca, will you go out with me tonight? There will be no wine and no drinking, but I can promise you supper and a nice quiet evening where no one will barge in on us." He smiled for the first time.

"I'd love to go with you. What can I bring to help with supper?" She returned his smile.

"Not one thing. I make a real mean ham-and-cheese sandwich, and I've got just the hideaway spot for us to visit." He stood up. "We could leave from here when you get off work at five."

"I probably should go home and get cleaned up if this is a date," she told him.

"If you want to, you can lose the apron. If not, then you look pretty damn gorgeous in it." He extended a hand to help her up.

Her fingers tingled the moment they touched his. One date, and then she'd make a decision and never look back with regrets whichever way it went. After the way she'd acted the night before, he deserved that much. When she was on her feet, he pulled her to his chest and kissed her—long, hard, and passionately.

Well, maybe two dates just to be sure, she thought when the kiss ended and he walked out of the winery without saying another word.

Chapter 8

BECCA WASN'T SURE WHAT TO THINK WHEN DALTON CAME to get her for their date. He was driving the beat-up old ranch work truck. When he had told her she should just take off her apron, she hadn't expected that they would go to a five-star restaurant or a dinner theater, but she did think maybe he would spring for his fancy club-cab vehicle.

"Where are we going?" she asked as she fastened her seat belt.

"Somewhere secluded and so quiet you can hear the tree frogs singing," he answered. "Do you trust me?"

"Yes," she answered.

"I promise you're going to love it, and before you ask, I've never taken anyone, male or female, there before. It's my hidden place where I go to think," he told her.

"I feel special," she said.

"Darlin', you are far more than just special," he whispered softly before he closed the door.

This wasn't her first rodeo when it came to pickup lines. She had worked in bars all over Nashville and fended off lots of guys when they brought what they thought was a game good enough to sweet-talk her into bed. What Dalton said didn't affect her as much as his tone, and the way his warm breath caressed her neck when he spoke.

He drove through Terral, passing the elementary school on the right, Mama Josie's café on the left, and then he crossed Highway 81, and drove through a cattle guard with HT welded onto the gate.

"What does that stand for?" she asked.

"Hard Time Ranch," he answered. "The owner is a friend of mine, and he doesn't mind if I cross his property to get to my hidey hole down by the river."

She envisioned a place where they'd have to crawl back into a cave of some kind and hoped to hell there were no spiders or field rats in it. "The river, huh?" She pulled her phone from her purse, found the song they'd listened to the night before, and played it.

"Yep, and I do love that song," he answered. "We're going to the river to sail our vessels. I've got them ready in the back of the truck, along with our supper in a basket."

She turned around and looked out the back window, but all she could see was a big basket and some chunks of wood. Maybe he was speaking symbolically instead of having a real vessel to sail.

The truck rattled and groaned when he drove down a rutted path toward the river. She was amazed when they passed a herd of white-tailed deer and a wild hog with a dozen little piglets following behind her. They flushed a covey of quail out of the path, and she watched them fly away, and then a bobcat with a couple of kittens watched them go by.

"Aren't they the cutest things ever? I wonder what Grammie's new babies would think of one of those," Becca said.

"I'm not sure you could tame one of those any better than a cowboy can a wild Irish lass with a temper." Dalton grinned.

"So, you think I'm a wild lass?" she asked.

"I saw a little of that in you last night, and truth is, I kind of liked it," he admitted.

"I'm glad you like me just the way I am," she said, nodding.

He braked and brought the truck to a stop. "Honey, I wouldn't change a single thing about you. We'll walk from here. It's not far. I'm taking my boots off. I like to feel the sand beneath my bare feet like when I was a kid."

She kicked off her shoes and tossed them in the bed of the truck along with his boots. He shoved the wood and some string down into a paper bag and picked up the basket. "See that willow tree over there with the limbs hanging in the water?"

"It's beautiful," she gasped.

"That's where we'll have supper. Would you bring the quilt? I've kind of run out of hands." He pointed toward the cab.

She reached over the side and picked up the patchwork quilt. This just might be the most interesting date she'd ever been on in her entire life. The river was peaceful, flowing along, just like it had been since the beginning of time. A pungent aroma filled the whole area, and the willow branches swayed in the warm evening breeze.

When they reached the huge tree, Dalton set the basket and sack down and parted the thick limbs. "Welcome to my secret place, Becca McKay."

She carried the quilt inside the opening and spread it out on the sand. "It's lovely, Dalton. Thank you for trusting me enough to bring me here."

He picked up her hand and kissed the knuckles. "Thank you for trusting me, period. Have a seat and we'll have our supper, and then we'll go sail our vessels."

"Are you serious?" She eased down on the quilt.

"Yep, I brought homemade sailboats and string so we can guide them down the river. Sometimes I fish right here, but tonight, I want us to float our little boats and think of that song about the river." He sat down and opened the basket. "Another confession. I haven't dated much. Last time I actually asked a woman out was probably for my senior prom in high school."

"Really?" she asked.

"I want us to be open and honest with each other," he told her.

"I've dated a lot, but I've never been picked up in a bar," she told him.

"Then we've had two different lifestyles." He handed her a cold bottle of root beer and then laid the rest of the food out between them on the quilt. "The sugar cookies from last night and the bananas are for dessert."

Supper was a ham-and-cheese sandwich, a small bag of potato chips, and sweet pickles that they ate with their fingers right out of the jar. Every bite tasted better to Becca than if she had been eating filet mignon in a five-star restaurant.

"I can see why this would be your favorite place," she said. "It's so quiet that I really can hear the tree frogs."

"Sometimes they argue with the owls and the other birds roosting in the trees for center spot," he said.

At that moment Becca could feel peace surrounding

her heart, much like the drooping branches of the weeping willow tree circled around her and Dalton.

"If this works out between us, we should come here once a week and leave all our troubles, arguments, and disagreements in the river," she said.

Dalton leaned over the food between them, cupped her face in his hands, and brushed a sweet kiss across her lips. "That's what I do when I float my little boat down the river. I put all my worries on it and give them to the current."

"Then why the string to control the boat?" She touched her lips to see if they were as hot as they felt and was surprised to see that they were actually cool.

"Because sometimes I'm not quite ready to let go of my worries, but when I am, I drop the string," he answered.

"What worries are you going to put on your boat today?" she asked.

"I'll tell you mine if you tell me yours," he replied.

"You first." She nodded toward him.

"My first worry is that this will be our one and only real date."

You kissed me on Sunday. According to Grammie, that makes it a real date, she thought.

"My second is that my wild past will always hang around to haunt us both."

Not if we work at squashing it every time it rears its ugly head.

"My third is that I won't have the courage to tell you how I feel about you, and make you believe me."

I think I already know because I'm listening to my heart.

"Now, it's your turn," he said.

"You cited three, and that's a lot to put on one little boat. My worries are number one"—she held up a finger—" that if we did enter into something serious, you'll get tired of me and break my heart." The second finger went up. "That I might regret not giving Nashville one more year." The third finger shot up. "And that you'll never bring me back here again."

"I would never get tired of you, darlin'"—he took her hand in his—"and if we get really serious about each other, I will love you so much that Nashville will never enter your mind again." He brought her hand to his lips and kissed each knuckle. "And Friday or Saturday night can be our official weeping-willow-tree date night. Are you ready to sail our vessels down the Red River?"

"This is crazy to think about this right now, but I just remembered that Austin scattered her grandmother's ashes on this very river. Do you think she'll destroy our worries for us?" Becca put all the trash and leftovers back into the basket and then stood up.

"Rye told me that the first time he laid eyes on Austin, she was at the edge of the river giving it her grandmother's ashes, and it was love at first sight," Dalton said. "I bet her granny will be glad to drown our worries for us."

Dalton got to his feet and picked up the paper sack. In a few long strides, they were beyond the willow tree, and he took two small pieces of wood from the bag. He'd drilled a hole in the top of each one that held a tiny paper sail affixed to a dowel rod.

"They really do look like little sailboats," Becca said.

He tied a long piece of twine to each of the dowel rods and handed one to her. She set her boat in the water and mentally loaded it down with her worries. Dalton did the same, and soon the river gently took them both downstream. Within a few minutes, the strings got tangled up together and tightened in their hands.

Becca took a deep breath and let go. Dalton held on for just a second longer and then turned his vessel loose. The strings were so tangled up with each other that the little boats floated side by side on down the river, forever touching each other.

"Think that's an omen?" she asked.

He slipped an arm around her shoulders. "I hope so. We've known each other almost six months, Becca. We've worked for the same folks and gone to the same church, so we know each other pretty well. I don't know where the future will take us, but I hope that those little boats with their strings all tangled up together mean that wherever our life journey takes us, we are together in it. I would never rush you, but will you be this old cowboy's lady?"

Without hesitation, she wrapped her arms around his neck and whispered, "Yes, Dalton, I will be your lady."

About the Author

Carolyn Brown is an award-winning *New York Times* and *USA Today* bestselling author. She is the author of more than one hundred novels and novellas, and her books have been translated into twenty foreign languages.

She was born in Texas but grew up in southern Oklahoma where she and her husband, Charles, a retired English teacher, make their home. They have three grown children and enough grandchildren to keep them young.

When she's not writing, Carolyn likes to plot new stories in her backyard with her tomcat, Boots Randolph Terminator Outlaw, who protects the yard from all kinds of wicked varmints...like crickets, locusts, and spiders. Visit Carolyn at carolynbrownbooks.com.

Also by Carolyn Brown